Hellfire

Hellfire

KARIN FOSSUM

Translated from the Norwegian by Kari Dickson

Harvill *Secker*

LONDON

1 3 5 7 9 10 8 6 4 2

Harvill Secker, an imprint of Vintage,
20 Vauxhall Bridge Road,
London SW1V 2SA

Harvill Secker is part of the Penguin Random House group of companies
whose addresses can be found at global.penguinrandomhouse.com

Penguin
Random House
UK

First published with the title *Helvetesilden* in Norway by Cappelen Damm in 2014

penguin.co.uk/vintage

A CIP catalogue record for this book is available from the British Library

ISBN 9781846559402

This translation has been published with the financial support of NORLA

Typeset in India by Thomson Digital Pvt Ltd, Noida, Delhi
Printed and bound in Great Britain by Clays Ltd, St Ives plc

Penguin Random House is committed to a sustainable future for our business, our readers and our
planet. This book is made from Forest Stewardship Council® certified paper.

MIX
Paper from
responsible sources
FSC
www.fsc.org   FSC® C018179

My darling Finn.
Thank you.

Chapter 1

5 July 2005

Women and children sweated in the heat, but the men knew better and stayed in the shade with the peaks of their caps pulled down over their eyes. In a hollow in the fields up by Skarven, an old Fendt caravan stood in a cluster of dark pines. A torn curtain hung in one rusty window, a fine net of nylon threads and white lace where insects had got caught and trapped. A child was lying just inside the door, a child of around four or five. And on the narrow sofa under the window, a woman. She had a great gash in the corner of her mouth and the blood had run down her neck. The inspector stood in the doorway, his heart hammering.

The caravan was dilapidated; surely they hadn't lived here, the mother and child? No, he thought, they couldn't have. Maybe they were just here for fun. They had gone for a walk over the fields in the lovely weather, perhaps, and had seen the rusty little house standing there. Let's sleep in the caravan tonight!

Geirastadir lay to the west and Haugane to the east, but here, in the dark cluster of trees, lay the mother and child. Sejer climbed into the caravan. The adrenaline made his mouth dry. He stepped over the child, careful to avoid the blood, then spotted a knife lying on the floor over by the sofa. A knife with a riveted wood handle and a long, thin blade – the kind of knife used to fillet meat or fish. There were streaks of blood on the shiny blade – it had clearly run thick and fast – and the air smelt raw. On the worktop he found a handbag with a purse in it; it was red, with several compartments. A backpack and a half-eaten pizza; some clothes on the shelves. A thousand kroner in cash in the purse. In other words, this was not a robbery, but then he had never thought it was. There was always some kind of relationship, he believed, a reason, a motive. A seed from way back. The person who had killed the mother and child knew who they were. And where they were. He had tracked them down, pursued them over the fields and found their hiding place. If it was a hiding place. It was certainly a dismal place to be found, full of stains and damp and that foul smell. Rain leaking through the roof, dead insects. The child was wearing a tracksuit in red, white and blue, the Norwegian colours. It wasn't possible to tell if it was a boy or a girl. Lying on its back with its arms outstretched, as though it had been pushed back by something at the door. Some fair curls caked to its brow. The head twisted back at the neck, a thin, white throat.

Sejer opened the purse again and took out the driver's licence. Bonnie Hayden. So that was the mother's name. But for the moment, the child's remained unknown.

'Not yet,' he said to the others who wanted to get in. 'Don't touch anything. It's not long since this happened, it's still wet. Call Snorrason at forensics and ask him to come immediately.'

He had to go out to get some fresh air; he stood for a while on the grass and breathed in deeply. He registered that some things were crystal clear: the birds were still singing, a light wind played with the black fringes on the branches, a thrush pulled and tugged at a worm it had found in the field. A huge area had been sealed off already and the plastic tape fluttered on the breeze like colourful bunting.

The men followed the dusty path up towards Geirastadir. Their conversation was limited to short, hushed comments. He had presumably walked this way, trodden this path after doing the deed. 'One of them must have seen the other die,' Sejer said, turning to his younger colleague. He didn't know which was worse. If the child had witnessed the mother's death, or if the mother had witnessed the child's death. The most horrific thing possible had happened to them both. Evil incarnate had snuck across the field and stabbed them with a knife. There was something methodical about the murders, something determined; he couldn't see it any other way.

I only hope to God it was quick, he thought.

He exchanged a few words with Randen, the farmer who had found the bodies. Robert Randen stood, frightened, at a respectable distance, unable to move forwards or back, didn't want to leave, didn't want to stay. He owned the caravan, which hadn't been used for a few years; it had stood there empty and rusting among the pine trees.

'We'll need to take a statement from you later,' Konrad Sejer said. 'But for now, have you noticed anyone in the area in recent days? Anyone who doesn't belong?'

'No,' he replied. 'I haven't seen a soul. I've got some Polish workers on the farm,' he added, 'and they knew that the boy and his mother were staying in the caravan. But it was only one night – they came yesterday. I refuse to believe that any of my men are involved. And if that is the case, it'll break me, they're my people.'

'There's a knife on the floor inside,' Sejer continued. 'Did you see it?'

The farmer caught his breath. Almost imperceptibly.

'I want you to take a closer look at it. See if you've seen it before.'

'Do I have to go in again?'

He was reluctant.

'Yes.'

He climbed the two steps and peered in.

'It's not our knife. Can I go now?'

'Yes, we'll follow you up later. Don't talk to the press.'

Sejer was about to go back inside the caravan when something in the grass caught his eye. It was an overturned cake plate by the narrow door. The cake had slid off the edge and was now lying on the ground, untouched. The discovery puzzled him, and he made sure that it was photographed. The fat crows would undoubtedly dive in and finish it off in no time if they didn't take it with them. The technicians took their pictures. Bent over in the cramped caravan, hunkered down. There were several bloody prints on the linoleum floor, the sole of a big shoe; most were faint or incomplete, but one was clear. Sejer moved carefully between the dead bodies. The pungent smell of meat and blood tore at his nose. But his brain was clear. Through the window, he saw a thicket of ripe raspberries.

Chapter 2

December 2004

The snow finally came just before Christmas.

'Do you really have to go out?' Eddie asked. 'There's a storm blowing.'

They had said on the radio that it was icy, that driving conditions were bad and they advised people to stay indoors. Visibility was virtually zero.

Mass put her hand on his arm; her voice was calm and decided.

'Eddie,' she said kindly, 'I've got winter tyres. And I'll drive like a snail, I promise. I want to come home to you in one piece. But I have to go to the shop, we need food. Or do you want to try going without?'

Eddie shook his heavy head at the thought of having no dinner.

'You stay at home with Shiba,' she said. 'What do you want from the shop? I'm sure you're hungry.'

Eddie Malthe wiped his nose with the back of his hand. He was the shape of a giant pear, with thin, spindly legs, and he was wearing the same heavy boots that he always wore, which were narrow at the heel and broadened out towards the toes. He had the feet of a big goose. His hands were huge, white, with short, stubby fingers.

'Cinnamon rolls,' he said without hesitation.

'Cinnamon rolls it is,' his mother replied. 'I'll be off then. And be nice to Shiba: don't pull her tail. I know that's what you do when you're here on your own.'

'Cross my heart and hope to die,' Eddie said, as he planned with glee to do just that. When he pulled her tail, Shiba always started to whine and scratched the floor with her long claws as though she was trying to escape.

'Remember your seat belt,' he said with authority.

His mother pulled on her coat.

'And don't forget your mobile. If you run off the road you must call the emergency services. That is, if you're not unconscious.'

'Eddie, stop it. Now go and sit down on the sofa and I'll be back in three-quarters of an hour, no more.'

Eddie looked at his mother long and hard.

'When you go out, it'll get cold in the house,' he complained. 'You know what it's like. Don't forget the cinnamon rolls. If they haven't got them, get some biscuits. Lemon creams.'

He stared out of the window; the glass was shiny and clean – his mother kept things neat and tidy. His eyes felt sore. He watched the car reverse out of the garage and turn onto the main road. The snow was coming down and swirling around in the wind, ending in great drifts on the roadside. He said a quiet prayer that everything would be all right. That his mother would come back unharmed with the shopping. The dog was sleeping in front of the burner with her head on her paws. He went straight over to her and pulled her tail hard, as he always did. Shiba scrambled to her feet, whining, and ran out into the kitchen.

Eddie sat down on the sofa, picked up the newspaper and turned to the second-last page, where the crossword was. He normally managed to solve it. It wasn't that he was stupid. He found a pencil and started to read. *Across, possessive, seven letters.* He wrote the word 'jealous' in the seven squares.

The burner was roaring, and the dog had settled down on the floor in the corner of the kitchen. She was an overweight, eight-year-old Labrador, and his mother had said she didn't have long to live. Her body was full of lumps, he could feel them under her golden fur, but she wasn't insured, so they couldn't afford to take her to the vet.

'We'll just have to let life run its course,' his mother would say. 'Nothing lasts forever, you know.'

'I know,' Eddie would answer. Then he'd think about his mother's death, because it was going to happen one day. And even though she was only fifty-six, and he was twenty-one, it still terrified him to think about her demise and he got all hot and bothered. He often had to put his hand on his heart to calm it down. *Romany*, he read, and he got the fourth letter 's' from jealous. He wrote the word 'gipsy' in the five squares. He always did the easy ones first. Then he looked at the clock on the wall and watched the seconds tick by. His mother would be back with the cinnamon rolls in twenty minutes. He could already taste them in his mouth. He really, really hoped they had some! And that they were good and fresh! *Direction, five letters*; could be north. Or south. Either way, he had the next word for *circle, five letters*. It must be 'round'. Then he got on to the more difficult clues, and decided to take a break. He went back to the window and stared out at the driving snow. 'Let Mum make it through the storm,' he prayed to Jesus, wherever he was. 'Because I'm sitting here all alone waiting for cake. There's only the two of us. You have to look after us!'

He went out to see Shiba in the kitchen, pulled her tail hard again, and then laughed when she shot up and ran into the living room, where she scooted under the sofa and collapsed, panting.

'Stupid dog,' he said, and laughed again. 'You don't fight back. Haven't you got any teeth?'

Then he sat back down with the crossword, sucking on the end of the pencil. The clue *cease* made him uneasy, as the word had only three letters.

Forty-five minutes had passed and his mother had not returned. He grabbed his mobile and tapped in her number with his fat fingers. But all he got was a voice saying, 'The person you are calling is unable to answer the phone right now.' He paced over to the window again and stared out at the snow, thick and white, the sun only managing to produce a pale, modest light. He knew that his mother would send him out to clear the snow later, and if there was one thing he hated, it was clearing snow. He tried her number again, but once more heard the disembodied voice telling him she was unable to answer the phone. It was fifty minutes now. This is it, he thought in desperation, she's driven off the road and crashed into a tree. She's sitting with her nose buried in the airbag. For a moment he considered throwing on his jacket and walking along the road to look for her. But then, as he stood there by the window, anxiously wringing his hands, he saw her car swing in through the gate. The headlights shone into his face and he ran out into the hall and down the front steps.

'You said three-quarters of an hour,' he complained. 'I was scared.'

'Don't be such a drama queen,' she chided. 'I can't answer the phone when I'm driving, and I was almost home.'

'Did they have cinnamon rolls?'

'Yes,' she said. 'I got two packets. See, here you are, plenty for you to enjoy. Put the milk in the fridge, I'll have to clear the snow from the steps. And when you've finished, you can come out and clear the rest.'

Inside, she counted out seven cinnamon rolls and put them on a plate.

'You can have some more this evening. I think you're putting on weight, my love. I know that you're a big boy, but a hundred and thirty kilos is too much. Being overweight is dangerous, Eddie. The milk and cake settle in your arteries like clay. And then a big clot comes loose and is carried towards your heart – or your brain, for that matter – and then there'll be no more crosswords for you.'

'But I can have the rest of the cinnamon rolls this evening, can't I?' he asked.

'Yes, I promise,' she said. 'But you do understand that I have to be strict, don't you? Someone has to keep an eye on you, we agreed on that.'

'We have to go to the shopping centre,' he said. 'I need new clothes. I want one of those sweatshirts I saw in the paper. *I Love New York*.'

That night he dreamed about chicks. Yellow, fluffy and soft, running around on stick legs. He picked them up and dropped them in a pan with melted butter and garlic. He dreamed that they lay there simmering, then peeped and squeaked when he added boiling water. He woke up abruptly at the end of the dream, listened for sounds in his mother's room. Sometimes she talked in her sleep, other times she moaned, but mostly it was quiet all through the night. He didn't like it when his mum was asleep. When she wasn't there to look after him, when she didn't answer if he spoke to her, when she was out of reach, breathing in the dark.

He always woke up first and lay there listening for his mother, to hear if she was awake. He didn't move until he heard the toilet flush, then he rolled out of bed and went into the living room, pulled open the curtains and looked out at the new day he was now part of. He walked into the kitchen, one hand down his pants, the other opening the bread bin. He cut two slices of bread, spread on a thick layer of butter, then reached for the sugar bowl. He wiped some crumbs from the easywipe tablecloth. His mother came out of the bathroom and saw him sitting there with the bread and sugar. Always the same thing: nag nag nag, how many times do I have to tell you to wash your hands before you eat? – you haven't even been to the bathroom yet. Your hands have been everywhere.

Eddie kept his thoughts to himself. He knew that she often slept with a hand between her sweaty thighs; he could hear her moaning at night. I'm not a bloody idiot, he said to himself. And even though his mother chivvied him into the bathroom to wash his hands, he felt superior. His mother looked out at the snow that was still falling thick and fast. 'We'll take the bus today,' she said, looking at her son. 'It's just as easy. And we really need to get you to the hairdresser's, you look like a girl.'

Eddie snorted. How could she say that? He was one metre ninety tall and his voice was as coarse as a grater.

There was no way he looked like a girl. His hair was curling at the neck, thick and brown and soft, but he didn't like it when the scissors snipped around his ears.

Soon after she was sitting on the bus seat beside him, with her hands folded round her brown handbag.

'We'll go to the Suit Store,' she said with authority. 'They have XXL. You really must stop putting sugar on your bread,' she added. 'You'll get diabetes.'

He didn't answer. He sat on the seat beside her and breathed in the scent of soap. He liked sitting like this on the bus, swaying, the low, drowsy humming of the engine, the smell of the new red plush seats. The smell of strangers he didn't need to interact with.

The Suit Store was on the first floor of the shopping centre, so they took the escalator up. There were racks of sale items outside the shop, old stock that had been reduced.

'I want a pair of trousers and a sweatshirt,' he said, loud and clear, to the young assistant who came over. 'The trousers have to be black. With lots of pockets, front, back and on the legs. Not denim, it has to be some other material. I hate stiff clothes. Extra large, because I'm a big boy.'

The sales assistant smiled and showed her white teeth. Her skin was dark as chocolate and her hair was black.

'You're not Norwegian,' Eddie said, more a statement than anything else.

'I am too,' she retorted. 'My dad's Ethiopian, but I was born and brought up in Norway. Look, these trousers have lots of pockets. Six in front and two at the back, how's that?'

'They're not black,' Eddie said, dissatisfied.

'No, but it's the closest I've got. In your size. If the pockets are so important. We do have other trousers that are black, but they're jeans. And you just said you didn't want jeans.'

'Ah well,' Eddie said. 'I guess I'll be going home with dark blue trousers today then. To think you can't even satisfy such a simple request. And the sweatshirt,' he continued. 'Black as well. Have you ever been to Ethiopia to look for your roots?' he asked out of curiosity.

'Don't be so nosy,' his mother interrupted. 'Why don't you just go to the fitting room and try on the trousers? I'll look for a sweatshirt. You shouldn't ask people where they come from – it's none of your business. How would you like it if people asked and went on about your origins?'

'I wouldn't mind; I'd like it,' he said.

He pulled open the curtain and went into the narrow changing room, took off his old trousers and tried on the new ones. His mother came back with a sweatshirt she had found with *I Love New York* on it, but he didn't even want to try it on, he could see it would fit. Mass paid 720 kroner for the clothes and Eddie carried the bag out of the shop.

They stood in front of the counter in Christiania Cafe on the first floor.

'You can have a sandwich and a cake,' Mass said. 'I'm going to have waffles and jam. Listen, Eddie, you really mustn't ask people where they're from.'

'But Ethiopia's a nice place,' he said. 'It's not anything to be ashamed of.'

They sat down at a table by the window. Eddie pressed his custard slice down on the plate, tried to break the top layer into small pieces.

'Do you remember when we came back from Las Palmas? Do you remember the Negro who fell on the escalator at

Gardemoen?' he asked. 'He broke both his legs. In several places. It was terrible.'

'You shouldn't say Negro,' Mass corrected him. 'What made you think about him anyway?'

'Well, we have to go down the escalator too. We'd better be careful. Hold onto the handrail. I'll carry the bags.'

He licked his lips.

'I'm going to watch *Tracker Tore* tonight. I wonder who he's going to help this time, and if they'll find who they're looking for,' he said. 'It always starts me thinking about Gran and Grandad. And all the others on Dad's side. Where they came from. And everyone before them. And how they lived. And what they did.'

Mass took a sip of coffee.

'But they're dead,' she objected. 'It doesn't matter any more. It's you and me now, and I think we manage very well.'

She ate some of her waffle.

'Perhaps you should get a girlfriend,' she said. 'After all, I'm not going to be here forever.'

Eddie looked up with a horrified expression on his face.

'Why do I need a girlfriend when I've got you?' he exclaimed. 'Were you upset when Dad left?'

'No,' she replied. 'Not really. I think I was expecting it. He was a womaniser, Eddie, just so you know. He found someone else – someone much younger than me, of course; that's just the way men are. But then he got ill and died, so she didn't get much joy from him either. I don't know if they had any children, maybe they did. But we've talked about all this before, Eddie. There's nothing more to tell.'

'It sounds like you think it's all OK,' Eddie said, offended. 'Didn't you think about me?'

'Of course I did. I just didn't want you to grow up with a father who didn't want us.'

Later that afternoon, Eddie sat on the sofa with the newspaper. He liked to read the deaths and obituaries, savouring them like sweets. Lots of old ladies who tasted like camphor. Some, like all the little children, were sweet as toffee. And some were stronger than Turkish pepper. It might be a murder or a suicide, or the many who lost the fight against cancer. His thoughts started to wander. Then he returned to the crossword. *Corona, five letters*, and the last one was 's'. He knew that Corona was a beer; he knew that it was a town. And it also had something to do with the sun. He went to look it up on the Internet and discovered to his great surprise that it was also a virus. The things I know! he thought to himself happily. I've got my eye on the ball.

Chapter 3

Blåkollen, December 2004

Her son was asleep beside her, a damp lock of hair on his forehead. Four and a half years old, with big blond curls, and small white hands with nails like mother-of-pearl.

'Simon,' she whispered, 'are you awake? The day has begun and we have to get up.'

The boy wriggled and turned over; he wanted to carry on sleeping.

'I'll get up without you then, and make the porridge,' she said, with some resignation, putting one foot down on the floor. 'With butter and raisins and sugar and cinnamon.'

What sounded like a sigh came from the child, as though the thought of buttery porridge had penetrated his sleep. She kissed him on the cheek; it was warm and covered in the finest down. Then she pulled on a thick sweater and crossed the cold floor into the kitchen. She poured some milk into a pan, added oats and a teaspoon of salt. And finally a handful of raisins. Then she went back into the bedroom and lifted the boy up from the bed. He opened his eyes drowsily and put his arms round her neck. He weighed next to nothing. She carried him out into the bathroom and helped him get dressed while he leaned against the sink. Eventually he sat down on his Tripp Trapp chair by the kitchen table. And like every other morning, he threw a tantrum. 'I don't want to go to nursery,' he screamed, banging his spoon on the table and making the porridge bowl jump. Bonnie felt like crying.

'But you'll have a great time,' she said as enthusiastically as she could. 'You can play with Märta. And you might get hot chocolate with marshmallows.' She stroked his cheek. He kept on banging the table with his spoon. All he wanted was to be with his mother, and more than anything, he wanted to be back in bed under the warm duvet. Bonnie poured milk onto his porridge and sprinkled some sugar over.

'I'll be home this afternoon, so we can have fun together then,' she said. 'We can make a tent with the blanket and two chairs, and we can pretend you live in the tent, and I can give you supper in there. That would be fun, wouldn't it?'

At nursery, the children each had their own picture by their coat pegs. Simon's was of a snail, carrying its little house around on its back, its tentacles standing up like two antennae. Simon sat down heavily on the pine bench as his mother took off his jacket, then his hat and scarf, mittens and toasty boots. He collapsed in a little heap, didn't have the energy to protest any more; he knew that his mother had to go. She took him by the hand and led him into the other children, who were milling around.

This can't be right, Bonnie thought, leaving him with others. Being away all day. It should be him and me all day long. Her child next to her body, her child within arm's reach, so she could comfort him if anything should happen. They only had a meagre three hours together in the evening. Her guilty conscience gnawed away at her, but she had to work. She was a home help who washed, scrubbed and polished for old people; she beat carpets, shook out rugs and served food. Today she was going to Erna first, and Erna was always a challenge.

'Good morning, Simon,' said Kaja, who was the head of the nursery. 'And what would you like to do today?'

He didn't have an answer. The little boy wasn't used to having his wishes fulfilled. He slowly wandered across the room, sat down on the big corner sofa, and picked up a picture book. He started to turn the pages with his thin fingers. He could read a few words – his mother had taught him – the word 'ice cream' and the word 'ape', and his own name. As his mother's back disappeared through the door he got up and ran over to the window. He watched the tail lights disappear through the gate and down the road. Now he had to wait for nine hours. He walked slowly back to the sofa and started to look through the book. Kaja sat down beside him.

'You're on kitchen duty today,' she said with a smile. 'You'll enjoy that, won't you? We're going to make bread rolls. And you can knead the dough.'

Simon didn't answer this either. The sight of the unhappy little thing who was only four and a half years old nearly broke Kaja's heart. No one should have to leave a crying child. It was wrong and she really felt for Bonnie Hayden. She tried to think about all the positive things: he didn't go hungry or get cold; he was a much loved child. And that couldn't be said for all the children in her care.

Once in the car, Bonnie took a moment to pull herself together. It was the same pain every morning, the same terrible feeling of guilt that she had to push back down.

She drove out through the gate, on her way to Erna, who was incredibly demanding. She cursed her mean little life, the fight she had every morning with her crying son. Everyone else seemed so much happier than she was, had more energy and plans and dreams for themselves and their children. She often wondered if Simon would manage to get by in life, worried that he would also fall short and be left on the outside. Life was an endless succession of obligations and demands. He had to manage on his own at nursery, had to make friends. Get on with the staff and other children. Then he'd have to do well at school, get good marks and learn to socialise. He would eventually grow up and have to get a job – preferably a well-paid one – something secure. And she hoped he would get a girlfriend and that they would have children. And if they didn't have children they would have to explain why. No, we don't want children or we can't have children. And if they did have children, they would have to manage the endless expectations of society. My little Simon, she thought with smarting eyes. How will things turn out for him?

The car spluttered when she changed up to fourth gear because there was a hole in the exhaust. It was about to fall to pieces, and if it did, she couldn't afford to buy a new one. And if she didn't have a car, she couldn't keep her job as a home help. Her heart got stuck in her throat at the thought. She gritted her teeth and put her foot on the accelerator. She knew that Erna would be sitting by the window watching out for her.

Erna's profile looked like it had been carved in stone as she sat waiting by the window. Bonnie could see the sharp ridge of her nose through the glass. The old woman took her time opening the door as usual, and only with great reluctance let her in: she always liked to make a point. As soon as Bonnie was through the door she breathed in the familiar smell of old people who are no longer able to look after themselves.

'It's cold today,' Erna complained. 'You'll have to put the heating on. My legs are like ice. What about you?'

'Thank you for asking,' Bonnie said. 'Simon was completely blue with cold when we left for nursery.'

'You mothers today, you just abandon your children,' Erna said sharply. 'We didn't do that in my day; we were at home with them all day. And why is it you don't have a husband? Was he not getting what he wanted? You know what men are like.'

'He left, I've told you before,' Bonnie replied, upset. 'He met someone younger, there was nothing I could do. You should have seen him, he was completely obsessed. And I don't want another man, one was enough.'

Once she'd hung up her coat, she went into Erna's bedroom. In the corner of the room there was a basket full of odd socks. Bonnie felt exhausted just at the sight of them. She stood for a while by the bed, her head hanging. If only she could lie down on the soft mattress. Her head ached with tiredness, but though she couldn't bear the thought of starting to clean, she picked up the basket of socks and went back into the living room. On the way out, she looked up at the wall briefly to study a photograph that hung there. It was of Erna at her confirmation, wearing a long dress. Every time Bonnie saw the picture, she was astonished. Could that really be Erna? It was hard to believe because the young girl in the picture was beautiful and beaming.

Erna was sitting in a wing chair with a blanket over her knees, watching her every move; Bonnie could feel her gimlet eyes on her back. She took a sock from the basket and bent down, lifted the heavy oak coffee table and put the thick sock on one of the legs. Then put a sock on the second, third and fourth. She did the same on the armchairs, which were also heavy as lead. Erna had an enormous dining table and six chairs at the other end of the room. Soon all of Erna's furniture was wearing white tennis socks with a red-and-blue stripe. Then it was time to get the heavy vacuum cleaner from the cupboard. The furniture was now protected from the vacuum head, which might otherwise bang against the legs and dent the wood. Erna was worried about wear and tear and the socks were a fixed ritual. Her eyes followed Bonnie as she worked. Her hands lay like claws in her lap and she moved her face from side to side like a bird of prey.

'We have to wash the windows today,' she commanded. 'There are marks all over them. Will you never learn to use the squeegee without leaving stripes?'

Bonnie answered loudly over the noise of the vacuum cleaner.

'It's too cold, Erna,' she said in a tired voice.

But Erna had an answer for that.

'Put a little methylated spirits in the water,' she said. 'It's in the cupboard under the sink.'

Bonnie didn't have the energy to reply. She coaxed the head of the vacuum cleaner in between the table legs, terrified of hitting the precious woodwork. Because then Erna would flare up, call the office and complain, say that Bonnie was sloppy and didn't care. Not that Ragnhild in the office ever listened to her, but it was still unpleasant. Erna's radio was on; she was listening to the news. A case worker in one of the jobcentres in Oslo had been threatened with a knife.

'It was probably a foreigner,' Erna said. 'An African, no doubt. Those people don't know how to behave decently, they just come here to sponge off us.'

Bonnie straightened up to release her back. She had waited in a queue at the jobcentre herself when she was unemployed and on the dole, and had noticed that there were a lot of foreigners there. She was not proud of her bitter thoughts at the time. She bent down to carry on vacuuming. Simon, where are you now? Are you sitting inside the little house in the play corner, or are you on the sofa with a book? Or maybe you're outside sledging with the others. Don't cry, I'll be there soon, I just have to clean. Every day I have to clean. And maybe if I work really hard and save as much as I can, we can buy a plane ticket. To the Mediterranean. And then you can swim in warm water and play on the soft white sand.

'I hope the African is sent home,' Erna announced from the wing chair.

'If it was an African,' Bonnie said. 'Norwegians can threaten people too, if they think it's necessary.'

She moved the standard lamp and a basket of newspapers, and glanced over at the windows as she did so: they were polished like a mirror. Methylated spirits in the water? She wasn't going to get away with not doing it. She would have to stand on a stepladder in the snow to do the outside because the big living-room windows couldn't be opened. She put the vacuum cleaner back in the cupboard, closed the door and sat down on a chair; she just wanted to rest a little. Organ music poured out of the radio. Erna had closed her eyes.

Now she had to wash the floor. She went to get the bucket, filled it with warm water, but not too warm as that might damage the sheen on the oak parquet. Erna was pernickety about that. Then she did the kitchen and the bedroom, and finally the bathroom. The grout between the tiles was grey and Erna had suggested that she use a toothbrush to clean it properly.

Bonnie shook out the rugs. She did the laundry and changed the bed. Then she sat down at the kitchen table and polished a five-armed silver candelabra that Erna had once bought in Egypt. According to her job description, she wasn't supposed to do that kind of thing, but it was a job she liked, a welcome relief. She could sit still and rest her back. The candelabra sparkled when she was finished. But then she had to balance in the snow outside the living-room windows, while Erna stood inside and made sure she did a thorough job. She mustn't leave any stripes from the squeegee, or she was done for. Her hands were freezing inside the rubber gloves, and her ears were cold. When she was finished, she carried the stepladder inside and put it away. She watered the plants and dusted, carried old newspapers out to the recycling bin, changed a light bulb that had blown in the kitchen, and put five white candles in the newly polished candelabra. Next she went through the food in the fridge. Quite a lot was past its sell-by date, including the milk, cheese and ham. Eventually she collapsed onto a chair. Half a day's work done. Now she had to go to Marie's, which was a lot easier, as Marie lived in a small flat in a sheltered complex for the elderly. Erna got up from the wing chair and shuffled across the floor to her bedroom. Bonnie thought about Marie as she sat and waited. After a while, Erna came out again with a shoebox, which she handed to Bonnie.

'This is for you,' she said briskly. 'I've been saving it. I used to get them for Christmas. And I don't have use for them any more.'

Bonnie looked at the box. It was quite light, the lid tied down with a piece of string. Erna had never given her anything. She was a real miser. The most she would do was gather up her crumbs and give them to the birds. Bonnie thanked her warmly for the gift and carried it to the door where she said goodbye.

Marie sat on a chair while Bonnie gave her a shower.

She had a plastic overall on over her clothes, but still managed to get soaking wet, as she always did. The hardest thing was getting the temperature right, as Marie was so sensitive. She had to test it on her feet first. First it was too hot, then it was too cold, then it was too hot again, but eventually she got it right. Afterwards, once she'd dried Marie's thin body and she was sitting on the edge of the bed, Bonnie rubbed in some cream. Marie's old skin was so dry that it flaked. While Bonnie massaged her, Marie sat and mused about how evil people were, as was her wont. A man had strangled his wife with some rope. Then he had rolled her up in a carpet and put her in the car, and driven to the edge of a quarry and thrown her over.

'Do you think he'll come here?' Marie asked anxiously.

Bonnie had to smile. She had worked her way down to Marie's feet, which were as small as a child's.

'No, dear Marie, why would he do that? They'd probably had an argument,' she assured her, 'and you never argue. Anyway, he'll be sentenced to years in prison.'

'But he'll get out again,' Marie said. 'And then he'll look for someone else. I'm not going to open the door. Give three short rings when you come so I know it's you.'

*

Simon sat and waited for her by the window.

Bonnie swung in and stopped in front of the nursery. She was happy, because now it was just the two of them, all evening and all night. She would give him everything he hadn't got during the day; she would buy a bottle of ginger beer and a bag of dinosaur biscuits. As soon as she opened the door he came running towards her. His cheeks were red; he must have spent a long time outside in the cold. He sat down under the snail picture straight away and she helped him put on his coat.

'Shall we build that tent when we get home? We'll make a big one, we can use a sheet and blankets and I've got lots of pegs.'

Simon climbed into the back seat of the car and she fastened his seat belt.

'Marie asked me to say hello,' she told him. 'She never remembers how old you are, she thinks you're already at school.'

'What's in the box?' he asked curiously. Bonnie had put the box tied with string on the back seat. She got in and started the engine, and as usual the Opel had to cough and splutter a few times before it started.

'No idea,' she said. 'Erna gave it to me. What do you think it could be? Shall we guess?'

Simon reached over and put the box in his lap. He shook it first, but heard nothing.

'Is it shoes?' he asked in surprise.

Bonnie had to laugh.

'No,' she said, looking at him in the rear-view mirror. 'I couldn't wear Erna's shoes, her feet are too big.'

She paused for a moment, looking right then left to make sure it was clear, then pulled out onto the road.

'I wondered if it might be a vase,' she said, 'or some coffee cups that she doesn't need any more. She said she got it for Christmas and that she doesn't need it. That she's too old.'

'Do you get too old for coffee cups?' Simon wondered.

'No, of course not, that was silly of me. Perhaps it's chocolates, that's what old ladies get for Christmas. And then they'll probably be hard and mouldy and we won't be able to eat them.'

'They also get slippers,' Simon said, like a little grown-up. 'Granny has lots of pairs and she got them all from us.'

'It might be a smart little handbag,' Bonnie said after a while. 'That would be nice. Erna never goes to parties. And so maybe she thought that I might have more use for it than she does.'

Simon leaned forward and grabbed hold of the back of her seat. 'You don't go to parties either,' he said.

She looked at him in the mirror again.

'No,' she replied. 'I don't. I'd much rather be with you.'

When they got home and had taken their coats off in the hall, Bonnie asked if they should eat or open the box first. Simon had to think about it.

'What are we having?' he asked.

'Pasta twists,' Bonnie replied. 'With tomato sauce.'

Simon sat down on his knees on the sofa and Bonnie put the box down on the table in front of him. He lifted it up again and started to shake it.

'I think maybe it's a lamp,' he said, wisely.

'Well, then it must be a little one,' Bonnie said. 'Or perhaps it's a torch. I'm sure that Erna wouldn't have much use for that. Although actually, if there's a power cut, and she has to find the fuse box . . . I can just see her stumbling around the house, banging into her horrible furniture, knocking over the lamp and tearing the curtains.'

Simon chuckled.

'Pasta twists first, because then the secret will be even bigger. Race you to the kitchen!'

He grabbed hold of the footstool he needed to stand on to reach the work surface as he raced past. He liked to watch his mother making food, liked her thin fingers with no rings.

'That's good, you can watch and learn. One day you'll grow up and move away from home, then you'll have to cook your own food.'

Simon shook his head.

'But I want to live with you; I don't want to leave home.'

Bonnie filled a pan with water and put it on the hotplate. After a while it started to boil and she opened the bag of pasta and the tomato sauce. Simon got some dry pasta to play with. He lined the pieces up on the worktop, end to end like a string of pearls. She asked what he wanted to read when he went to bed.

'*Where the Wild Things Are,*' he said without any hesitation.

'But we read that yesterday.'

'I know, but I want to hear it again and again, a hundred times.'

Bonnie put the food on the table and sat down. Simon kept glancing into the living room at the box that was waiting there with only a temptingly thin piece of string round it. He ate as fast as he could and afterwards helped his mother to clear the table. She rinsed the plates in warm water and stacked them on the side. Finally she wiped the table and then came into the living room. She put the box on his lap, and Simon started to struggle with the string. Erna had tied a really tight knot, but Bonnie didn't help him, he had to do it himself. That way they could eke out the precious moments.

'Maybe it's money,' he said, full of hope, because he knew that was something his mother never had enough of.

'Banknotes don't weigh much,' Bonnie said. 'This is heavier.'

'What about coins?' Simon suggested. 'Ten-kroner coins.'

'No, then we would have heard them clinking. And anyway, Erna's a miser.'

Bonnie was getting a bit impatient now too; it was exceptionally rare for someone to give her a present. Simon had finally managed to loosen the double knot. He threw the string down on the floor, sat for a short while with the tip of his tongue peeping out of the corner of his mouth.

'Shall we do a fanfare?' Bonnie laughed. 'Then you can take off the lid.'

She put her hands in front of her mouth to make a trumpet. Then she performed a long, jubilant fanfare and finally Simon lifted the lid off the box. For a while they just sat there and stared, Simon's face reflecting his disappointment.

'It's just newspaper,' he said, throwing the lid down onto the sofa.

'That means it's something fragile,' Bonnie explained. 'You have to unwrap it. Be careful.'

Simon took out a small package. He quickly saw that there were several of them and his curiosity was piqued.

'It must be trinkets,' Bonnie guessed. 'She has so many of them.'

'Trinkets?'

'Decorations. Little figurines and things like that.'

He opened the package carefully, which wasn't easy because he was so excited, but soon he was sitting there with a small bottle in his lap.

'Perfume!' Bonnie exclaimed. 'Just what I've always wanted, but could never afford.'

Simon admired the bottle. His mother was happy and that made him happy too. She took the bottle from him and took off the top, then held it under his nose.

'Oscar de la Renta,' she said. 'Very expensive.'

'Who's Oscar?' Simon asked.

'Oscar is the man who makes the perfume.'

'But why is it so expensive?'

'Perfume is made from flowers,' Bonnie explained. 'And you need an awful lot of flowers just to make a small bottle. Can't you just picture Oscar walking through his garden picking flowers and putting them in a big basket?'

'Does he pick them himself?'

Bonnie had to laugh.

'No, the perfume is made in a factory. Open another one, there are more.'

She put the perfume down on the table, where the gold cap sparkled in the light from the lamp. Simon took out another package. He dropped the paper on the floor in front of the sofa; they could tidy it up later.

'Gucci,' Bonnie said enthusiastically. 'We have to smell this one too.'

She let Simon smell it first, then she took the bottle from him and sniffed. The bottle was different, but it was also beautiful. She put it down next to the Oscar de la Renta. The third bottle was shaped like a woman's body. The cap was where the head should have been, and they each sniffed it. The fourth was small and round like a bauble, about the size of a tennis ball, and then there was only one left. It was square, simple and boring. Simon sat with it in his hand; he thought the other bottles were much nicer. But Bonnie clapped her hands with joy.

'I don't believe it!' she cried. 'This is the best of them all, Chanel Number 5.'

'Are there lots of flowers in that one?' Simon asked.

'Yes, loads and loads of flowers. You know, Simon, this is the world's most famous perfume. All the film stars wear it.'

Suddenly she hid her face in her hands and started to sob. Simon was horrified. He took the bottle from her and put it down beside the others. He didn't know why she was crying – she'd been so happy a moment ago. She dried her tears and stroked his cheek.

'I'm just so touched,' she said. 'I would never have dreamed that I'd get all this from Erna.'

She picked up each bottle and looked at them one by one from every angle.

'You'll get a present tomorrow as well. We'll go to the toy shop.'

Simon clapped his hands.

'But can we afford it?' he wondered.

'Yes, tomorrow we can afford it. I've been given a present, so you should have one too. And now I'm going to put on a drop of Chanel Number 5.'

She unscrewed the square cap from the bottle and dabbed her index finger on the top, and then she rubbed it lightly on her left wrist.

'Why do you put it on your arm?'

Bonnie put the bottle down and explained: 'Well, because the skin is so thin there. And under the skin there's a big vein, so the skin is very warm just there. And when it's warm, it smells better. Come on now, let's build a huge tent.'

Four chairs and four sheets later, Simon had his own beautiful tent in the middle of the living room. He took some cushions from the sofa and crept inside. Bonnie got down on her knees and crawled in after him. For a while they sat there in silence.

'I'll go and get *Where the Wild Things Are*,' she said. 'You stay here. And we have to have a torch.'

She found the book on the shelf and went back in, chose a cushion.

'Can we get a real tent one time and sleep out in the forest?' Simon asked hopefully.

'Yes,' she said. 'I promise. But it may be a while before we can do that. Here, you hold the torch.'

She read the whole of *Where the Wild Things Are*. Her voice rose and fell and Simon could vividly imagine all the scary monsters. He loved it just as much as always, it was only a story, after all, and it had a happy ending, little Max always got home safely.

'Can I sleep here tonight?' he said suddenly. 'I want to sleep in the tent.'

'But the floor's stone hard; that won't be very comfy, will it?'

Simon was adamant. After his evening snack, he went to the bathroom and brushed his teeth, especially carefully. Bonnie got his duvet and pillow, found the cushions from the garden furniture in the cupboard, then crawled into the tent and made up a simple bed for him. He said goodnight and crept in, lying on his side with a hand under his cheek. She could see the light of the torch through the sheets. She then sat down in front of the TV and watched the news. She knew that he wasn't asleep, but she pretended he was. We'll get by, she comforted herself. I must thank Erna. I suppose she'll pooh-pooh it, because that's just the way she is.

She turned the TV off at ten o'clock. Simon had switched off the torch and she sat there listening. She smiled at the thought that he was lying there holding his breath, because he was listening too. Then she got up and turned out the light, thinking as she did that it would now be pitch-black in the tent. But he had asked to sleep there, inside the warm den with all the cushions. She went into her bedroom, but left the door ajar, and lay in bed listening for a long time, because she knew that he'd be there soon enough. He wouldn't want to go to his own room. He would creep in when he thought she was asleep, and she would hold open the duvet for him, and hug him to her.

Chapter 4

July 2005

The dog, Frank, lay down under the desk, where he had an old duvet, but before lying down, he turned round and round, making a kind of nest. Sejer went over to the window. From his office he had a view over the river, which was now busy with big and small boats, and the odd keen kayaker. He spotted a family of swans and an old man feeding bread crusts to the ducks, and he saw some children swimming in the strong, ice-cold current.

Sejer was fifty-five, but women still turned to look at him when he walked through town. He was tall, lean and grey with strong features. He knew that he would have to step down in a few years, that others were waiting, ready to take over. The thought of becoming a pensioner irritated him beyond reason. What was he going to do? Sit on the balcony with a generous whisky? Listen to Monica Zetterlund and go for walks with Frank? He crossed the room and sat down at the desk, opened the top drawer and took out a pile of photographs of the two victims, the mother and child. He knew that the pictures would plague him, that they would reappear in his thoughts when he was old. The first photograph showed the old caravan from a distance. It was white with a dark stripe under the window and the name *Fendt* written in silver letters across the back. A couple of the Poles who worked on the farm had slept in it in the past, but now it was too dilapidated, and this year they were staying in one of the outhouses, where there was room for four. They came in May every year and went home again in November. Sejer had never owned a caravan. He had a cabin on Sandøya and spent a few weeks there every summer, but he had always thought that caravans were something good. A little house on wheels, the people inside them like snails, happy to be on their way to the sea, and sun and summer. He would never think like that again. From now on, whenever he was driving behind a caravan, he would think about the woman and her child.

Somewhere a killer was sitting, listening out for his pursuers. Or he might be standing by the window looking out. Or following the news, perhaps discussing the case with his neighbours. He was most probably over twenty, and possibly under forty, but almost certainly of Norwegian descent. It was in all likelihood his first murder. All the same. He had without a doubt some behavioural disorder, although that would not necessarily be apparent to those around him. Perhaps he had a job, perhaps not. Family? No, he didn't think so. Nor any close friends. And he was pretty sure the man would have had some previous contact with the psychiatric services.

Sejer was still of the view that the murders had been planned, because nothing of value had been taken from the scene of the crime. The killer had made no effort to remove any clues. The knife was left lying on the floor. The deed had perhaps given him some kind of satisfaction, and he was less bothered about what happened afterwards. His mission was accomplished, whatever it was. To punish them or to get rid of them. He had walked across the fields with awful intent. In his hand, presumably the right hand, he had carried a knife. He had approached the woman and child with determination; perhaps the door had been left open, it was warm. Maybe the woman had looked out of the doorway to see who was coming. Maybe nothing had been said, maybe he'd just forced his way in, thrown them to the floor and killed them in cold blood. Or maybe it wasn't cold at all, maybe his blood was boiling. No one had heard a thing. The farm was too far away. He must have been covered in blood, but had obviously not met anyone. And Sejer guessed he had come from Haugane or Geirastadir.

Frank chewed the toe of his shoe; he wanted attention. Sejer leaned over and patted him on the head.

'Soon,' he said. 'I'm busy right now.'

He moved on to the next picture. The forensics technician had taken it from the doorway, looking in at the two victims. Even the torn curtains were sprayed with blood. Some bloody playing cards lay on the small Respatex table; they might have been playing Crazy Eights, if the boy was old enough to understand the rules. On the worktop: a handbag, an empty pizza box and a bunch of wild flowers. At the other end of the caravan, two beds had been made up on the narrow sofas. Flowery duvet covers and pillowcases, and a teddy bear in one. He looked at the next photographs. The first was of the child, lying on his back. His tracksuit, which was red, white and blue, was far too big for him and lay in folds. He had blond curly hair and his trainers looked new. There were no wounds on his hands or arms to indicate that he'd tried to protect himself, he hadn't had time. Sejer thought the child had been killed first, as his body was closest to the door. The next picture was of the woman, who was the child's mother. There was just the two of them, Bonnie and Simon Hayden, no father who lived with them, no brothers or sisters. The mother was also blonde, but she didn't have curls, so perhaps the child had inherited his mop from his father. Her white summer dress was wet and stained with blood from the stab wounds. Sejer carried on to the close-ups, which were taken under the instruction of Bardy Snorrason, who was responsible for the autopsy. Her feet were bare, the toenails varnished. On and on through the photographs, until finally he sat staring at the last one. The worn, grey linoleum floor covered in considerable amounts of blood. And over by the worktop, a clear footprint. He studied the picture, holding it up to his eyes. This, he thought, is all we have for the moment.

He leaned back in the chair to process the images. Frank started to chew the toe of his shoe again and there was a knock at the door. Snorrason came in with the forensics report. He was also close to retirement age. He gave Frank a pat and pulled out a chair, put a pile of paper with dense text down on the desk in front of him.

'The preliminary report,' he said. 'I've been thorough.'

Sejer started to read the report while Snorrason sat beside him and commented on the findings.

'The boy, Simon, had four stab wounds. All to the stomach; he presumably bled to death. And sadly, it may have taken some time. His mother, Bonnie, was also stabbed four times – he made quick work of it. Once through the carotid artery, so her death would have been swift. The three other wounds were to vital organs, the heart, liver and kidneys. And then the gash by her mouth –

he slashed her face. What are your thoughts so far?' The Icelander looked at the inspector.

'He must have known that they were in the caravan,' Sejer said. 'They've been carefully selected. He may have planned this for some time. I'm guessing that he feels no remorse; this is a deeply disturbed individual.'

He leafed through the pile of paper, didn't understand all the terminology, but Snorrason explained it to him.

'Maybe he tortured a cat, that's how it often starts,' Sejer said. 'Or someone has done him wrong. And this is his revenge. But why a mother and child? I don't understand. There's certainly plenty to piece together.'

Frank came out from under the desk and Sejer bent down to stroke his head.

'We won't leave this case unsolved,' Snorrason said, 'if it's the last one we work on. So, let me tell you what else the bodies told me. They had just eaten. There was undigested food in both their stomachs, and the boy had had a fizzy drink. Both were otherwise healthy, but the mother had broken a bone, presumably as a child. She is one metre seventy tall and weighs fifty-four kilos. The boy is of a slight build. Otherwise I haven't found anything out of the ordinary. The wounds are deep. The blade was twenty-three centimetres long, but very narrow. And the knife handle was eleven centimetres.'

Sejer clasped his hands round his neck. He thought of all the people he would have to talk to.

'Bonnie Hayden didn't have colleagues as such,' he said. 'She was a home help and they work independently. But I'm going to talk to all her clients. Her parents are still alive, but she had no siblings. I've already been to see her mother, Henny Hayden, but she was not in any fit state to say much, so we'll wait until after the funeral. Although we don't really have time to wait. Bonnie had practically no contact with the child's father any more; they had only lived together for a couple of years. The boy went to nursery, so I will talk to the staff there, and there's Bonnie's boss at health and social services. I'll also go back and talk to the farmer at Skarven and his Polish farmhands. They've been coming here regularly for a while now and know the area well.'

'Is that what you're thinking?' Snorrason asked.

'To be honest, my thoughts are all over the place,' Sejer replied. 'I'll keep you posted. You carry on with what you're doing, and I'll swing by later.'

Snorrason left and immediately Jacob Skarre appeared in the doorway with his golden locks.

'Shall we get started?' he said. 'Tell me what you've got.'

He sat down on the chair that Snorrason had just vacated and looked through the papers.

'The only thing we have is a right foot,' Sejer commented, 'but it's a big one. We're not talking about a small man. And he was furious.'

Chapter 5

December 2004

The snow was wet and heavy and stuck stubbornly to the spade, so after Eddie had been shovelling for half an hour, he had to straighten up and stretch his aching back. His hair was slick with sweat, but there was still some way to go down to the road. And then he'd have to clear the snow around the bins. Otherwise they wouldn't be emptied, his mother said, there were rules for things like that. He rested for a while, breathing heavily as he stared at the snow. He knew his mum was hovering at the window to make sure he was doing the work. So he put his back into it again, tried to find a rhythm, chanting heave-ho in his mind as he threw the snow to the sides. The edges were high now. As he worked, he tried to decide what he wanted for supper, because his mum normally asked, and it was best to have an answer. It eventually stopped snowing and the sky that had been grey as lead started to clear. The horizon was blushed pink by the setting sun, and it looked like the valley was covered in a white veil, like something out of a fairy tale. He was wearing his new top under his jacket, *I Love New York*. His mother had asked why he wanted that one. Because New York is a good city, he'd replied. But you've never been there. No, but we could go there. And then we could go for a walk together in Central Park. His mother had turned her back and said, I couldn't cope with the jet lag. And he knew then that they would never go to New York, and he would just have to be satisfied with the sweatshirt.

Finally he was finished and he leaned the spade up against the wall. It was dusk, beautiful and blue, but soon the dark would settle over the small house. Inside, his mother would turn on all the lights, which always put him in a good mood, he felt safe and secure. On a sudden impulse, he waded through the drifts of snow and over to the wall. He stood there by the window where his mother could see him. The snow was wet, so he could form it into whatever he liked. He made a hard, compact snowball, which he then put down on the ground. Then he made another one, and placed it beside the first. And just as he had thought, his mother opened the window.

'What on earth are you doing?'

He glanced up at her, and carried on making snowball number three. They were as big as oranges.

'I'm making a snow lantern,' he told her enthusiastically.

'Gosh, you haven't done that since you were little.'

'No. It's for you, so you have something to look at.'

He hadn't lost the knack. The first circle was perfect, and he worked the snowballs for so long that they were as hard as possible and would last a long time. As he worked he hummed the song 'New York, New York', which he had heard so many times on the radio. He hadn't travelled much, except one holiday to the Mediterranean and the odd day trip over to Sweden, where his mother bought meat and red wine and he would select heavy boxes of

Cherry Coke and carry them out to the car. He was on row number three, but had still not started to slope the walls in, because now that he was making a lantern, it was going to be a big one. He worked without stopping, and every now and then his mother appeared by the open window.

'Goodness, you're good at this, that's the best one I've seen.'

Eddie brushed the hair from his brow. He liked it when his mother praised him, he couldn't get enough of it. The snow had never been so good! Strange that he hadn't thought of it before, the snow had been on the ground for a long time and it would soon be Christmas. Roast ribs and candles and presents. Having worked long and hard, he took a few steps back to admire the lantern. The top was still open, of course, because he had to put the candles in. It was already getting dark, but he worked in the light from the window. Then he waded back to the door, opened it and shouted into the house: 'A candle! Matchsticks!'

He could hear his mother opening the drawer. Seconds later she appeared with the things he had asked for.

'Actually,' he added, 'I need more than one. It's a big lantern.'

She disappeared inside and returned with two more candles. He took them and stuck the three candles in at the bottom of the lantern. He checked that they were steady, careful not to touch the walls when he put his arm in, as they might topple. Then he lit the candles one by one, made the last snowballs and held his breath as he closed the lantern. If the snow drizzled down, it might extinguish the candles.

They stood side by side at the window and admired Eddie's incredible handiwork. It was a big, beautiful snow lantern, and the light from the candles flickered and shimmered on the surrounding snow. They said nothing as they stood there, it was hard to pull themselves away, and throughout the evening Eddie went to check that the candles were still burning.

Mass made spaghetti and meatballs, and while they ate, they chatted about this and that. Eddie was good and put the plates in the dishwasher – it was the only thing he could do. Afterwards, he took Shiba for her evening walk. On his mother's advice, he wore a hi-viz waistcoat and put a flashing blue light on Shiba's collar. They saw the odd car as they walked, and each time he pulled back to the edge of the road and waited until the car passed. He thought about his mother's promise, that he could have the rest of the cinnamon rolls. He loved the white doughy inside, spread with cinnamon. Later on in the evening he would watch *Tracker Tore*. It was just as overwhelming every time someone found their lost relatives. Mothers, fathers, brothers and sisters, often in different countries, sometimes even on the other side of the world. Some only found a grave they could visit, but that in itself was something. This led his thoughts once more to his father, who was buried in Copenhagen. He had never been there.

When Shiba had squatted to pee a few times, he turned round and walked back to the house. The dog immediately padded into the kitchen and lay down in the corner.

'Those clay layers you were talking about,' Eddie said. 'In our blood vessels. That can come loose and go to your heart. Do you think I've got a lot of them? I mean, I am fat.'

Mass shook her head.

'No, let's just hope that everything's OK. It's a good thing you don't smoke. And you don't drink either, you're actually very healthy.'

Eddie leaned his elbows on the table.

'And what about you?' he asked. 'Have you got any of those layers? Can you see them on X-rays?'

'I don't know,' she replied. 'Maybe. Why do you ask?'

He gave it some thought.

'Well, because if you did, we could do something about it. There are medicines that thin the blood so that it flows better. You know, you need to keep the system moving!'

His mother looked at him and smiled.

'Why give it so much thought? Are you scared of dying?'

She pulled out a chair and sat down at the table, took his big hand in hers and patted it gently; it was white and soft, the nails bitten to the quick.

'I want to die long before you,' Eddie said, 'because I don't want to be left on my own.'

Mass looked pensive.

'Eddie,' she said, 'I'm fifty-six. And you're twenty-one. You can work out for yourself what that means.'

His heavy head sank and he looked despondent. Mass, who was christened Thomasine, a name she couldn't stand and had never used, wanted to comfort him.

'Don't think about it, it won't happen for a long time yet. We're both fit and healthy, we'll live for many more years, so we should just enjoy every single day of the time we have left.'

'What stops first? Your heart or your breathing?' Eddie asked.

'Depends,' Mass said. 'But I don't really know about things like that. Come on, let's go into the living room, *Tracker Tore* is about to start.'

The light from the screen flickered across Eddie's face. The blue and white shadows illuminated his heavy features and brought his face to life. He chewed the cinnamon rolls slowly, sipping from his can of Cherry Coke every so often. He loved the sweet, sickly, prickly cold feeling on his tongue.

His mother sat beside him with her feet on a footstool and a blanket over her knees. She glanced over at her son from time to time and wondered what would become of him, because Eddie was special. He didn't fit in with society. He had once got a job sorting post, but gave up after only fourteen days. He had struggled to get there on time in the morning, and found it hard being around strangers. There was no doubt that he had talents. He had once built a church with sugar lumps and icing sugar, which took him several weeks, it even had a spire. He was brilliant at doing crosswords and his memory was impressive. It was often he who had to remind her of things. When they sat together in the evenings, watching quizzes on TV, he knew more than she did even though she was thirty years older. Presumably he had gathered a lot of knowledge from the Internet, which she couldn't make head nor tail of, whereas he could sit in front of the computer for hours at a time. If she made the mistake of promising him something, he would never forget about it, and would not stop nagging until she had done what she promised. Like when he started to beg for a puppy eight years ago. She had said, let's see, but not right now. Well, when then? he wanted to know. In the summer maybe, I don't know, she said wearily. But is it more than a year? He pestered her like a horsefly. Eddie, she said, let's not talk about it any more. But when can we talk about it then? he wanted to know. Can we talk about it this evening? Or tomorrow perhaps? They had the same conversation at regular intervals. She had to give in eventually. And so Shiba arrived in the house, a soft, champagne-coloured puppy who chewed everything she could find: wires, several pairs of shoes, the book spines on the bottom shelf. An old thirteen-volume encyclopaedia, bound in red leather, had been stripped of its spines. But Eddie soon grew bored with the dog, and she knew for a fact that he taunted Shiba when she wasn't looking. But he still did some duties. He had to take her out for a walk three times a day. They were short walks, as both he and Shiba were overweight and slow.

She looked sideways at him now. There was something else that Eddie had begged for. He had wanted them to go to Copenhagen to look for his father's grave, and she had given her usual reply: we'll see. To be honest, she didn't even know where he was buried.

Eddie reached out for the last cinnamon roll; it was fresh and soft. He was glued to the screen, where Tore had boarded a plane for Lahore, together with a dark-skinned teenager called Susann. They were going to look for the girl's mother.

Every time Eddie saw someone, either on the road or at the shops – or simply on the television – his imagination ran wild. He could see that they had their own smell and taste, their resonance, like an instrument, or he would match them to an animal or a fruit or vegetable. He loved to play this game, he always had. He made a snap decision and never changed his mind. Their neighbour Ansgar, for example, was a sneaky hyena. Knut Nærum, who he saw on the telly every Friday, was a chirpy little meerkat. And the old lady in the house next door, Irene, who had Parkinson's, reminded him of jelly-like *lutefisk*, the way she wobbled. His mum sounded like an alto saxophone, and he himself was a beautiful, sonorous bassoon. Almost no one could master the bassoon. But

Mass, who was also woodwind, always managed to get him to make a sound.

But now, Tracker Tore. Tore was a turnip. Or a half-baked baguette.

'Do you think they'll find Susann's mother?' he asked, bright with anticipation.

'Of course,' Mass replied, 'otherwise they wouldn't have made the programme. But what's the point really? She's got such lovely parents in Norway. I'm sure she's much better off here than she would have been in Pakistan.'

Eddie didn't agree at all.

'But she's not the same colour as us. Of course she wants to see where she comes from, that kind of thing is important.'

'But things will just get more complicated with two sets of parents,' Mass continued. 'I mean, who should she listen to? Maybe they won't even want to see her; after all, there must be a reason she was adopted.'

'Maybe they didn't want to give her away,' Eddie said. 'Maybe she was taken from them.'

'In that case, her mother isn't a good mother,' Mass retorted. 'If she let them take away her child. And there's no reason to get in touch with a bad mother.'

The plane landed in Lahore, and Tore and Susann and a television crew found a taxi to take them through the hot streets. The sheer volume of traffic and noise, people and heat took their breath away. It seemed inconceivable to Eddie and Mass that they would be able to find Susann's mother at all in the chaos. But Tracker Tore knew what he was doing, he'd done his research. Susann's parents in Norway had given him the address of the children's home where she had been left sixteen years ago. When she was but a baby with no name.

They were met at the children's home by a friendly woman with a scarf over her head. She showed them into an office, where she opened a large book and started to read in good English.

'"Seventeenth of August, 1989,"' she read. '"A woman came in with a baby wrapped in a blanket. The baby had more or less just been born, and she didn't even have a name, so we christened her Adelina. The woman had had four children, and given them all up for adoption. We know nothing about the father."'

'But why?' they wanted to know. 'Why did she give them away?'

The principal of the children's home closed the big book and put her hands down on it, as though she wanted the secret to be kept there. Now that it was out in the open, she hoped that it would lead to some good, but she doubted it. Adelina, who had been given the name Susann in Norway, was a thin and beautiful girl in expensive clothes. She had been fortunate, she had everything a child could wish for. The principal looked into the nearly black eyes, wide open with anticipation, and felt a weight on her heart.

'Her mother was poor as a church mouse,' she said. 'She had nothing. It simply wasn't possible for her to keep any of her children.'

'But where does she live?' they wanted to know.

'In a village, some way from the city; you'll have to find a boat. I'll write down all the information you need, name and everything. Find a helmsman who can speak English, you'll need an interpreter.'

'God,' Mass exclaimed from her chair. 'How's it all going to end?'

Eddie sat leaning forward on the sofa; he was so excited that he was sitting with his mouth open, because now they were so close, so close. Back out on the street, Adelina-Susann bought a beautiful, colourful shawl that she wanted to give to her mother. It took some time to find a man who was willing to take them up the Ravi in a big flat-bottomed boat. He pushed his way upriver, while Tore and Susann explained in English why they were there. He didn't seem to be particularly interested; he was more concerned about the money he was going to get for the trip. They passed several small villages as they travelled, where lots of children sat on the bank and watched them pass. Some of them shouted and waved, jumping up and down in sheer delight.

'Imagine living like that,' Eddie said, chewing his cinnamon roll. 'They're cut off from the rest of the world. No TV, no phone, no computer. How's it possible?'

'It's perfectly possible to live a good life without all those things,' Mass pointed out. 'But they don't have enough food or medicine, and that's far worse.'

They followed the boat's progress. Mass poured some more coffee and Eddie clutched the now empty Cherry Coke can in his hand. Finally the boat moored at a small jetty, and some children immediately came running to meet them. Susann had the shawl on her lap, wrapped in brown paper. They clambered out of the boat and walked up a gentle slope full of lush green plants and beautiful trees. They were asked to wait. The helmsman disappeared over the top of the slope, leaving Tore and Susann sitting on the grass, with the half-naked children standing in a ring around them. Susann clutched the shawl in one hand, Tore held the other. After what felt like an eternity, the helmsman eventually came back. He had with him a very thin woman, barefoot and dressed in rags. Her face was dried out and wrinkled, and her eyes downcast. Susann got to her feet straight away, stood there staring at her mother. She tentatively held out her hand and the woman took it. This beautiful young girl in expensive clothes was the baby she had once given away, the last of the four children she had not been able to support. Susann gave her the present. But her mother made no move to open it; she was simply bewildered and desperate. She did try to smile, and Susann saw to her dismay that she had no teeth. All she could see was pale, bare gums in the middle of her wrinkly face. Poverty and destitution had made her old before her time.

'Oh, that's terrible!' Mass cried. 'Imagine finding your mother in that state. I'm sure the poor girl won't be able to sleep for years now. And it's just opening an old wound for the mother. Then pouring salt on it. Mark my words, Eddie.'

Eddie hung his head. He had hoped for a joyful reunion – touching scenes on the riverbank, with the children clapping their hands in delight. He was deeply upset by what he had seen. But he still believed it had to happen. Everyone had the right to know their origins. He got up, went over to the window and looked out. The snow lantern was still flickering silently in the dark. It would probably blow out in the course of the night. He just hoped it wouldn't be ruined by a new snowfall.

Chapter 6

The next day at nursery, Simon told Kaja about the five perfume bottles. He sat on the bench under his snail, with a bag full of spare clothes – in case he got wet in the snow – on his lap. Simon seemed happy and that was unusual. Kaja tried to prise the bag from him and hang it up on his peg, but he protested and wanted to keep it with him. Kaja liked Simon Hayden. He was quiet and shy, and she knew that he was often difficult in the mornings. He found the daily separation from his mother hard to accept.

'You're looking very secretive,' she said, and patted him on the head. She had to talk loudly to be heard over the noise of all the children. Simon opened his bag and took out a small parcel wrapped in pink paper. There was a blue ribbon round it, which his mother had curled.

'Is that for me?'

Kaja was surprised. Even though the walls in her kitchen were full of the children's drawings, she wasn't used to getting presents.

'You have to open it now,' Simon said.

His eyes were wide with anticipation. Kaja had to find some scissors to cut the ribbon. Some of the other children had gathered round to see, including Märta. Kaja tried to remove the ribbon and tape without spoiling the paper, but in the end she had to give up and tear it. Inside was a bottle of perfume.

'Oh, Simon,' she exclaimed in delight, 'you've given me one of the bottles? That's so kind of you, because the one I've got is almost empty.'

'I wanted to give it to you,' he said proudly. 'Mum's got so many. She's got enough perfume to last years.'

Märta leaned forwards and grabbed the bottle.

'I want some perfume too,' she said enviously.

'Maybe you could put it on your Christmas list,' Kaja suggested. 'You can ask your mum.'

'We're going to the toy shop today,' Simon said. 'I'm going to get a present too. So long as it doesn't cost more than two hundred kroner.'

Bonnie had parked the old Opel outside Ingemar's house. She thought it was a good day, even though the snow was falling heavily. But it was always a challenge, because Ingemar was not easy to help. They give me all the difficult ones, she thought, it's not fair. They could have divvied it up better. She steeled herself and opened the door. Ingemar never bothered to lock it, it was left open overnight. He had worked in the police all his life and didn't worry about burglars. People could just come and go as they pleased. Bonnie stopped in the small living room for a moment, even though she knew he was sitting in the kitchen, because he always did. The smell of old man and old food hit her as soon as she went into the kitchen.

'Hello, it's just me.'

He grunted something incomprehensible in reply. He was looking out of the window, busy watching two horses wandering around in the white snow. All his food was out on the worktop and table – he never put it back in the fridge – and it had all gone off. The jam was mouldy and the liver pâté was changing colour. He lifted a bottle of cod liver oil and took a few slugs. Ingemar was eighty-six and had been a widower since he was forty. He had children who couldn't bear coming to see him and in a way she could understand them, because he was cantankerous and downright unfriendly. He lived his life in filthy chaos. Bonnie sat down on a stool. It was a good day, but she still felt unmotivated. It was always hard to get started, and no matter what she tried to do, Ingemar always protested: surely that's not necessary. The Hoover is too noisy, I don't like it. But she carried on regardless. The rug under the furniture in the living room was heavy, it was impossible to carry it out onto the snow, even though she should probably have done that. She straightened up and started to move the furniture out of the way. It weighed a ton, just like Erna's furniture. She got the vacuum cleaner out of the cupboard. It was an old Volta and wasn't much good. Still, she had to do something to fill the hours. She was soon finished, and started to wash the floor. Ingemar didn't budge from his chair in the kitchen, so she had to mop around his feet. Suddenly he looked away from the window.

'You have to change the bed,' he said abruptly.

Bonnie looked at him in surprise. He never asked her to do anything, so in a way it was an improvement. She finished what she was doing, put the bucket back in the cupboard, and went over the furniture with some polish.

51

She liked the smell of it, and it made everything shiny and bright. Then she went to the bedroom and pulled up sharp in the doorway. A nauseating stench hit her. The bed had been stripped and there were big brown stains on the light-coloured mattress. It took a while before she realised what had happened. He had soiled himself in bed. And then he had stripped the bed himself. Bonnie put a hand over her mouth. This can't be true, she thought. She stood there, surrounded by the awful smell, wondering where to begin. On an impulse she went out into the bathroom and found the bedclothes in the bath, just as she had thought. He had left the duvet cover, sheet and pillowcases to soak in cold water. The water was brown and she could see lumps of shit floating around. She sat down on the toilet seat and pulled at her hair. She didn't know how long she sat there, all she could think about was old Ingemar in the kitchen drinking cod liver oil. Pretending that nothing had happened. Then she made a decision. She called Ragnhild at the office.

'The whole bath is full of shit,' she explained. 'And his mattress is soaking wet. He can't sleep in that bed. Everything has to go!'

Ragnhild heard the desperation in Bonnie's voice.

'I'll talk to his daughter; we have to get him into a home. Things can't go on like this.'

'I know,' Bonnie said. 'But it takes time, and right now I have to help him.'

Ragnhild thought for a moment. She was a nurse and had experienced most things.

'Tell Ingemar that you have to go out. Go to the Bed Store and get a new duvet and pillow. Have you got enough money to pay for it? I'll make sure you're reimbursed by social services.'

Bonnie said that was fine.

'But what should I do with the mattress?'

'He'll just have to carry on using it for the moment,' Ragnhild said. 'But you might want to wash it with chlorine, and turn it.'

Bonnie thanked her for her help. She went back into the kitchen and explained to Ingemar that she had to go out, but would be back soon to sort everything out. He was obviously bothered by what had happened during the night and was still staring defiantly at the horses outside the window.

She drove into the centre of town. She used her card to pay for the parking and then walked the two blocks to the Bed Store. When she got there and started to look around, she discovered that a feather duvet cost a lot of money, and she didn't have much in her account. So she had to buy a thin synthetic duvet that only cost two hundred kroner. She found a pillow to match, paid for the whole lot and put the receipt in her purse, then hurried back to the car. She had to get a move on; her other clients would be waiting. When she got back to the house, she nodded to Ingemar as she passed through the kitchen and set to work. She found some yellow rubber gloves and two black bin liners in the cupboard. She pulled the plug out of the bath and tried to wring as much water as possible out of the soiled duvet cover, but it wasn't easy. Because it was wet, it weighed a ton and it was hard to get it all into the bin liner. She put the dirty sheet and pillow in the other bag. She tied them closed and carried them out into the snow, because if they were left in the house they'd stink the place out. She went back in and got started on the mattress. Even though she didn't manage to remove the stains completely, she got rid of a lot and the smell faded. Then she turned it. She found some clean bedlinen, which she had washed a while before in Ingemar's old machine down in the cellar, and made up the bed and washed the floor. Finally, she went back into the bathroom and scrubbed the bath.

'That's me finished,' she told Ingemar. 'Everything's done now.'

He didn't want to look at her. Maybe he was ashamed after all. She went out to the car and called the office.

'I've done it,' she said to Ragnhild. 'It wasn't as bad as I thought. The rubbish bags are standing in the snow outside. His children can deal with them. If they bother to show up.'

'Bonnie, I have to thank you,' Ragnhild said. 'I'm pretty certain that none of the others would have done that, but then none of the others are as dedicated as you.'

Bonnie put the key in the ignition and started the car.

'You can go home now,' Ragnhild said, all of a sudden.

'I'm sorry?'

Bonnie was so surprised her mouth dropped open.

'You earned some extra time off. You're invaluable.'

When Bonnie appeared in the doorway to the playroom, Simon jumped with joy. He ran across the floor into her arms as fast as his little legs would carry him. She squeezed him tight.

'Was Kaja pleased to get the perfume?' she whispered.

Simon nodded happily.

'But Märta was jealous.'

Bonnie smiled and said not to worry. She carried him in her arms to the office, where Kaja was doing some paperwork, exchanged a few friendly words with her, then took him out to the car.

'The toy shop,' she said. 'I promised you yesterday. Have you thought about something you'd like that isn't too expensive?'

Simon beamed from the back seat. Oh yes, he had thought about it a lot. Because he'd once gone Christmas shopping with Granny Henny and had seen something that he really liked. But it wasn't what he got that Christmas and he'd never forgotten about it.

The car park by the shopping centre was full, so Bonnie waited patiently, and soon enough she saw a van reverse out of a parking place.

'That was lucky.'

She slipped the Opel into the space, and they got out. Simon was so excited that he climbed the high escalator steps. They went into the toy shop and started to browse along the shelves, but it was clear that Simon was looking for something in particular, because he was patient and systematic. Every now and then he lifted something up, stood for a while admiring it, but his mind wandered back and he continued his search. He finally found himself in front of a shelf with all kinds of animals in all shapes and colours. There were lots of cuddly fur toys, but he already had a well-loved teddy bear with black glass eyes. No, he was looking for something else. He picked up some big bags of colourful plastic animals, each containing different things. One of them was full of rubber snakes with beautiful zigzag patterns on their backs and red, poisonous tongues.

'Ugh, you don't want snakes, do you?' Bonnie shivered. 'They're horrible.'

Simon liked them, they were soft and nice to touch, but he put them down again. He lifted up another bag, this one full of Norwegian farm animals: sheep and cows and horses, a goose with orange feet, some hens and a spotty dog. He put these animals back too. And when he lifted up the third bag, he had found what he was looking for. Wild animals from the African savannah. A lion with a great mane. An elephant, a giraffe, a rhinoceros and a hippopotamus. An ape and a beautiful flamingo, a gnu and a hyena and a vulture.

'One hundred and ninety-eight kroner,' Bonnie said. 'We've got just enough.'

They paid for the animals, and Simon carried them out in a carrier bag. As they approached the car, Bonnie suddenly stopped. On the windscreen, under the wipers, was a piece of yellow paper. For some reason, she'd been given a parking ticket. With slow steps, she went up to the car and snatched up the piece of paper; it was like plastic, weather-resistant. She had parked in a handicapped parking place. The low sign showing the disabled symbol was buried by the snow, so she hadn't seen it. Seven hundred kroner, she sobbed. Simon could see that his mother was upset. And even though he was happy to have his animals, this alarmed him. Bonnie put the yellow piece of paper in her bag and made light of it. She didn't want to ruin the day.

Once they were home, Simon asked for some scissors. He cut open the bag and let all the wild animals fall onto the floor. With great respect, he placed them in a big circle with the lion in the middle; only the buffalo was walking away.

'Scar?' Bonnie asked.

'Mufasa,' Simon replied. 'We should get a jungle.'

Bonnie looked around the living room. She had pot plants on two windowsills, so she lifted them down, one by one. She made a lush green ring with them round the animals.

'Which one do you like best?' she asked.

'All of them,' Simon said without hesitation.

He knelt on the worn wooden floor and admired the wild animals, lifting them up one by one, smelling them. Bonnie went out into the kitchen, where she opened her handbag. Found the yellow slip and dried a tear.

Chapter 7

July 2005

Frank was lying with his head on Sejer's feet. Sejer liked the feeling of being close to something warm and alive, even if that generally meant he got wet socks because the dog slobbered. He was holding a glass of whisky in his hand, with no ice. On the table beside him was a pouch of tobacco, which he rarely opened, being a man of moderation.

He thought about Bonnie Hayden. The long knife had pierced her body four times. In a fury, or more methodically? He was certain that the murder had been planned, that there was a motive behind the evil act, a motive that he could not yet see. He had studied the photographs of the naked bodies for some time, Bonnie slim, Simon thin as a beanstalk. Both of them washed clean of blood, leaving the sharp wounds gaping, strangely narrow and precise. Bonnie had a tattoo on her shoulder. And over her breast, three moles in a gentle arc, which reminded him of Orion's Belt. He could just picture a man, perhaps Simon's father, stroking a finger over them, counting them solemnly. He could not imagine the fear and terror that must have filled the old caravan. But sometimes his imagination ran riot and then he struggled to breathe. When the glass was empty, he got up and switched off the lamp, and on his way to the bathroom, he passed a photograph of his late wife, Elise.

'I'll never get over it,' he said to the picture. 'Time passes, but this is not what I'd hoped for. Just so you know.'

Chapter 8

Robert Randen saw the car through the kitchen window. He had been expecting the police, so he immediately went out to meet them and ushered them back into the kitchen.

'We can talk in here.'

There was a long, sanded wooden table with eight chairs, each with a simple pattern carved on the back. Randen himself stood by the worktop.

'I can't sleep,' he said. 'I keep remembering the smell. It smelt like a slaughterhouse.'

Sejer thought to himself that it would be impossible to live with the scene that Randen had discovered. He would remember even when he was sitting in an old people's home. It would haunt him until the end of his days.

'How many people live here on the farm?' Skarre wanted to know.

'My wife Solveig, myself and our four girls in the main house. My mother lives in the cottage on the other side of the yard. And there are four Poles in the outhouse. So that's eleven in total.'

'Could the killer have walked through the farm?'

'Well, of course. I mean, we're not always standing at the window, but I'm pretty sure he didn't, as there's practically always someone outside here. Certainly in summer. No, I reckon he crossed the fields. From the woods. If he had a car, he might have parked it at Geirastadir. Lots of walkers do that: there's plenty of room for cars there. In the autumn, people come to pick berries to sell at the market, but they usually come on mopeds. And most of them are from Lithuania.'

'Can you tell me about your four Polish farmhands?' Sejer asked. 'Do they come back every year?'

Randen had decided that he wanted to sit down after all, and he pulled out a chair. Like most farmers, he was strong, lean and weathered. His thick hair was the colour of sand, and he would never lose it.

'This is the eighth year that they've come, so I know them well. They all have families back in Poland and they all have children. They've also got jobs to go back to in the autumn, and all four of them work hard and well, without complaining. We've never had any problems with them and they're never ill. They get up before us and go to bed late. I understand why you have to ask, but I would vouch for all four of them. Why on earth would they have anything to do with this? It's out of the question.'

Skarre shook his head.

'We don't think they're involved either, but we still have to question them. Could they manage in English?'

'Woiciech speaks Norwegian. He's pretty good.'

'Tell me about Bonnie Hayden and her son,' Sejer said. 'In as much detail as possible.'

'Well, they just appeared here on the steps. They were holding hands. The mother had picked a bunch of wild flowers, and she seemed a bit embarrassed, as if she was reluctant to ask. It was obvious that she was doing it for the boy, he was practically hopping on the spot. She asked if I owned the old caravan at the bottom of the field, and when I said yes, the boy could hardly contain himself. She told me that they'd walked past it and the boy wondered if they could spend the night there. That's all she said, and she squeezed the boy's hand while they waited for an answer. I said of course they could.

'To be honest, I was touched by the pair of them, but I did tell them that the caravan was in a terrible state – it's practically uninhabitable. But then they said that they'd already been inside and that it was good enough for them for just one night. They would go home to get some food, and bring their bedding back with them. I said that was fine, and the boy really did jump for joy. "How much would you like for the night?" she asked. I almost laughed. "My dear," I said, "I don't want anything for it. The caravan hasn't been used for years, and should really be taken to the scrapyard." They looked around at all the farm buildings. Asked if they could park here, and I showed them a place behind the outhouse, where the car wouldn't be in the way. And then they set off towards Geirastadir, to drive home and get all they needed. They waved to me before they disappeared. "We'll be back this evening then," the mother called to me. She seemed happy enough. And then they were gone.'

Randen folded his hands on the solid table.

'When the men came back in that evening, I told them that the pair of them were coming, so that they'd know. The Opel drove into the farm around seven o'clock. It was barely holding together, in a worse state than the caravan. I went out to greet them and to see if they needed any help carrying things down. The mother had a couple of duvets over her arm and the boy was holding a pillow and an old teddy bear. No, they'd manage themselves, they said.

I watched them walk down across the fields; there was something quite sad about them.'

'What do you mean by that? Sad in what way?'

'I'm not really sure how to put it. Like they were two lonely souls in a big world. They came back again about an hour later and disappeared round to the car, only to reappear a few minutes later carrying a pizza box and a bag, which they took down to the caravan. Then I forgot about them and got on with other chores – there's always plenty to do on a big farm like this.'

He focused on a knot in the table; they could hear his breathing.

'Why did you go down to the caravan the next day?' Sejer asked. 'You found them at 2 p.m. What were you doing down there?'

'I just went to say hello. To ask how the night had been.'

He told them that his wife had been busy baking all morning. An apple cake and an almond cake. The girls wanted the almond cake, and they decided to give the apple cake to the pair in the caravan. Emilie, aged ten, was allowed to put the thin slices of Pink Lady apples in the bottom of the tin like brickwork, and Solveig rolled the dough into thin sausages which she then wove in a pattern on the cake and covered it with generous helpings of nib sugar and almonds. 'So I took the apple cake and went down across the field,' Randen explained. 'The door was open. I knocked on the wall and called out hello so they wouldn't get a fright when I suddenly appeared in the doorway.

'This might sound a bit dramatic, but I don't think my life will ever be the same.'

The four Poles were waiting outside the house and were all clearly affected by what had happened. Two of them had seen Simon outside the caravan, carrying his teddy bear. His mother had been standing in the doorway and waved to them as they passed, and they had touched their caps with their brown working hands and waved back. Beautiful weather, they had called, and she had smiled and nodded.

'Think carefully now,' Sejer urged them. 'Did you see anything that might be of importance? I mean, people or cars in the vicinity of the farm in the days beforehand?'

They looked at each other. They had talked about this. The oldest of them, Woiciech, who was in fact a butcher back home in Poland, had seen an unknown car on the road up to the farm. On 4 July. It might have been following the Opel, but it had stopped some distance from the farm.

'Can you describe the car?' Skarre said.

'Definitely not new,' Woiciech replied. 'Red.'

Skarven Farm had been in the Randen family for four generations, and Robert Randen and his wife Solveig were used to working hard from morning to night. Their four daughters also had duties, and Randen hoped that the eldest girl, Johanne, would take over the farm in a few years' time. The family were sitting around the table eating supper in silence. Eventually, Solveig put down her fork and turned to her husband.

'When can we get rid of the caravan?'

'As soon as the police give us permission.'

'Will they wash it?' she asked.

'I very much doubt it. That's not the way it works. We should ask the boys in this evening, we need to talk.'

The youngest daughter, Emilie, looked at her father.

'Are we going to the funeral?'

'No, sweetheart,' Randen said. 'We won't be. We're not family.'

'But they died here. In one of our fields.'

'Yes, Emilie. But we should leave the family in peace.'

'Will they be in the same coffin?'

'No, sweetie, they'll each get their own. One big, one small.'

Ma, the cat, wandered in through the open door. She was a beautiful grey cat, well preened. She jumped up onto Emilie's lap, and curled up in a ball. Emilie's mother wanted to push the cat down, but she stopped herself. Everything was topsy-turvy on Skarven Farm, nothing was as it should be, and she felt it might never be again.

The girls cleared the table and put everything in the dishwasher, then they pushed all the chairs back in under the table. Randen lay down on the sofa in the living room and the cat came running over and jumped up onto his chest. The cat was heavy and made it harder to breathe, but he let the animal lie there. He felt Ma's warmth through his shirt and it calmed his nerves. Randen was a level-headed man, but now his thoughts were racing, because whoever had used that knife in the caravan was alive somewhere. He lived, he breathed, he ate, he slept. He talked and interacted with people who knew nothing, who smiled and laughed. While he waited for his pursuers. And in no way regretted what he had done.

I hope it will rain before too long, Randen thought. The farm needs rain. Perhaps we *should* go to the funeral. They did die here after all, on our property, in our field.

Chapter 9

December 2004

Mass had a full-length mirror in her bedroom, and she was standing there now, twisting and turning in front of it, with a dissatisfied look on her face. Everything had started to droop: her jowls, her breasts, her stomach, a great roll over the top of her pants like rising white dough. As she stood there, looking at her reflection, she felt a dull pain at the base of her spine. There, you see, she said to herself, that'll be all the cleaning I did yesterday, getting ready for Christmas. She had carried the heavy rugs out onto the snow, cleaned the floors. She had washed everywhere in every room, she was thorough. Eddie was no good at cleaning, all he could do was clear the snow. But the pain in her back – well, she wasn't actually stiff, it was more of a pulsing ache. The pain came in waves, running up and down her spine. She had never felt anything like it before. She turned her back to the mirror as if to look for an explanation. But there was nothing to see, of course. And as she stared into the glass, the pain disappeared just as suddenly as it had come. She pulled a brush through her thick hair, got dressed and went out into the living room.

Eddie was sitting at the computer, as usual. She stood and studied his broad back. She often wondered about her grown son. He had never been given a diagnosis, and so had fallen between all the stools in the system. She had managed to fight her way to a small allowance for him, after many visits to the GP who knew him well. And she had sent endless forms to NAV and the jobcentre. What will happen to him when I'm no longer here? she fretted. Even though he did have some skills, he was still helpless and so dependent on her, it was exhausting. He clung to her, nagged her, was on at her constantly. But he was all she had, so she accepted it without complaint, because he also brought her a lot of joy.

'What are you doing?' she asked as she sat down and reached for the paper.

'On the Internet,' he said, without turning round. 'Google.'

'What are you looking for? Seems to me that you're always sitting there.'

Eddie's fat fingers bounced on the keyboard. He muttered quietly at regular intervals. Mass was now very curious. She put down the newspaper, got up and went over to him.

'What have you found?'

Eddie read: '"The authorities in Ohio are now planning to try the new method using only one injection, after the execution of one felon took a full two hours, as they had great difficulties finding a vein. The usual method comprises three injections: the prisoner is first injected with a dose of barbiturate, then something to paralyse the muscles, and finally, an injection to stop the heart."'

Mass had her arm round Eddie's shoulder. She put her hand against his warm neck; she loved his wonderful soft, curly hair and played with it as often as she had the chance, and he never tried to stop her.

'Or,' Eddie continued, 'the electric chair. Two thousand volts to the head, with a big wet sponge under the helmet. They can choose how they want to die. What would you choose?'

Eddie Malthe looked at his mother and smiled.

'I'm curious about everything,' he explained, 'and it's fun finding out about stuff.'

'Death and destruction are hardly fun,' Mass scolded. 'Find something else.'

'Did you know,' Eddie continued enthusiastically, 'when you're hanged, everything goes black after seven seconds? It's an underrated method, I think.'

He finished what he was doing and got up from the chair, walked heavily across the room, plonked down on the sofa and picked up the paper. He turned to the crossword on the second-last page and started to chew his pencil as he read. He liked the taste. He was well trained after all these years, and he seldom needed to rub anything out, and when he did, he sat there and sniffed it, it smelt sweet. He knew most of the compilers, knew what they were interested in: science, history, geography and politics, the human body. Astronomy. The odd abbreviation, every now and then a made-up word that didn't actually exist. Cheating nonsense, was what he thought then, no fun at all. But now he was stuck. *Gas escape, two words, fifteen letters.* Was a gas explosion the same as a gas escape? Only twelve letters. Volcano explosion? Sixteen letters. He wrote it down with some uncertainty, but soon realised that it had to be wrong. Because that involved magma, which turned to lava when it ran down the mountainside. But where would you find gas? In nature. And presumably in heavy industry. He carried on with the crossword and got the first letter of the second word, which was a 'p'. And the last letter was 'r'. Then he got an 'm' and an 's'. Solar prominence. The great flames on the surface of the sun that can reach for thousands of kilometres into space. He pondered the next clue: *seam*. Six letters, the second of which was 'u'. Suture. *Thread, six letters*; that was hard. The first was 'c' and the fifth was 'u'. Catgut. When he was halfway through the crossword, he decided to keep the rest for later. So he turned to the obituaries. *Fredrik was only twenty-two when he chose to leave life. The service will end at the grave. No flowers please.* Twenty-two, he thought. He must have had a miserable life. Eddie couldn't understand why anyone would choose to take their own life, to die when they didn't need to.

'Don't forget to take Shiba out,' his mother called from the kitchen, where she was peeling root vegetables. Eddie went out into the hall to get his jacket and pulled a hat down over his curls. He put a lead on the fat dog and went out into the snow. Before he turned out onto the road, he stopped and admired his snow lantern; it was still standing. Every evening after dark, he lifted off the top snowballs and lit a new candle.

Shiba stopped as soon as they were out on the road. She went down on her haunches and did her business. When Eddie tried to make her carry on, she resisted, but he hauled her over to the mailbox all the same. He opened it and took out the post; two bills: electricity and telephone. Just as he was about to turn round, their neighbour, Ansgar, came out of the house. His cat, Kennedy, slipped out behind him, a dirty yellow, scraggy cat with slit eyes. Eddie didn't like Ansgar at all, and he didn't like the cat either, it was horrible. That cat, he often thought to himself; one day

I'm going to lure it inside. And I'm going to boil it in a large pan on the cooker until the meat's falling off the bones. Then I'll leave the carcass on Ansgar's step. I'll hide behind a tree and watch his horror. No doubt there'll be uproar, and Ansgar will call the police and the local paper.

'Hi,' Ansgar said merrily. 'You walking the dog? I guess it's good to have something to do; the days must drag when you don't work.'

Eddie didn't answer. He started to pull at Shiba's lead, but she'd sat down and wouldn't budge.

'There was a job advertised in the paper yesterday,' Ansgar carried on. 'I don't know whether you saw it. A maintenance company were looking for people. And I thought of you, you know, because you don't really need a degree to change a light bulb.'

'They do more than just changing light bulbs,' Eddie muttered. 'Anyway, I'm not fit for work, the doctor says so.'

Ansgar grinned. His teeth were small and sharp and rather yellow.

'But most people can do something. You clear the snow like a professional. You could clear snow for me as well, if you like,' he added. 'I'd pay you.'

Eddie jerked the lead violently, pulling Shiba to her feet, and tramped off down the road without saying a word. When he got back inside, he undid the lead and took off his jacket, then he went into the kitchen and put the two envelopes down on the table. Mass looked at them despondently, then turned back to what she was doing. Eddie sank down onto a chair and Shiba collapsed in the corner and fell asleep.

'She can hardly walk,' Eddie stated. 'There's something wrong with her back legs.'

Mass turned to her son.

'I know. I keep meaning to take her to the vet and then I put it off.'

'Well, I think I know what's going to happen,' Eddie said, and put his great hands down on the table.

Now it was Mass's turn not to answer. She wearily brushed the hair back from her forehead. Eddie got up and went over to Shiba. He lay down on the floor beside her, despite his size. The dog moved uneasily and wanted to get away, but didn't have the energy. Eddie edged his hand in under her chest. He could feel her little dog heart beating softly.

Chapter 10

July 2005

'Take all calls seriously,' Konrad Sejer said. 'Write down all the details: names, places, times, cars and people. And for that matter, any random suspicions. People who are simply curious, or who have a fertile imagination. Divide them up among yourselves and be vigilant. I want to know every little thing. And if you're in doubt, talk to Skarre; we can't afford to overlook anything. Put everything else to one side.'

He went over to the map on the wall and pointed.

'We are assuming that he got there via one of the three following routes. One: from the parking place at Geirastadir, down over the fields, presumably along the edge of the woods. Jacob and I will walk that route. It takes fifteen minutes. Route two: he came from Haugane. Again, he might have parked a bit further away – we're assuming that he got there by car, even though we probably shouldn't. It's a shorter distance and perhaps more likely. The third alternative is of course that he walked through Skarven Farm, but that's unlikely. What's more, he was carrying a knife. He may have hidden this on his person, but the chances of being seen were greater, considering that eleven people live there.'

He left the map and sat back down at the table.

'One of the Polish farm workers said he saw an old red car some way down the road to the farm. On the fourth of July. He had never seen the car before, but it stopped there for a few minutes, before it disappeared. He thought that perhaps they'd taken a wrong turning. But the car is clearly of interest. He may have been watching Bonnie and Simon for some days before he killed them. At some point he must have seen them disappear into the caravan. God only knows what he thought.'

He looked at the people around him; there were ten of them, seven men and three women. They took notes, listened carefully and with great respect. They met in this room every morning at seven o'clock, when the day's tasks were assigned. All of them had their own field.

'He's left no fingerprints,' Sejer said. 'So we have to assume he was wearing gloves. Which is why it's strange that he left the knife behind. That's quite something to forget. So it's chaotic. Planned, but still a bit chaotic. This didn't happen in the heat of the moment, this was intentional.'

Sejer and Skarre sat in the canteen at lunchtime. It was warm outside, and the long-term forecast was that the heat would continue. Sejer had only taken a mineral water, whereas Skarre was working his way through a prawn-and-egg sandwich. When they were finished, they went down to the car park under the station. Skarre reversed the patrol car out, and they set off towards Geirastadir, which was a popular area for walkers.

'We'll get him,' Skarre said. 'But he's psychotic and he won't go to prison. He'll end up in psychiatric hospital and will be released after a couple of years, with the help of medication. He'll say he can't remember anything. I suggest we throw him into the cell head first. And throw the key away in deep water.'

Sejer stared out of the car window.

'I'm sure plenty would agree with you. But our system's not like that. Yes, he'll be out on the streets again in a few years, living among us. He'll get a house, he'll get a job, he'll get a life.'

'You can't atone for something like this.'

'Probably not. But you work for the police, you just have to swallow it. Here, don't forget to turn, we're going to the right.'

The road was full of stones and potholes, and Skarre piloted the car as carefully as possible along the final stretch to the parking place. There were a number of other cars there, and a young couple were busy putting their toddler, a thin little body with a sun hat, into a blue child carrier. There was a wooden signpost at the far end. Saga 9 kilometres, Svarttjern 4 kilometres, Haugane 3 kilometres. The man had got the child in place and now lifted the carrier up onto his back, while the woman put on a pair of sunglasses. But they stayed standing where they were when the two men approached.

'Do you come here often?' Sejer asked.

Yes, they told him that they did, but no, they had not been here on 5 July. They hadn't noticed anything out of the ordinary. They chose the path up to Svarttjern, and Sejer and Skarre set off along the path over the fields to Skarven Farm. Skarre took his time. As they walked, they kept an eye out for the Polish workers. Even though Randen said he could vouch for them, there was no getting round the fact that they had been near the scene of the crime. They had seen the woman and child at close hand, followed them with their eyes. No one knew about their past in Poland, and the eldest, Woiciech, was in fact a butcher. But it was perhaps a bit unfair to hold that against him. For a while they walked in silence under the baking sun. Skarre was sweating in his uniform. He was firing on all cylinders.

'At the very least we're talking about a behavioural disorder,' he said, 'and there're all kinds of them. Maybe he's been deeply offended by something, maybe he was high.'

They walked in silence again. Skarre checked the time. 'Thirteen minutes,' he reported. 'And there's the caravan.'

They stopped and stared, then ducked under the red-and-white police cordon and walked over to the small house on wheels, surrounded by the dark trees. From a distance, it looked idyllic, but as they approached they both got a knot in their stomach. The narrow door was closed and they stopped at the step. Skarre sat down. He had a bag of jelly babies in his inner pocket; he picked out a green one and popped it in his mouth, it was still quite fresh. As he chewed, he looked up at the farm. They saw a man coming down across the field and recognised Robert Randen in his blue boiler suit.

'I saw you from the window,' he said when he reached them. 'How's it going?'

Sejer stood with his back to the caravan.

'I heard you found a footprint,' Randen continued. 'Can you deduce anything from that? From just a shoe?'

He dug his hands into his pockets.

'How did you know that?'

'I heard it when you were working down here, that there was a print on the floor.'

'You must absolutely not mention that to anyone,' Sejer ordered. 'If that information gets out to the press, he'll have ample opportunity to get rid of the shoes.'

Randen understood.

'What I really wanted to know is when I can get rid of the caravan,' he said. 'It's the wife who's asking. We can see it from the bedroom window, you know; it upsets her. She stands there in the evening looking down here, can't find peace. I've forbidden the girls to come anywhere near the caravan – not that they want to anyway. But their classmates are clamouring for all the details. The local paper was at the door yesterday, wanted to hear my version. Though I chose not to tell them.'

'We support you on that one,' Skarre said from the step.

'Will you be going to the funeral?' Randen asked.

'Yes,' Sejer said, 'it's a matter of course. We'll have a lot to do with the family, for quite some time possibly.'

Randen made to leave, but then turned round once more.

'Yes, that was it, I was wondering if I can get rid of the caravan. Soonish.'

'No,' Sejer confirmed. 'I'm afraid it's going to have to stay here for the moment.'

They then drove on to Haugane. They stood for a while surveying the landscape. They could see down to the farm from here too, and once again, Skarre timed how long it took them to walk there. It was shorter, but rougher underfoot, and it wasn't easy to know which way he might have walked. But they still wanted to walk it themselves, and as they did so, they kept their eyes peeled. They found nothing and they saw nothing. On the way back to the station, they stopped at a petrol station and Sejer went in to buy the local newspaper. Then he sat in the car and flicked through it. He eventually found the death notice. Bonnie's mother, Henny Hayden, had written it with the help of the funeral directors.

Our dearly beloved daughter Bonnie and dearest grandchild Simon were suddenly and brutally torn from us today. Haugane, 5 July. Henny and Henrik.

Chapter 11

December 2004

Bonnie was due to go to Kristine that morning, but she went to the office first to talk to Ragnhild. She handed over the receipt for the bedding she had bought for Ingemar, and Ragnhild promised to have the money transferred. They sat for some time talking about the situation; Ragnhild had been in contact with the family and they seemed to understand how serious it was.

'We'll try to find a quick solution,' she promised, 'because it can't go on like this. Who's first on your list today?'

'Kristine.'

'Grit your teeth.'

Kristine lived at Reistad with her husband and two children. The house was luxurious and well positioned, with a big double garage and pillars by the front door, with decorative hop vines growing up them. There was an iron horseshoe under the nameplate. Every time Bonnie went there, she was struck by all the wealth, so unlike her own world. She went up to the door – a carved oak door – and when she put her finger on the bell, she heard a quiet ding-dong inside. She opened the door and went in, stood for a moment in the hall – it was almost as big as her living room. The stone floors were covered with rugs, which Kristine had told her were Persian Hamadan carpets. Bonnie didn't really know what that meant; she had a rug from IKEA that cost nine hundred kroner, with a deep, pepper-coloured shag. No doubt knotted by children with tiny fingers. She went upstairs to the main floor and found Kristine and the children in the kitchen. The children, who were eight and nine, were eating sandwiches. They both suffered from allergies, were oversensitive in every way to food and pollen and dust – and animals, of course. So it was Bonnie's job to keep the dust at bay. Kristine was only thirty-two, but she had still been given a home help for an indefinite period. Following a visit to a chiropractor, she had suffered temporary paralysis in her legs and she moved slowly and with great difficulty around the huge house. She couldn't do the housework, so she spent most of her time making food that Thomas and Tale could eat. She was a flight attendant for SAS and her husband was a pilot.

'Daddy's in Bangkok,' Thomas told her.

'How exciting,' Bonnie replied. 'Maybe he'll bring you back a present, I'm sure you'd like that.'

'When you've eaten, you can go and tidy your rooms,' Kristine said.

'The home help can do that,' Tale said, chewing her chocolate spread sandwich.

Her mother didn't correct her. Bonnie went into the little girl's room and stood there gathering her thoughts and her energy. Tale had hordes of cuddly toys on her bed. Bonnie had once counted them and there were nineteen in all, big and small. She thought about the one teddy bear she had given Simon. She went to get the vacuum cleaner out of the cupboard and set to work. When she had finished, she went into Thomas's room. There were no cuddly toys here, but he had shelves and shelves of model planes, cars and ships that his father had bought him on his long journeys. When she was finished there, she put the vacuum cleaner away and went back to the kitchen.

'I've thought of something,' Kristine said. She was standing by the worktop, hands on hips. 'Maybe we could go through the bookshelves today, I've had an idea.'

Bonnie accepted the order without saying anything.

'All the books have got covers,' Kristine explained, 'and as a rule they're pretty awful. But underneath they're faux leather, some are even real leather, and they're mostly black or red. So if you take down all the books, take off the covers and then put them back according to colour, that would be rather smart, wouldn't it?'

Bonnie nodded mechanically. As so often before, she thought that it wasn't strictly speaking a job for the home help, but she always went that little bit further for her clients. And who knows, sorting the books might be nicer than cleaning the floor, even though that was probably what she should be doing, given all their allergies. She went into the spacious living room and looked at the bookshelves. They were also made of oak, three of them along one wall, and they were relatively low. At least she wouldn't need to stand on a chair. She took all the books out of the shelves. *The Price of Love*, she read, and *Hunger of the Heart*. *Death of a Swallow* and *Rebecca's Choice*. Bonnie stacked the books in piles on the floor, not too high as she was scared they might topple over, so it was better to have a good system, just in case. Her back got tired bending over to reach the lowest shelves, and sometimes she got down on her knees. She could hear the children out in the kitchen; they were quarrelling. She carried on taking the books out, and when the shelves were empty, she went to get the polish. Just like Kristine had said, most of the spines were either black or red, but there were a few brown and green too, which she put back on the bottom shelves. Then the black ones, and finally the red books on top. She worked slowly and systematically, putting the books back one by one, all the covers lying in a big heap on the floor. Kristine came in when she was almost done. She had a black rubbish bag with her and asked if Bonnie could go down and throw it all away in the paper collection by the road. She stepped back and admired the shelves from a distance, pointed with a red-polished fingernail.

'Super.'

Afterwards, Bonnie drove to the By the Way cafe, where she bought a cheese-and-ham roll and a cup of coffee. She sat at a table by the window and planned the evening in her mind. Britt, who had been such a good friend over the past few years, especially since she had been alone with Simon, was coming to visit and she was looking forward to it. Whenever she came round, they sat for hours chatting, and once Simon had gone to sleep they would swap secrets. She watched the traffic outside as she ate her roll. There were a lot of lorries. Rows of trailers were always parked up outside By the Way, many of them foreign, from Germany and Poland, the Netherlands and Denmark. When she had finished, she got up from the table and drove over to Gjertrud.

Gjertrud was the highlight of the week. The kind-hearted old lady made Bonnie's job worthwhile, despite all the other hard work. She was by no means her oldest client: Jørgen was a hundred and one whereas Gjertrud had just turned eighty-five. She was bright and lively for her age, but suffered terribly from arthritis; her fingers were bent like claws and she was in a lot of pain. But she never complained. When she stood in the doorway and greeted Bonnie, her face lit up. Her white hair looked unkempt and Bonnie decided to do it for her today. They sat for a while in the comfortable armchairs in her living room, and Gjertrud raised a glass of eau de vie and took a sip.

'I have a little glass every day,' she said. 'Do you think that matters?'

'No,' Bonnie replied firmly. 'I'm sure it's good for you.'

The old woman smiled gratefully. She only just managed to hold the glass with the arthritic fingers. Bonnie leaned back in the chair, all she wanted to do was close her eyes, but she knew that she couldn't because then she would fall asleep. Still, she allowed herself a few moments of peace and quiet.

'Well, I better get started,' she said, and pushed herself up.

'No, sit a while longer,' Gjertrud protested. 'It's so nice to have some company, and you're not much company when you're busy washing, all I can see is your behind.'

Bonnie burst out laughing, they both laughed, and outside the old house the snow fell silently. Gjertrud's cat was lying in front of the stove.

'What are you doing for Christmas?' Bonnie wanted to know. 'Have you got people coming?'

'I'm going to Edith next door. She helps me with everything, with shopping and the post.'

Gjertrud didn't have any children and Bonnie had never asked why, it was none of her business. She knew the old woman had been widowed early and had lived alone for many years. She only had the white cat, and worried whenever it went out for a prowl as there was a lot of traffic on the road outside. Eventually Bonnie got up and went to look for the bucket. But Gjertrud wasn't concerned about the dust; she was simply glad that Bonnie came once a week. When she had finished cleaning, Bonnie helped the old woman into the bathroom, sat her down on a chair and washed her soft white hair in the sink. Gjertrud had to sit with her back to the sink and tilt her head over the edge, which was not a good position for an old body. So Bonnie worked as quickly as she could, rinsed her hair well and dried it with a towel, then they went out into the kitchen for the rollers. Gjertrud's lovely white hair was very thin and she tried not to roll it too tight. When it was done, she put a thin scarf over the rollers and tied it at the neck.

'My little scrubber woman,' Bonnie said affectionately. 'You'll be beautiful now.'

When she finally got ready to leave, they stood out in the hall and Gjertrud put a hand on her shoulder; it was trembling.

'You are coming back, aren't you?' she said hopefully. Her eyes were watery.

'Of course I am,' Bonnie said. 'I'll be back next week.'

She opened the door and the cold blasted in. The cat ran past them, wanting to get out.

Chapter 12

July 2005

'Do you think he said anything?' Jacob Skarre asked.

They were on their way to the home care services office. They had phoned to say they were coming. Someone called Ragnhild Strøm was there, waiting for them.

'When he came into the caravan, you mean?' Sejer prompted.

'Yes. Did they beg for their lives? Did he give them some kind of explanation?'

'For all we know, they may have been expecting him,' Sejer said. 'He may be someone they knew, it's often the case. Or maybe they fled the house at Blåkollen to go into hiding. In which case the caravan was a good choice. But he found them all the same.'

As they drove, Sejer sat and thought. The case required that they talk to a lot of people, and he ran through the questions he was going to ask in his mind. Now he wanted to hear about Bonnie's time as a home help, he wanted to get an insight into what she did and how she did it. His own mother had had a home help for a while, before she went into the nursing home. She was dead now, and he had no siblings.

Ragnhild Strøm's office was on the ground floor, third door to the left. As they came in, she stood up and welcomed them. She had already put out two chairs in front of the desk, which she had borrowed from the office next door.

'I'm not sure I can really help you,' she said. 'The truth is that I don't know much about Bonnie, she never gave much away. So I can only tell you about her work. On the other hand, I know a lot about that. She was exceptional.'

'So you don't know much about her private life?' Sejer pressed. 'Nothing at all?'

'Not a lot. She had a small house up at Blåkollen, where she lived with her son, Simon. There was no man in the house, as the boy's father had left them, so she brought Simon up on her own. He had a place at nursery. It was just the two of them. She talked about Simon all the time and I know that she hated having to drop him off every morning. It's a hard way to start the day, if only people knew.'

'How long had she been doing this job?' Skarre asked.

'For more than eight years. When Simon was born, he went to a council childminder to begin with. But I'll tell you this, and it's important, not many people last as long in this job, so it speaks volumes about Bonnie, the fact that she stuck to it.'

'And presumably she didn't have the same clients all the time?'

'No, it changes all the time. Some die, some get places in homes. She had a total of ten clients, that's two a day, so she was packing a lot into a day's work. It's a terrible thing to say, but I'll say it all the same: a lot of our clients are very demanding, or difficult in other ways. Home helps aren't always made welcome. I feel so bad,' she said, all of a sudden.

She closed her eyes. After a short pause, Sejer had to prompt her. 'Why do you feel bad?'

'Well, like I said, many of them are extremely difficult. So the truth is that a lot of the home helps come to me and say, I refuse to go to Erna, or I refuse to go to Ingemar, I can't bear being in that house, which puts me in a terrible dilemma. On the one hand, they've been offered help from home care services, and in that sense, the home helps are duty-bound to go to the addresses they are given. I've worked as a home help myself, and I know how it feels having to go to a client you don't like. Many of them don't want any help – it's their family who insist on it, they need someone else to take responsibility. A difficult and ungrateful client is like a knot in your stomach, you dread it all week. Some of the old people ring their home helps at home, they phone to nag them. Bonnie was always the solution. It wasn't in her nature to protest, she did what she had to do. In other words, she ended up with all the difficult clients. And not only did she go to them, she did an excellent job and never complained. I think she was actually quite fond of them, in her own patient way. And she has barely taken a day sick in all these years. A lot of our employees are off sick, they get bad backs. And then everything has to be rearranged, and others have to take on their clients. And again, it was Bonnie I turned to. How could I have done that to her?'

'Do her clients know what's happened?'

'Well, of course, some of them know – certainly those who are able to understand,' Ragnhild said. 'We've spoken to all the families and left it up to them to tell their relatives in the best possible way.'

'I would appreciate a list of all the people she went to,' Sejer said.

'Do you want to talk to them?'

'Yes. Don't you think we owe it to them? It might even be their right. We'll be gentle,' he promised.

Ragnhild's fingers tapped on the keys and she soon found a list of Bonnie's clients and their addresses. The printer hummed.

'Do you think any of them will come to the funeral?'

She nodded.

'I should think so, but not all of them. They're close to death themselves, it's only a matter of time, it could happen at any moment. In bed, or in the bathroom. Goodness knows what it's like to be at that stage.'

Chapter 13

December 2004

Britt came to Blåkollen at eight o'clock, after Bonnie had put Simon to bed. He was in his own room that evening. But he hadn't gone to sleep, he lay awake listening. Not many people came to the house, only Britt and Granny Henny. He only saw Grandpa Henrik occasionally, as he generally didn't come.

He heard voices out in the hall, then later they went into the kitchen. The door was ajar and he saw shadows.

'I've been Christmas shopping,' he heard Britt say. 'The little one is for you and the big one is for Simon.'

Simon's heart beat faster. It wasn't long until Christmas now, but time passed so slowly. The four of them always spent Christmas together. Grandpa would sit silently in his chair, he never took part in the conversation, but he ate with a healthy appetite.

'My, you smell good,' Britt said.

'Chanel Number 5,' Bonnie said. 'I got it from Erna.'

'Well, it's nice that one of them appreciates you,' Britt replied. 'You certainly deserve it.'

Then Simon heard footsteps, and the door was slowly opened a little wider. The light from the kitchen extended across the floor.

'Are you asleep?' Britt whispered.

Simon sat up in bed. He was full of the knowledge that she had a Christmas present for him. And she had said that it was big.

'Can I get a hug?'

He didn't answer but remained sitting upright, and she crossed the floor without a sound in her stockinged feet, bent down over the bed and gave him a hug.

'Be nice to Mummy,' she ordered in a kind voice. 'No fuss when you go to nursery, because if you don't go to nursery, then Mummy can't work, and then you'll have no money. And without money, there won't be any Christmas.'

He nodded.

'Now go to sleep,' she said, and went back out to Bonnie. She had put a Tupperware dish with stew in it on the worktop. And standing beside it was a bottle of good red wine. It brought tears to Bonnie's eyes. Britt thought of everything, she meant so much to her. And she was so busy herself, with a husband and three children, and a full-time job with the air ambulance.

They went into the living room, while the food was heating, and Bonnie set the table. Britt noticed the plants standing in a circle around the wild animals on the floor.

'You're getting thinner,' Britt said, when they started to eat.

'I've always been thin,' Bonnie retorted.

'Not as thin as now, there's nothing left of you.'

They ate for a while in silence. Britt filled Bonnie's glass as soon as it was empty. She only had one herself as she had to drive home.

'Tell me about the last job,' Bonnie asked. 'Was it dramatic?'

'It certainly was, but they always are. We had to pick up someone with burn injuries from Ringstad. A man, fifty-something; it was bad. Third-degree burns all over his body as a result of an explosion in his garage. He was conscious when we carried him out to the helicopter. He even had the strength to make a joke. I sat beside him on the way to the burns unit at Haukeland Hospital. The doctors can fix pretty much anything, he said, and put on a brave face. And I had to humour him and pretend nothing was wrong. I knew that he wouldn't survive with all those burns.'

'What?' Bonnie said, horrified. 'Is he dead?'

'He only lived for a few hours. Left behind a wife, four children and three grandchildren. There's something about men, they're always a bit lax when it comes to safety. We see it all the time at New Year with the fireworks, always a few fingers lost.'

She topped up Bonnie's glass.

'Now, what about you? How much time are you getting off at Christmas?'

'Fourteen days,' Bonnie said happily. 'Heaven! How about you?'

'I'm going to work. It doesn't bother me though. Jens will sort everything out at home.'

'You're so strong.'

'Yes,' Britt said, 'I am, but so are you. And I know you hate it when I say this, but I think you should find yourself a man. Simon needs a father figure, all boys do.'

'So you think I should go out on the town then?' Bonnie said. 'And who's going to look after Simon when I'm out there flirting?'

Britt had to smile.

'Don't be silly, we've got the Internet now. Lots of people seem to find their partners that way these days, there's no shame in it.'

'That's not what I mean; I just haven't had a good experience. Remember?'

'Not everyone is like Olav,' Britt said. 'Maybe it's time you got over him. I'm sorry for saying it, but there are good men out there, I found one.'

'I know,' Bonnie assured her. 'You're lucky. You haven't been through what I have.'

She got up and cleared the table, went into the kitchen and put on some coffee. Then they sat on the sofa and chatted until midnight. There was a thin layer of fresh snow on the red Volvo when she followed Britt out to the car.

'Ring me if there's anything,' Britt urged and gave her a hug. 'I can look after Simon if you want to go out and flirt.'

'You've got three of your own. It would be better to prevail on my mother.'

'Remember what I said,' Britt insisted. 'I've got a husband, and when I ask him to, he looks after the children, because he always does what I say.'

Bonnie tiptoed into Simon's bedroom and switched off the light. He was sleeping deeply, and had kicked off the duvet. She pulled it over him gently, then started to think about tomorrow. The wine had made her sleepy. Christmas soon. She had to do everything she could to make those days as special as possible. Simon was so excited about it he could hardly sit still. And she hoped there wouldn't be too much snow, because then she would have to clear it, which was heavy work. Her back ached enough as it was from all the cleaning. She got into her own bed, turned towards the wall and fell asleep, her worries running out like sand in an hourglass.

Simon was standing there pulling at her duvet. It surprised her, she was always the first one up. But the wine had made her heavy and tired. Simon buried his nose in her neck, and smelt the lovely perfume from the night before. He was excited, because he had been into the kitchen and the two presents were lying side by side on the worktop. There was also a big Tupperware dish that he hadn't seen before. Bonnie threw the duvet to the side and got up. She went into the bathroom to get dressed. Simon stood in the doorway and waited, and when she was ready they went into the kitchen. She spotted the two presents that she had forgotten to hide. She gave Simon a stern look.

'You haven't touched them, have you?' she asked, pretending to be strict.

'Just a little bit,' Simon mumbled guiltily. 'They're very hard.'

Bonnie had to laugh. She gave the little one a squeeze; it was a box. Then she climbed up on a chair and hid the presents away on the top shelf where Simon couldn't reach them.

'What's in the Tupperware?' he asked, pointing.

'Some food that Britt brought. There's plenty left, so you'll get it for supper. It's good.'

She made him some porridge, as she always did, and he was strangely calm. Not as reluctant as he normally was when he was going to nursery. He remembered what Britt had said, that without money there would be no Christmas. He sprinkled sugar on his porridge. His fair hair was getting long at the neck. She should really take him to the hairdresser, Bonnie thought, but he had such lovely hair that maybe it should be left to grow. Her mother thought differently, she said it made him look like a girl.

'What are you and Märta going to do today then?' she asked in an enthusiastic voice to bolster the boy's mood, which was such an improvement on normal.

'Märta's gone to the Canaries,' he said, his mouth full of porridge. 'They're swimming.'

'Is that Gran Canaria?' Bonnie asked. 'I'm sure it's nice there.'

'Can we go sometime?'

'Maybe. When we can afford it. It costs a lot of money to go there.'

She felt a pang in her heart when she thought of all the things she would never be able to give him.

They put on their coats and went out into the snow, which had obviously fallen heavily during the night, and the sight of the drifts by the driveway made her anxious. She strapped Simon into the back seat and brushed the snow off the roof of the car, then she got in and started the engine. Just as she feared, the wheels spun and went nowhere. Three times she pressed the accelerator, but the car just sank deeper into the snow. She put her forehead to the wheel and groaned in desperation.

'I can push,' Simon piped up from the back seat, undoing his seat belt.

'No,' she said. 'That won't work. We'll have to think of something else.'

She got out of the car to have a look and it wasn't good. Maybe she could put something under the wheels, but what on earth would that be? Some planks would have done the trick, but she didn't have any. Disheartened, she looked up at the road as the seconds ticked by. Then suddenly she had an idea and disappeared into the house. She had two rag rugs in the hall, which she now rolled up and carried outside. Simon looked on from the back seat. He didn't like it when his mother was upset, it scared him. Bonnie unrolled the rugs and put them down in front of the wheels. She tucked them under as well as she could and then got back in. She said a silent prayer and put the car in gear. She could feel immediately that there was traction, but not enough. Twice she tried, but the rag rugs were just pushed away, so she got out of the car again. She went to get the spade that was on the step, bent down and pushed the rag rags as far as she could under the tyres. She used all the strength she had, swearing and cursing to herself. She threw the spade down on the snow and tried again. It worked on the third attempt and she whooped with relief.

Once she'd dropped Simon off at nursery, she drove at top speed to Jørgen's tiny flat. Jørgen was a small, round man, but in good shape. His cheeks were incredibly smooth and he had lovely thick hair, and was always immaculately dressed in trousers and a shirt. He got up at five every morning and made breakfast, and he cooked himself a warm meal every afternoon. He went to bed at around eight, after the news, and as far as Bonnie knew, he always slept well. Jørgen had a daughter who was seventy-five, who was now in a home. She had dementia and needed round-the-clock care. Every Friday he went to visit her; he took a taxi both ways, and sometimes brought flowers which she didn't even notice. Jørgen had eight siblings, but they were all long-since dead.

Because the flat was so small and easy to keep clean and tidy, Bonnie had plenty of time to chat with him when she was finished and he was always happy to tell her about his life and experiences. He had driven a car, an old Lada 1500 S, until he was well over ninety, and he had never been ill. When he was sixteen, he went to sea as a deck boy on the *Flying Dutchman*. There was a painting of the ship over the sideboard, a very amateur piece, but the details were no doubt correct. Lovely boat, Bonnie said when he got to that part of his story. Then Jørgen told her about the sea serpent he claimed to have seen in the fjord several times, with its glowing red eyes and shark-like fins. This was followed by the story of the wolf. A poor maid had given birth to a daughter out of wedlock, and they lived in a small hut in the forest far from any neighbours. She frequently trudged down to the nearest farms, long skirt, skinny legs and bare feet. And as a rule she got work, so they managed to survive eating berries, herring and bread.

Jørgen paused here – as he always did – he was getting close to the climax. Bonnie pretended to hold her breath, even though she'd heard the story many times before. Jørgen had his eye on her. He wanted to make sure she was listening.

One summer's day when it was very warm, he said, she had filled a tub of water and put it out on the grass. She put the little girl in the water to cool off, then went back into the house to make some food. As she stood there in the kitchen, she heard the little girl scream, and ran out of the house to see what was wrong. To her horror, she saw that a great wolf had come sneaking out of the forest and pulled the little girl from the tub and was eating her.

'Oh my goodness,' Bonnie said, 'that's terrible!'

'Isn't it?' Jørgen agreed. 'The mother lost her mind and was never the same again,' he concluded. He twiddled his thumbs in his lap, very pleased with his story, which he never tired of telling to anyone who would listen. Bonnie always shuddered in a special way. Jørgen's words conjured up gruesome images in her mind, and even though she doubted that the story was true, it was still a glimpse into another time, and she thanked him for his thrilling tale.

'You're so good at telling stories. I can picture it all so clearly.'

She got up and went over to the worktop, where he had left a modest shopping list for her, then drove to the local Joker shop. She bought milk and bread and cheese, drove back, stopped at the mailbox, and took the newspaper and shopping into the house and put the milk in the fridge.

When she was finished for the day she went out to the car and phoned Britt. She wanted to thank her for such a lovely evening and say that all was well. She told her about the episode with the car and said that she had to go home now and clear the snow. She picked Simon up from the nursery, put on his winter clothes, exchanged a few words with Kaja, then drove home to Blåkollen. She parked out on the road, not daring to drive up to the house. She rolled up the rag rugs and took them back into the hall.

'Well, they've certainly been aired now,' she said to Simon. 'You go into your jungle and I'll come as soon as I'm done.'

Clearing snow was never fun, but fortunately they only had a short drive, and it had never crossed her mind to buy a small snowplough. Not that she could afford one anyway, it was out of the question. When she had finished, she leaned the spade up against the wall and went in to Simon. They sat on the sofa and read *Where the Wild Things Are*.

As Simon was about to go to bed, the doorbell rang. This alarmed Bonnie, as it was so seldom that anyone came, and if it was a salesman she'd have to turn him away. She put the book down on the table and went to open the door. To her astonishment, she found Britt standing on the front step. She was holding something heavy. Bonnie stood with her mouth open.

'What on earth have you got there?'

'I talked to Jens,' she said. 'And he suggested we buy you a set of snow chains. Here you are. Now you won't get stuck any more.'

Chapter 14

The walks with Shiba got shorter and shorter, and every time Eddie went to the mailbox he was worried that he might bump into Ansgar. He would always make some sarcastic remark and Eddie was painfully aware that people talked about him. The slow, fat boy who lived with his mum. Shiba went no further than round the corner, then she dropped down onto the snow to do what was expected of her. He couldn't be bothered to pick up after her, he never did, and they gossiped about that too. He walked along the road hatching plans. He was always thinking about his dead father; in fact, he was always thinking about death, because it was such a great mystery to him. That one day all his thoughts would disappear, his body would be cold and white and he would be buried in the ground. And that all the creepy-crawlies that lived underground would eat him. But clairvoyants can contact the dead, he thought. He decided that he would find one of those clairvoyants, he'd seen them on the telly. He'd also heard stories about the dead visiting their nearest and dearest in the form of a voice or a grey light or a movement in the room. He hadn't heard anything from his dad, which disappointed him. It was as though he'd meant nothing to him, because he'd never bothered to show himself, not even once.

'How was she?' Mass asked when he got back. She was worried about the dog.

'Not good,' Eddie replied. He was standing in the hall with his jacket on. His heavy boots were wet with snow. Mass had said he should get them waterproofed.

'I have to borrow the car,' he said with force.

Mass looked at her son, alarmed. He practically never asked for the car. He didn't like driving; he had managed to pass his test, despite some hesitation, on the fourth attempt after fifty hours of driving lessons. And now he wanted to go out in the car, on the icy roads. Heavens above. She gave him the keys somewhat reluctantly and looked at him solemnly.

'You will take it easy now, won't you?' she said. 'Where are you going? Are you just going for a drive?'

'I'm going to the church,' Eddie declared. 'Up at Haugane. I like going there.'

Mass couldn't imagine what the point of that was, but then her son was a riddle that she only partially understood.

'Don't be too long. And only use the low gears.'

He slammed the door shut and struggled with the gate, which was heavy and creaked at the hinges. Mass had folded the side mirrors in as she always did to get more room, as the space was tight. He put the car into gear and reversed out. Before he turned onto the road, he looked at the two side mirrors, but couldn't remember how to open them again, it was so long since he had last driven. He thought it was a button, maybe between the seats. After a bit of trial and error, he managed. He indicated left and pulled out onto the road. Mass had had the snow tyres put on, so he felt safe. Still, he drove no faster than fifty and he was in control. It took him twenty minutes to get there, and as he drove, he thought about his father, Anders, and how nice it would be if he was buried at Haugane. Then he could go to the grave every week, with flowers and candles. He parked outside the gate, sat for a while staring out through the windscreen. The church was quite small, a pretty whitewashed building with a modest spire. Opposite, on the other side of the square, stood a chapel with arched windows, and behind that, the parsonage with two large outhouses and a big barn. The priest, Oscar Berg, who he sometimes met in the shop, lived in the parsonage, and was always friendly. He even remembered Shiba, and always said to say hello to his mother. Eddie left the keys in the ignition. He had parked beside a Toyota, which he thought was familiar. On the wall beside the gate, he saw a green metal sign, 'Commonwealth War Graves'. He went through the heavy wrought-iron gate and straight over to the ten military graves by the chapel. They were all pilots. He had often stood by their graves, because there was something dramatic about their demise. He studied the white stones, each decorated with an eagle in flight, surrounded by a circle with a crown, and some words he couldn't understand.

Per Ardua ad Astra. The pilots were British and had been killed on 9 April 1940, the start of the Nazi occupation. The oldest of them was thirty and the youngest only twenty-one, the same age as Eddie. Their planes had been shot down by the Germans, and he thought to himself that they had come here to save this little country in the far north. He walked from grave to grave, stood a while in front of each stone, as though to honour them. I see you, he said quietly in his mind. Then he read the solemn words that were carved there.

What we know not now we shall know hereafter.
Memories live longer than dreams.
He giveth his beloved sleep.
His sun went down while it was yet day.
God gave and God had taken.

Then he turned his back on them and went over to the church. This one had been built in 1851, but there had in fact been a church here since the Middle Ages, dedicated to St Hallvard and St Margaret. Eddie had learned that at school, he'd done all right there actually, simply because he had a good memory. He walked on to the big tree by the water tap. The tree had stood there for a long time, but now it was dying. The dry, thick trunk was hollow and opened up to the sky. He couldn't resist going inside, there was just enough room. He lifted his head and looked up, saw heavy clouds warning of more snow. As he stood there like this, musing, he heard footsteps crunching on the snow, and a dark shadow reared up in front of the opening.

'Are you playing hide-and-seek, Eddie?' he heard.

Ansgar peered in at him with a mocking smile. Eddie pushed his way out, his cheeks burning with embarrassment. He didn't know what to say and his neighbour was clearly expecting an answer.

'Do you know someone who's buried here, Eddie?' he probed.

But Eddie didn't. His father was buried in Copenhagen and his maternal grandparents were buried at Geirastadir Church, and he went there on Christmas Eve with his mother to light candles and decorate the graves with a wreath of pine branches, baubles and cones. In spring she planted pansies, and watered and weeded and kept it looking nice.

'I've got an old friend here,' he mumbled.

Ansgar nodded, satisfied.

'I see,' he said. 'Well, it's good to have friends.'

Eddie wanted to get past him and away; he stepped down onto one of the well-trodden paths.

'How's Shiba?' Ansgar called after him.

'Fine, thanks,' Eddie lied. He walked with long strides round to the back of the church. When he ventured out again a few minutes later, the Toyota was gone. Damn him. Sticking his nose into everything. Idiot. I'm going to kill that bastard.

The old gravestones were always the best, tall and beautifully decorated; he studied the dates of birth and death, and worked out in his head how old they'd been. There were kneeling angels on some stones and little birds on others. On one of them it just said Martin and Helene, with no dates. The stone was shiny and black, like an arrow into heaven. Waldemar Enger, who was buried not far away, had a beautiful text. *Peace be with your dust.* I want something like that, Eddie thought, and carried on. He found the grave of a baby boy, only three months old. What a sad story, he thought, but I bet they had another baby; he certainly hoped so. Charles Østbye, the priest, had a healthy juniper bush leaning over his grave.

He went back to the parking place and stood for a long time looking at the high birch trees that edged the church and chapel. Fourteen in all. Now they only sported sharp, bare branches, but in spring they wore a delicate green. He looked at the path that led up to the church, lined by eight maple trees on each side. He sat quietly in the car for a few minutes. This is where I'm going to be buried, he thought, and fantasised again about what would be carved on his gravestone.

We will remember you forever.

Yes, that was the best one yet. But who would sort out the stone? When Mass died he would be on his own, he didn't know another living soul. There was his aunt in Bergen, to be fair, but he never saw her. The thought of what lay ahead made him shudder.

Chapter 15

July 2005

Bonnie and Simon Hayden were buried at Haugane Church on 15 July, some ten days after they were murdered. Sejer and Skarre drove up the avenue of trees in an unmarked car, looking for a parking space. A lot of people had come. Many of them had to drive back down and park along the roadside. Skarre had changed out of his uniform into a dark suit, and shorn the curls for which he was so well known. Sejer glanced at him sideways and thought that he looked like a stranger. They sat in the car for a while, looking up at the church, and the steady stream of people. Then they noticed a white minibus edging its way closer. At first they couldn't understand what a minibus was doing at the church, but then Sejer realised it was Bonnie's clients. Presumably the council had put on a bus. The doors opened and he saw the driver release two steps and Ragnhild Strøm climbed out. Ingemar Kroken was the last person out. He had been collected from Hallingstad and had a nurse with him. The grey-haired procession progressed slowly across the car park to the church steps. Once they had disappeared inside,

Sejer and Skarre followed and found themselves a couple of places on the back row, whereas the pensioners were sitting closer to the front with Ragnhild. Henny Hayden was sitting in the front row, together with Bonnie's father, Henrik.

'Our man,' Skarre whispered. 'Do you think he's here?'

'No, it's not very likely. Mind you, the whole case is pretty unbelievable, so who knows.'

The congregation were all dressed respectfully in black. The two coffins lay side by side at the front, one big and one small, and a brown, well-loved teddy sat on top of the small one. Sejer thought about the two bodies. Presumably Simon was wearing his finest pyjamas, and Bonnie was in a beautiful dress. The priest, Oscar Berg, who had been at the Norwegian Seamen's Mission in Antwerp for many years, had come to Haugane Church with his wife and four children, and was well liked in the parish. Even though he had a seemingly impossible task in front of him, he did not hesitate for a moment. There's something about priests, Sejer thought, they manage to find the right words for every occasion. And if they can't find their own, they borrow from the scriptures. But there was definitely something about Oscar Berg all the same, something genuine and sincere that made an impression, and unlike other priests who were often slow, heavy and solemn, he had an energy and strength in his voice. He was, quite simply, full of life and not afraid to show it. It was as if everyone woke up when he spoke. The service lasted an hour, then the church bells rang. Six strong men carried Bonnie's coffin and four carried little Simon. Henny and Henrik went first, though Henrik Hayden looked so lost that he wasn't much support to his wife at all, but followed the coffins with small reluctant steps. What was going on around him bore no relation to him. He knew it was about death, he could smell the lilies.

The birch trees that lined the churchyard were at their best, and the mother and son were buried side by side, in front of the chapel. They sang a final hymn. Sejer noticed that Henny was taking everything in, she wanted to see who had come. She seemed to forget the psalm and the priest, her eyes drawn to a man at the back of the group of mourners. She broke out of the ring and walked briskly towards him. He looked as though he could be around sixty and was wearing a leather jacket and jeans, dirty trainers on his feet with grey laces. When he saw Henny approaching he looked uneasy.

She leaned forward, right up in his face. But no one could hear what she said.

'How old are they?' Skarre wondered, talking about Henny and Henrik.

'She's seventy and he's seventy-five,' Sejer told him. 'Which isn't really that old these days. And as for you, you're just a whippersnapper. But not to worry, because you're a smart whippersnapper.'

He popped a Fisherman's Friend in his mouth, then tried to scratch his elbow through his jacket. He suffered from a mild form of psoriasis which bothered him sometimes.

Later, when he was back in the office, it felt odd to be at work in a dark suit. And yet he hadn't taken the time to drive home and change. He sat there at a loss for a while. He had plenty of things to do, it wasn't that. In the end he decided to drive over to the pathology lab and talk to Snorrason.

*

The doctor's office had a window into the autopsy room. The dead could teach the living. Sejer stared at the blinding white tiles. Tubes and drains where the last remains of life were washed away. Snorrason had spent most of his working life in this cold and sterile environment. For some reason, he had chosen a room where he was alone with the dead.

On the wall in his office, he had an enlarged black-and-white photograph, slightly out of focus, taken in Brentwood, USA. It was a portrait of a dead woman. Her head was tilted back, her face was puffy and formless with large, dark patches of discoloration, any features wiped out. Her eyes were swollen and closed, her mouth open. Her hair, fair stripes pushed back from the forehead. It was hard to discern whether she had been a beauty or not. But Sejer knew that she had been, because it was Marilyn Monroe. The picture had been taken a few days after her death in 1962.

'You're looking very smart today,' the doctor remarked. 'Designer suit?'

'Now that would be something,' Sejer replied. 'Bog-standard high street.'

Snorrason knew why Sejer had come, he wanted to think out loud, as he had done so often before. They pulled the pictures of Bonnie up on the screen, and even though the inspector had seen them before, he leaned forward. He studied the tattoo on her left shoulder, a small lizard that looked as though it was creeping over to her collarbone. It had probably been there for a few years – it wasn't black any more, more bluish-green.

'In a way, a tattoo is the same as self-harming,' Snorrason said.

'In what way?'

'Well, it hurts. It shows a need to be noticed. And it's permanent. Like when young girls cut themselves and then later sit there running their fingers over the scars.'

Sejer liked the little lizard and the three moles on her breast.

'The knife was clearly not blunt,' Snorrason went on. 'Look, the edges are even and sharp. He was aiming for her face, but she turned her head to the side. I talked at length with the funeral directors. I wanted to make sure that they wouldn't let the parents see her – some people simply insist. Think they can take it. Feel they should, for the dead person's sake.'

He moved on to a picture of Simon. They were both silent for some time.

'Have you found anything?' Snorrason asked, looking up at the inspector.

'Well.' Sejer chewed on it. 'There have been lots of phone calls, mostly about cars that have been seen at Geirastadir and Haugane. We're working our way through them at the moment. The men who phone in can give the car make, and often the model, whereas the women don't see the details, just the colour. But they spot things that the men don't. You know how it is. Someone must have seen him on his way there on the fifth of July, it was a lovely day. People would have been out in their gardens or sitting on their terraces.'

'Do you think he's a local man?'

'I assume so, because he managed to find his way to the caravan. We've gone through the criminal records for the area, but we haven't found anything that would point to something like this. But all the same, we think he must have stood out in some way from an early age, we just don't know how.'

'How many people are you taking in for questioning to begin with?'

'At the moment, seventeen. Everyone who had dealings with her in one way or another. Then we'll widen the search.'

'What do you console yourself with when you lie awake at night?'

'Our clear-up rate. It's unbeatable.'

In the evening, he put on his trainers and went for a run along the path behind the block of flats. Frank ran alongside him, with his tongue hanging out. The dog was a little overweight and Sejer was doing all he could to slim him down. Even so, on occasion, he was tempted to give him something tasty, a sausage or a chop that was left over from dinner. If they met a bitch on their way, Frank was like the possessed, pulling at the lead, while Sejer tried to explain to the fat dog that he didn't stand a chance, not with a long-legged greyhound or a small white poodle.

He ran with a light step and relaxed shoulders. He had always been fit and hoped that he could keep age at bay by staying in good shape. He sometimes went to the gym and no one had yet beaten him at arm-wrestling, not even the young guns there. He was strong, lean and had stamina, he never got stressed, but he was a serious man and sometimes prone to deep melancholy. Occasionally, when the weather was good and there was no wind, he would drive down to Jarlsberg airstrip and climb into a Cessna, go up to three thousand feet and then jump out, with a French-made parachute on his back.

He turned round after five kilometres and ran back. As he ran, he thought about Henny Hayden and the man she had spoken to by the grave. He had the feeling that it was significant. It was always the small things, the links between people and where they could lead. Frank started to flag on the stairs up to the twelfth floor, so Sejer scooped the dog up and carried him in his arms.

Chapter 16

December 2004

Bonnie opened her eyes. Today she was not going to clean or shake heavy rugs. Margot needed new shoes and they were going to drive into town and look at the shops. Then they would go to a cafe and then the bank. After that she would go to Nelly. Nelly had to be taken to hospital for some tests. Simon grunted sleepily when she woke him.

'It's nearly Christmas,' she whispered, 'and this afternoon we'll go into town to buy presents.'

Buoyed by what was to come, Simon bounced out of bed, and as they ate breakfast, they discussed what they would buy for Granny and Grandpa. He wolfed down his porridge and came up with several dazzling suggestions, so Bonnie made it clear that it couldn't be anything expensive.

'I'll pick you up as soon as I'm finished with Nelly,' she promised.

The wind was stronger outside and the snow was falling thick and fast; it was turning out to be a harsh winter. Bonnie drove slowly and carefully; she felt safe with the snow chains Britt had given her in the boot. When they got to the nursery, Kaja came out to meet them, said goodbye to Bonnie and took Simon inside with her. Bonnie drove over to Margot's, a little white house with a small front lawn that her grandchildren looked after in summer.

Margot was a frail old lady with thick, steel-grey hair. Bonnie followed her into the kitchen. There was a basket of bananas on the table and Bonnie gladly accepted one. Margot had a personal alarm around her neck and she pressed the button at regular intervals to make sure it worked. Within minutes she would get a call from the switchboard and Bonnie would have to explain that it was just a test.

'What kind of shoes are you looking for?' she asked, as she ate her banana.

'I would like two pairs,' Margot said. 'One for special occasions and one for every day. I thought we could go to Magnussen's, they've got the best selection. I have to have shoes with laces, otherwise I can't get them on. And I've got a wedding to go to,' she explained happily, 'my granddaughter is getting married. They've already had a baby, so it's high time. It's a little girl.'

'So you're a great-grandmother?' Bonnie was impressed. 'Have you seen her yet?'

'No, only a photograph. But they've promised to come and visit me. They've called the baby Vilde. What do you think of that?'

'Lovely.'

Margot had put on a good frock as she was going into town, but her hair was greasy, which Bonnie thought was odd. Old people generally had dry hair.

'When we get back I'll wash your hair for you, if you like.'

'No,' she replied. 'That's not necessary. I washed it only yesterday.'

Bonnie couldn't believe that. She stroked Margot's hair; it stuck to her hand.

'What kind of shampoo do you use?'

'Wella,' Margot told her.

Bonnie went into the bathroom and on the edge of the bath was a bottle of Wella conditioner. But there was no shampoo to be seen.

'You've washed your hair with conditioner,' she explained to Margot. 'It's an easy enough mistake to make.'

Margot gave a sheepish smile and reached for her coat.

'We can buy some shampoo when we get to town,' Bonnie suggested. She helped Margot get into the passenger seat and fastened the seat belt. When they got into town, she parked in the big car park over the shopping centre, got a ticket, and then helped Margot into the lift and they went down to the shops. It wasn't easy to get Margot's feet into a pair of smart shoes, but the young girl who helped them was very patient. She knelt down and eased the shoes onto Margot's old feet. Then she helped her up to try them out. Margot took a few steps across the floor and then sat down again, and gave her verdict on each pair. Too tight. Too big. Too high. Too stiff on the sole. Eventually she found a couple of pairs she was happy with, one white and one brown, and they went to the till to pay. After that they carried on to the bank. It was a rare visit for Margot and she had some bills she wanted to pay in the old-fashioned way, even though Bonnie had warned her about the fees. She also withdrew some cash and on the way back to the car they bought a bottle of shampoo.

In the afternoon Bonnie drove to Nelly, who was sitting ready and waiting. She had the letter from the hospital in her hand; Bonnie read it and found clear directions for where they were supposed to go. In through the main entrance, the lift B up to the fourth floor. Follow the blue line on the wall until you get to reception.

'Are you nervous?' Bonnie asked.

'No, not at all. It's just some X-rays. And if they find something, they find something. After all, I'm eighty-six.'

While Nelly was in getting her X-rays, Bonnie sat in the waiting room and flicked through a women's magazine. She always felt despondent whenever she browsed through magazines like that, the pictures showed a glamorous world she would never be part of, and after a while she threw the magazine down and sat there thinking instead. Maybe she'd get a scarf for Mum and gloves for Dad. She knew she had given them that before, so it would be doubling up, but they might be glad of a bit of variation. Her mother would be happy with anything. It was important to show how pleased you were, for Simon's sake. When Nelly finally came back, she was relieved. Her coat was buttoned up wrong, so Bonnie gave her a hand. She put the receipt from the car park in her wallet so that she could claim expenses, and when they got back to Nelly's house, they sat for a while at the kitchen table for a natter. Nelly gave Bonnie a hug when she got up to go, and then she drove straight to the nursery to pick up Simon.

'We could buy slippers,' he suggested. 'You know, the ones with sheepskin.'

'We could,' Bonnie hedged. 'But it might be tricky to get the right size, and if they don't fit then we'll have to change them.'

'I want chocolate cake after,' he then declared. 'And Cherry Coke.'

'Chocolate cake and Cherry Coke you shall have,' Bonnie promised, putting the old Opel in gear. The snow was falling on the windscreen and visibility was poor. She heard Simon chatting away in the back, but only half listened, because she needed to concentrate on the road. As they drove past the big Kiwi shop twenty minutes later, Bonnie spotted an old woman walking along the road. She was wearing a brown coat and hat, and had a carrier bag in her hand. It was obvious she was struggling with the strong wind and ice. Dear God, Bonnie thought, that someone as old as that had to venture out alone in this weather. She instinctively slowed down. When the old woman heard the car coming up behind her, she stopped and turned round, and Bonnie saw to her surprise that it was Gjertrud. She put her foot on the brake and pulled in to the side, got out of the car. When Gjertrud recognised Bonnie, her face lit up, and at the same time she had to put a hand on her hat to stop it blowing away.

'Gjertrud,' Bonnie exclaimed, 'what are you doing out in this weather when I do your shopping for you?'

Gjertrud clutched her Kiwi bag.

'I ran out of cat food,' she explained. 'He's sitting in the kitchen miaowing.'

'But couldn't you have asked Edith?'

'She wasn't home.'

'Get in,' Bonnie ordered. 'I'll drive you home.'

Gjertrud shuffled round the car while Bonnie held the door open. She noticed Simon in the back as she got in, and told him what a lucky boy he was to have Bonnie as his mother. She was the best person in all the world.

'Now, is there anything else you need before you go home?' Bonnie asked as she started the car.

'Well, nothing that's important.'

'But there is something you'd like to get?'

'I don't want to trouble you, you've got your own things to do. And your son.'

She seemed embarrassed. Sat there with her eyes downcast, clutching her handbag. Bonnie didn't give up, not until Gjertrud said what she wanted.

'I don't have any eau de vie left.'

'Then off we go to the Wine Monopoly,' Bonnie said. 'I'll pop in and get some for you. The day's not quite the same without it,' she added, and laughed, then Gjertrud had to laugh too, and Simon leaned as far forward between the seats as he could. Gjertrud opened her bag and got out her purse with shaking hands. She took from it a crumpled note. Simon thanked her politely, just as his mother had taught him.

There was a queue at the Wine Monopoly, of course, as it was almost Christmas. Bonnie thought that as she was standing in the queue anyway, she might as well get herself a bottle of cheap red wine. When they got back to Gjertrud's house, the old dear wanted to pay for both bottles and the petrol, and she wouldn't let them go until Bonnie took the money.

'It's nearly Christmas,' she said. 'God bless.'

Then she said goodbye and went inside to her hungry cat.

Chapter 17

On the wall above his bed, Eddie Malthe had a photograph of himself sitting on his father's lap. It had been taken when Eddie was three, just before his father left them. Mass had refused to let him have it in the living room, and Eddie looked at it every night before he went to sleep. Only now it was morning. He sat up in bed and took the picture down. It had been taken on a warm day and they were both wearing summer clothes. His father was holding Eddie tightly in his strong arms. A thick fringe fell over his forehead and his smile was broad and happy, whereas Eddie looked very serious.

He stared at the photograph. Even though he had studied it countless times before, it was as new for him each time. His father looked so happy, so why had he left them? He hung the picture back up on the wall and went into the living room. Soon after his mother appeared in her nightie; he could see her body through the thin material. She checked the thermometer outside the window and shivered.

'Minus eleven,' she reported. 'We'd better light the stove. Put your coat on, you'll have to go out and get some wood.'

Eddie looked at her body; she was heavy, just like him, and he could see her big breasts swaying under the fabric.

'Let Shiba out so she can pee.'

She opened the door to the bathroom and disappeared inside, and he heard her turn on the tap. Shiba was lying in her corner and Eddie went over and pulled her tail. Then he hauled her up by the collar, pushed her from behind out into the hall. The cold hit him when he opened the door. He stepped into his heavy boots and pulled on a thick jacket. He wouldn't have to clear snow today, which he was pleased about, but the price was the extreme cold. Shiba immediately went round the corner of the house and peed, then she wanted to go straight back inside.

Eddie got out a couple of plates. He took the cheese, sausage and jam out of the fridge and got the bread, then set the table for a simple breakfast. Then he sat down to wait. He had slept heavily and could still feel the sand in his eyes.

'I dreamed about Dad last night,' he said, when his mother sat down. It wasn't true, but he wanted to hear about his father, and it was a way to start the conversation.

'But you can't even remember him,' Mass objected. 'You were only three.'

'I know.' He chewed his bread. 'But sometimes I think I remember things all the same.'

'What kind of things?' Mass sounded sceptical.

'His white shorts,' Eddie said with conviction.

'That's what you've seen on the photograph.'

He didn't answer.

'What did he die of?' he asked instead.

'I've told you before,' Mass said patiently. 'It was cancer. That's what we all die of these days. Sooner or later.'

'But you won't, will you?' Eddie asked anxiously.

'No,' she said, and laughed. 'I'm certainly not planning to do that. I'll probably live to a hundred. But I have got a pain in my back,' she admitted.

'Why?'

'It happens to ladies of my age. We scrub and clean all our lives, you know. There isn't much help to be had from you.'

'But I'm good at clearing snow,' Eddie retorted, offended. Mass had to agree with that.

'You're right,' she said, with a sudden smile. 'What would I do without you?'

Eddie Malthe crowed. They needed each other so much, it put him in a good mood. He said that he would stack the dishwasher. Mass stayed at the table; she studied the dog that was lying asleep in the corner.

'I'm worried about Shiba,' she said. 'She's not that old, but she's really not very well. There's something wrong with her leg. What do you think it is?'

'Hip joint dysplasia,' Eddie suggested. He put a tablet in the dishwasher and closed the door.

'No, never. I'll get an appointment at the vet. Do you want to come?'

Eddie nodded happily. The dishwasher started to rumble as it filled with water. Then he went out into the snow to get the newspaper, and luckily didn't bump into Ansgar. He went back in and gave it to his mother who was now on the sofa.

Eddie sat down at the computer. He looked up Copenhagen, the city where his father had moved to with someone else, and then died. Copenhagen had a population of 1.2 million and was the largest urban area in the country, comprising eighteen constituencies, Eddie read. It was situated on the east coast of Zealand, and the key institutions were the Danish Parliament, the Palace, the Supreme Court and the government administration. Twenty per cent of Denmark's population lived in Copenhagen. He sat and studied the map, telling himself that his father had lived in one of those streets. He turned to his mother. 'Where exactly in Copenhagen did Dad live?'

Mass sighed and lowered the newspaper.

'Goodness, I don't know. It's such a long time ago. I don't know that I want to know either. Sorry.'

'Are you sure you don't know?' Eddie persisted.

She shook her head.

'Eddie darling, do you think I'd lie to you?'

No, he didn't think so. He carried on reading about Copenhagen, a city he had never been to. Denmark's a small country, he thought, I'll find him.

Chapter 18

July 2005

Who, what, where? Sejer thought. With what? Why, how and when? They had answers to some of the questions. Bonnie and Simon Hayden had been killed with a sharp knife in a caravan on Skarven Farm on 5 July. Sejer went out into the corridor and found Skarre; in his hand he had a list of all Bonnie's clients. They knew that the police were coming, Ragnhild Strøm had warned them.

All morning they went from house to house and as considerately as possible ran through what had happened. The old people were all terribly upset – several of them were having problems sleeping. This evil thing that had happened was gnawing away at them all. And her little boy as well, it was unbearable. Sejer asked each of them if they had noticed any changes in Bonnie. Had she appeared different in the period before the murder? Had she mentioned anything that was bothering her or that she was being followed? Had she seemed to be frightened of something? They all thought about this, and answered no. In fact, if anything, she had seemed happier, as if something good had happened. He asked if she had confided in any of them, and some of them smiled, especially the women. Yes, now and then, maybe she felt it was safe because they were old and would soon move on to other pastures.

'What did she tell you?' Skarre asked.

Time after time they shook their heads sadly and said that she had talked about her husband, and that he had left her when the boy was very young. 'I told her she should find someone new,' Gjertrud said, 'but she just laughed.'

Marie sat with her hands on her lap, crying. She had a tissue tucked in her sleeve and her voice was thin and rusty, and she had to cough to get the words out at all.

'He'll go to prison, won't he?' she stammered helplessly. 'But then he'll just get out again in a few years' time.'

'Probably,' Sejer conceded. 'That's the way our system works. Do you think that's bad?'

She nodded.

'We can't have a man like that walking free. I don't know how I'm going to manage without Bonnie.'

'They'll get you a new home help as soon as possible,' Skarre assured her. Ragnhild had said: 'I'm not sure how much comfort that is though. There's only one Bonnie.'

Marie fished the tissue out from her sleeve and dabbed her eyes.

'I've got nothing to look forward to now,' she said. 'My son works in Kuwait and I never see him.'

'Do you know what a tear is?' Skarre asked, when they were back in the car.

'What it is? Salt water, isn't it?'

'Yes, water and salt,' Skarre replied. 'And proteins and fat and sugar and citric acid and enzymes and antibodies. Tears kill bacteria and lubricate the cornea. They're the body's way of getting rid of toxins. In other words, it's not a bad thing to have a good cry every now and then.'

'And it's tears that make us human,' Sejer added.

'We're not the only ones who cry,' Skarre corrected him. 'Some big animals cry as well when they're sad.'

They drove on to Skarven Farm.

Jürgen, Thomas, Stanislav and Woiciech were all in the outhouse, ready to play bridge. Woiciech, or the Butcher of Warsaw as the others called him, dealt out the cards. He had phoned home and told his wife Danuta about the gruesome killing. She was waiting for him in their simple flat in Krakow, but knew that he wouldn't be home again until November. Then he would once again swing his cleaver and slip in under the duvet with her at night. But they were in agreement about the arrangement, as it considerably boosted their income. For seven years in a row now he had come home with lots of money, and they dreamed of buying their own house. He worked as hard as he could. He harvested cabbage and leeks and lettuce and picked strawberries. The raspberries were ready in July, and then the apples, and red and yellow plums. They repaired machines and other equipment, and this summer they had painted the barn and fixed the windows on the old cottage.

The men fanned out their cards and held them tight to their chest. Thomas, who was the youngest, looked over at Stanislav.

'I saw you following them,' he said. 'You crossed the field just after they went down with the duvets.'

Stanislav put his cards on the table.

'And what of it? I thought they might need some help. She didn't look very strong.'

'You should have told the police,' Thomas countered. 'They need to know everything. Who was where and when.'

'Did you talk to them?' Woiciech wanted to know. He put his cards down on the table too and looked at his friend.

'Like I said,' Stanislav said. 'I asked them if they needed any help.'

'Well,' Woiciech said, 'you didn't hang around, did you? And she was quite something, that woman. What would your wife say if she knew you were chasing Norwegian women? My guess is that the police will come back, ask more questions, dig around. I'm annoyed at myself for not taking more notice of that red car. If I knew the make they could have traced it.'

'It's probably got nothing to do with the case,' Jürgen cut in. 'It was just a car that had gone the wrong way.'

'We don't know that. It was parked up on the road for a while. The police are always interested in cars, they're always looking at traffic movements.'

'A red car? I mean, Jesus,' Jürgen sighed, 'that says nothing. You're just trying to make yourself out to be important.'

They were interrupted by Randen, who appeared in the doorway. He said that supper was ready, and that Solveig and the girls were waiting. Randen walked with his head bent and his hands clasped behind his back, as was his wont. He would never get over what had happened on his farm, and wanted in some way to show that they were mourning. We should have gone to the funeral, Solveig had said. I regret that we didn't. Perhaps people thought it strange that we weren't there.

They all sat down at the table. Little Emilie put her hand on Jürgen's arm, on his impressive tattoo of a fire-breathing dragon.

'Did it hurt?' she wanted to know.

'Not at all,' Jürgen told her. He helped himself to some of Solveig's scrambled eggs.

'I want one too,' Emilie piped up, and looked at her father over the table.

'Absolutely not, young lady,' he said firmly. 'It's enough that you've had your ears pierced.'

The cat came into the kitchen to beg for titbits and Stanislav lifted it up onto his lap. After what had happened in the caravan, he longed for home, he needed to get away. And yet it was still so raw, so they sat and talked about it throughout the meal.

An hour later, the men thanked their hosts and went back to the outhouse, where they each had a bunk with a thin summer duvet. As was their habit, they chatted in bed before going to sleep. One by one their voices faded out, and it was quiet long before midnight.

The first time that Sejer and Skarre went to visit Henny Hayden, the day after the murder, it was with the sincere hope that she could help them. That something in Bonnie's life would give them a clue. But she had barely been able to speak. She just sat in the chair and stared out of the window, answering their questions in one-syllable words. She held on to the windowsill with both hands and leaned her forehead against the glass, and they could hear her laboured breathing. But then, she was the person who was closest to Bonnie. They were on their way back now, with renewed hope.

Her husband, Henrik, also liked to sit by the window; he turned his head when they came in, but made no move to get up, just stayed where he was. So they went over and shook his hand.

'He's just visiting,' Henny explained. 'He spends most of the time at Hallingstad.'

Sejer noticed a Post-it note on the television. There was one on the standard lamp next to the sofa as well. He went over to read what was written on them. On the lamp it said 'lamp' and on the television 'TV'.

'He's got Alzheimer's,' Henny continued. 'He can't remember things from one day to the next, and he's lost a lot of his long-term memory too. He comes home as often as I can manage. The kitchen is full of Post-its too, you know, cooker, fridge, freezer and things like that.'

'How has he reacted to what has happened?' Skarre asked, with some care.

'I have to tell him again every morning. He only remembers one day at a time. Sometimes not even that, it's impossible. I have to watch him like a child.'

'What does he say?'

'He doesn't know who Bonnie is any more.'

Henny Hayden lit a cigarette.

'I had to tell him why we were at the funeral, but he just seemed to be confused. People suffering from Alzheimer's live with a great deal of fear, each day is new to them and so are the people.'

She looked at them over the table.

'My retirement has not been what I hoped it would be,' she said. 'And I'm only seventy. What if I live for another twenty years with this misery?'

'Tell us about Bonnie,' Sejer said, changing the subject. 'From the time that she was little. What was she like as a girl?'

Henny managed to smile, but squeezed her eyes shut at the same time as if she was in pain.

'She was the best daughter in the world. But then all parents say that. She was kind and bright at school, lots of friends. Sometimes the house was full. The other girls in the class all wanted to be her friend, but she chose with care.'

'What were her dreams and aspirations when she was little? Can you tell us something about that?'

'Oh, she had lots of dreams. For a while she wanted to be a doctor and preferably work with geriatrics. She wanted to help everyone in need.'

She drew on her cigarette, tapped off the ash.

'She cared about everyone, really. When she was older, she did a lot of babysitting, often for her teachers. She was known to be reliable and kind and people trusted her. She earned money that way.'

'And what did she use the money for?' Skarre wanted to know.

'She saved it,' Henny told him. 'She was always very sensible. And she never nagged us for things like so many other children do when they're in a shop. She got a little pocket money from us, and in return she did certain chores around the house. She used to do the hoovering and cleaning, and I often thought that one day she would make someone a good wife, as they say.'

She smiled at this.

'And the boys,' she continued. 'Well, they queued up. But she wasn't really interested in them, she thought they were childish. She wasn't silly either, in the way that teenage girls can be. At least, we didn't think so.'

'And what about puberty,' Skarre asked, 'was that a difficult time?'

'Puberty came early. She was perhaps quieter than before. Sat in her room more, but she was never rude or difficult. She distanced herself from us a little, but that's only natural. We had an easy ride of it compared to so many other parents we spoke to – lots of girls stamp their feet and slam doors at that age. We were very proud of her. I knew that she would look after us well when we got old, at some point in the future. Now there's no one left, neither Henrik nor I have any other family.'

She stubbed out her cigarette.

'If you don't find the man who did it, I'll never forgive you. I want to know why. You have to find him. Find him and get him locked up!'

'We'll find him, I promise you,' Sejer assured her. 'But it takes time. It's important for us to get an overview of Bonnie's life. And everyone who was close to her. So it's important that you tell us everything you know.'

'Britt knew her best as an adult. They were very close.'

'So Britt is the one who can tell us about Bonnie's life?'

'Yes, I would think so. The break-up with Olav Nøklan, Simon's father, was a terrible time for her. He left them two years ago now, when Simon was three. Bonnie didn't want to find a new partner – although she was never short of admirers – because she wanted to protect Simon from what she called deceitful men. She said it was better that it was just the two of them, then at least she was in control.'

Skarre noted down the name.

'He works on the rigs in the North Sea. Gullfaks B. Two weeks on, four weeks off.'

'Did he come to the funeral?'

'No.'

She pursed her bloodless lips.

'It's a bit strange not to go to your own son's funeral, isn't it?' Skarre exclaimed in surprise.

'Yes,' Henny admitted. 'But after they split up, Bonnie didn't want to see him at all, she was very bitter. And she didn't want him to have any contact with Simon, who she clung on to with all her might.'

'But surely the father has rights too?'

'He never did anything to change the situation, so he must have been happy with it. He's a coward, if you ask me. The thing is, he ran off with Simon's babysitter. Can you imagine? She was only seventeen. Every time he and Bonnie went to the cinema or something, he would go to collect Kathrine, and when they got back, he would drive her home. So they had sex in the car.'

'How did she find out?' Sejer asked.

'He told her. He and Kathrine are married now and have a daughter. Ylva. I've never seen her.'

'A slightly different question,' Skarre cut in. 'What was their relationship like when they were living together?'

'I think it was good. I've never seen Bonnie happier. Everything seemed to be fine, and Henrik and I were proud grandparents. That was before he got ill, while he still had all his faculties.'

She looked over at the man by the window.

'There's one more thing we have to ask,' Sejer said tentatively. 'We were at the funeral and I saw you go over and speak to a man who was standing right at the back. Who was he? And what did you say to him?'

'Not much,' she said dismissively. 'But I couldn't help remarking on his clothes. Everyone else was wearing dark suits and white shirts, and he looked like a tramp.'

'Do you know him?'

'No. But I did take note of who was there and what people were wearing. I didn't know all Bonnie's friends and acquaintances; maybe he was interested in her at some point, there were so many of them. He's irrelevant.'

'Well, then all we need is an address for Simon's father,' Skarre said. 'Do you have it?'

'He's got a huge house in Nordhellinga. But I can't remember the number.'

'And Britt?'

'She lives with her husband in a flat in Oscarsgate. Her name is Britt Marie Bergan and they have three children. You should talk to her as soon as possible.'

They stood up and got ready to leave, but first they made it clear to her they would have to come back. Both of them went over to the man by the window to say goodbye.

'I can't face showing you out,' Henny said. 'I'm too exhausted.'

'Anything there?' Skarre asked when they were back in the car.

'Probably not,' Sejer replied. 'But it sounds as though Bonnie had quite a few admirers. Perhaps one of them was more insistent, and she rejected him. Some men can't cope with that. On another tack,' he added, 'would you go up to someone at a funeral and comment on what he was wearing?'

'No,' Skarre replied. 'I don't think so. She definitely said something to him, but I'm not sure how we can find out what.'

Chapter 19

December 2004

In the evening, Bonnie suggested they should drive down to the video shop, to find a film they could snuggle up and watch together. Simon was delighted and immediately ran out into the hall to put on his coat. They locked the door and went out to the car. No more snow had fallen and it would only take twenty minutes or so to drive there. She put the key in the ignition and tried to turn it. But the key wouldn't budge, it was stuck, and after she tried three or four times she sat back in the seat and stared nonplussed at the windscreen. It probably wasn't anything major and would be sorted soon enough. So she tried again, but the key still wouldn't budge. Oh no, she thought in desperation, I haven't got time for this!

'We have to go now,' Simon said from the back seat.

'Yes,' Bonnie replied. 'But I can't start the car.'

Simon sat up, an unhappy expression on his face. Bonnie looked at him in the rear-view mirror. His blond curls were hidden under a red woolly hat and he looked like a little gnome.

'Maybe we could take a taxi?' he said hopefully, but Bonnie said that would be far too expensive. She tried to turn the key again, and again it remained stuck.

'Bloody car!' she said out loud – she couldn't help herself. In frustration, she tried with all her strength to force it, but then realised that the key might break, which would be even worse. Simon panicked. A terrible thought struck him: if the car was broken, his mum wouldn't be able to get to work and if she couldn't get to work there would be no money, and if there was no money, there would be no Christmas. That was what Britt had said.

'We'll have to go back inside,' Bonnie said wearily. She closed her eyes and groaned. Took the key out of the ignition and trudged back through the snow. Simon trotted along behind her. There was nothing for it, they just had to open the door and go back into the warmth.

'I'm sure we'll find something on TV,' she promised. 'I'll check all the channels.'

Simon climbed up onto the sofa and she chose a channel for him, then she went into the kitchen and sat down at the table. She laid her head on her arms. As far as she could see there was no solution, and her heart was heavy. She looked around the kitchen and spotted the bottle of red wine standing in a corner on the worktop. She got up, opened it, took out the largest glass in the cupboard and filled it to the brim. Sometimes she thought the fact that everything was so difficult was some kind of punishment. There was no getting away from a guilty conscience. She drank the red wine. She gritted her teeth. She was indifferent. Ah well, everything could just go to hell, Erna and Ingemar and the others would just have to look after themselves. She drank in great gulps, and when the glass was empty, she phoned her friend Britt and told her about the damned car and all her problems.

'Jesus, it's all a bit too much for you right now,' Britt said.

Bonnie sat in silence at the other end and pressed her mobile phone to her ear. Just to hear Britt's voice was a comfort in itself.

'I'm going to go to bed early tonight,' she said. 'I'll call Ragnhild in the morning and explain. Right now I'm so tired; everything else will just have to wait.'

When she had put the phone down, she poured another glass of wine and went into the living room, to Simon, who was watching lions in Africa. They were resting under an acacia tree, having just killed an antelope, and were bloody at the mouth. He found it interesting, but his thoughts kept returning to his mother, and he realised that the problem with the car was not good. He thought about what she had said out loud. *Bloody car*. Sometimes he dreamed that someone would parachute into their lives, perhaps from the sea in a big helicopter, someone like his dad, Olav, for example. But he rarely mentioned it, because his mum just shook her head and wouldn't say any more.

When Bonnie switched over to the news, Simon sat down at the table with his African animals; he lifted the vulture and let it attack a lion.

'There's a car coming,' he stated.

Bonnie looked at him in surprise.

'Two cars,' he said, and pressed his face to the window. Bonnie went over to look, but it was dark so she could only see the headlights. The cars stopped out on the road, the doors opened. Two cars outside the gate, what could that mean? Simon watched his mother. Some of her tension spilled over into him. He had seen her like this before, white in the face with worry. They went out into the hall to open the front door, and there was Britt standing on the front step, her husband Jens behind her. They were both smiling. Bonnie looked at the two cars back on the road. She had never seen one of them before, but the other was Jens's red Volvo.

'The Ford belongs to my father-in-law,' Britt said, 'but it's just been rusting away in the garage, because he stopped driving after the heart attack. So you can borrow it while yours is getting repaired. It's probably just the lock cylinder and that won't break the bank. We'll tow your car to the garage, it's not a big job. Jens says it will be done in a minute.'

Bonnie started to cry. She was overwhelmed by her friend's ability to solve problems.

'You big softie,' Britt laughed. 'Stop your crying. Most things can be sorted, you just need to be creative. Where were you going?'

'The video shop,' Bonnie replied, looking down at Simon.

'Great, you take the Ford then,' Britt ordered.

Bonnie had to laugh at that.

'I've drunk half a bottle of red wine,' she admitted, 'so I'd probably better not.'

Britt looked over at her husband.

'Well, we'll just take you there in the Volvo then,' she said. 'What do you want to see, Simon?'

'*The Lion King*,' he said happily, because now the evening had been saved and his mum was smiling again.

She knew that it would be late by the time they got back. First they had to tow the Opel to the garage, then go to the video shop, and then back here. They would both be late to bed. But right now she didn't care, she was so relieved. She stood for a while and looked at them, filled with immense gratitude. She didn't see Jens very often. But when she did, he always gave her that special look: a glint in his eyes, which she had seen so many times before. She was used to men looking at her, but this was her best friend's husband. She didn't return the look.

Chapter 20

When they got home after speaking to Munthe the vet, and Eddie had carried Shiba from the car into the house, they sat down in the kitchen. Mass fiddled with a box of tablets that the vet had given her, Metacam, chewable painkillers for dogs. They were tasty and Shiba had eaten one without hesitating.

'Eight is quite old for a dog,' Eddie said. 'In human years she's actually fifty-six.'

'Yes,' Mass said, and looked straight at him. 'She's as old as me.'

Eddie hadn't thought about that. He followed his mother with his eyes as she got up and went over to the worktop, where she stood, at a loss.

'Whatever,' Eddie said. 'She's not exactly a puppy. And she's overweight, just like me.' He said this with a smile that his mother didn't see.

'I'll go and get the paper for you,' he soothed her, 'so you can relax a bit.'

He pushed his feet down into his boots and went back out into the snow. He didn't bump into Ansgar, which was a relief; the possibility of an encounter always added a touch of tension to his trips to the mailbox. Sometimes he thought that if Ansgar made any more sarcastic remarks he would break his nose. Ansgar was a bit of a wimp really, he was bigger and stronger. He collected the post and went back. Mass was sitting in a chair waiting, and she took the newspaper from him. Eddie went to the fridge for a Cherry Coke, then he sat down at the computer. He sat there thinking for a while, before starting to search. His dad had spent his final years somewhere in Copenhagen; he had to be buried in one of the graveyards there. It must be possible to find out which one. He did a search for graveyards in Copenhagen, and when a long list popped up on the screen he felt slightly sick. He hadn't imagined there were so many; where on earth should he start? He ran down the names and addresses, reading them quietly to himself.

Assistens Cemetery in Kapellveien. Holmen Cemetery in Østre Farimagsgade. Solbjerg Cemetery, Roskildevej. Vestre Cemetery in Vestre Kirkegård Allé. Vor Frelsers Cemetery in Amagerbrogade. And so it went on.

He slowly worked his way through them all. His mother didn't know where his father was buried, only his new family knew and they also lived in the city of Copenhagen, along with 1.2 million other people. But he still thought there must be a way to find him. Or his grave, of course, as he wouldn't find anything else. His mother did have some information; he knew his name, date of birth and the date he moved to Copenhagen.

'What are you doing?' Mass asked from her chair. 'What are you looking for?'

'Nothing in particular,' Eddie said tersely. His mother wouldn't like what he was doing, he was sure of that, and he didn't want to tell her about the plan he was hatching.

Mass lowered the newspaper. Once he had decided on something, he never gave up. Suddenly it occurred to her that he might be looking for a girlfriend – there were lots of people who met on the Internet these days, it was quite normal. He had said that he didn't want a girlfriend, but he could have changed his mind. And even though he was one of a kind and on the heavy side, she thought he was handsome, with his strong body and curly brown locks.

'Are you keeping secrets from me?' she teased.

'Yes,' was his reply.

She didn't want to ask any more questions, because even though they lived in the same house, he had the right to some privacy. After a while, he turned the computer off, and Mass went to the utility room to take some laundry out of the tumble dryer. Eddie picked up the paper and turned to the crossword, worked his way steadily through it, word for word. *Biblical fruit, two words, ten letters.* Adam's apple. *Central star.* Sun. Flame. Girlfriend. The expression 'deadly defence' was harder, eleven letters. He had an 'l' and a 'u', nine letters, so the word was leucocyte, a scientific term for killer cells. *Purification works.* That might also be something in the body, six letters and he had an 'e'. Spleen. *Ideology, eight letters.* Politics? Religion? Both fitted. After doing some more he got the letter 'm' and then 'f'. The word was manifesto. But now, he had to sort out this graveyard thing. The thought of his father's grave would not go away, he kept mulling it over in his mind. He would never forgive the woman who had taken his father from them, never. The audacity. He put the newspaper down and went into the kitchen, bent down over the dog and whispered in her ear: 'We'll be going to the vet again soon to have you put down.'

'Leave Shiba alone,' his mother said sternly. 'She's ill and needs some peace.'

'I know.'

She was standing with a piece of clothing over her arm, and she held it up for him. It was his black New York sweatshirt and it had shrunk to child-size in the warm tumble dryer.

'I want a new one,' he said, determined. 'We'll have to go back to the shop.'

'Aha,' she said, and laughed out loud. 'That's only because you want to see the Ethiopian girl again.'

Chapter 21

July 2005

After fourteen days on the rig, Olav Nøklan was flown back to the mainland by the helicopter service. Kathrine picked him up in the car, and their little daughter Ylva was in the back. He gave them both a good hug, he was happy to see them. But they didn't say much on the drive home. Olav knew what was waiting. Tomorrow, the police would be on their doorstep, and the thought of all the questions they would ask was eating at him.

'What are you going to tell them?' Kathrine asked, as she drove.

'Absolutely everything. I'll be honest and answer their questions as well as I can.'

'Do you think I should be there? I knew Bonnie as well, after all.'

'Don't know,' he said curtly. 'They might want to talk to me alone.'

Ylva sat babbling in her car seat behind them, and he tried to stay calm. He had a horribly bad conscience about all manner of things, and he would definitely be the first to admit that if they asked. He should be ashamed. He should do everything he could to make up for it, he should repent.

'Why did you leave Bonnie?' Sejer asked. 'Did you argue a lot?'

'No, we didn't actually,' Olav admitted. 'We had a good relationship. Especially after Simon was born. It was just that I fell head over heels for Kathrine. You can't control that sort of thing, can you? I'm only human.'

'Kathrine was seventeen?'

'Yes. It does sound a bit like cradle-snatching, but she was very mature. That was why we used her as a babysitter. And then what happened happened. It was a difficult time, and to be honest, I didn't know what to do. Kathrine and I had endless discussions, and I told her countless times that she could easily find someone else. And then we'd split up – we tried several times. But it didn't work. We couldn't end the relationship, it was almost impossible for me to think straight. So I decided to come clean and tell Bonnie.'

'How did she take it?' Skarre asked.

'Oh, it was unbearable,' he sighed. 'And I knew that she would struggle financially. She didn't earn much as a home help.'

'You could have helped her financially, couldn't you? With the money you must earn on Gullfaks?'

'Yes,' he said. 'And I paid my share for Simon. She accepted that of course. But she wouldn't take a krone more. She was as bitter as can be and I didn't want to pressure her. But I begged her to tell me if she ever needed anything, because I did want to make up for what I'd done.'

'It's hard to understand why she said no,' Sejer remarked.

'You didn't know Bonnie.'

Sejer looked around the living room, which bore witness to both good taste and good money. The house that Bonnie had lived in after the separation was another story: a tiny old place where they had gone from room to room without finding anything that might help the investigation. Sejer had stood in the doorway to one of the bedrooms and looked at the unmade bed: the duvets were still in the caravan.

'How often did you see Simon?'

Olav bowed his head. He looked both guilty and unhappy.

'Hardly ever,' he confessed. 'Bonnie always made it difficult. I think she wanted to punish me.'

'You didn't insist on more contact?'

'No. I guess I'm just a coward, that's all there is to it. And then Ylva was born. But I always gave him presents for his birthday and Christmas. I thought she might soften over the years, but to be honest, I didn't really believe she would, she was totally unforgiving.'

'Were you close when you were together?' Skarre asked. 'I mean, did you share secrets and dreams? From your childhood, for example, or when you were teenagers?'

'Not really. But perhaps we should have done. Though I have to say, my teenage years were pretty wild. And for obvious reasons I wasn't that keen to talk about it. Bonnie was pretty secretive about most things, not that I really wanted to know about her past – what did it matter?'

'But you had a good relationship?'

'Yes, in every way.'

'And the fact that she never got over the split, does that mean that she clung to you when you were together?'

'Yes.'

Kathrine came into the room with Ylva on her arm, and they asked her a couple of questions which verified what her husband had said.

As they walked to the door to leave, Sejer turned round one last time.

'Did you go to the funeral?'

'No,' he admitted.

Sejer stood for a moment, thinking.

'I find it very strange that you didn't go to your own son's funeral,' he said. 'Can you explain?'

'Yes,' he said, sounding wretched. 'I'm totally ashamed of it. But the fact is that I was scared of Henny Hayden. She wasn't just bitter, she was furious with me for what I'd done to Bonnie and Simon. So I chose to stay away. I was scared she would make a scene – she's not the type to hold back. And I didn't want that to happen at Simon's funeral. So I drove up to Haugane Church last night with red roses.'

They parked beside a red Volvo, then went in to see Britt Marie, who had been Bonnie's closest friend for many years. Her husband and children were sent down to watch TV in the basement. The dog, Sugar Man, was asleep in front of the fire with his head on his paws.

'I've helped Bonnie with a lot over the years,' Britt said. 'Now there's nothing more I can do. The only thing would be if I had some information that might in some way help you to find him. But I have nothing.'

'Do you know if she had any unfinished business with anyone?' Sejer asked.

'No,' she replied. 'It's hard to imagine – she was kindness itself.'

'Do you know if she had any enemies?'

'I can't think who they would have been. No, absolutely not.'

'Did she say anything that might indicate that someone was after her?'

'Men,' Britt said with a smile. 'I'm assuming you've seen photographs of her.'

'But she never mentioned anyone in particular?'

'No, not like that. Not after Olav.'

On the wall there was a picture of Britt and Bonnie standing close together. It was taken in the rain and both of them were wearing red raincoats, the hoods pulled up against the weather.

'Jens took that photo,' she told them. 'It's quite recent.'

'So your husband also knew Bonnie?'

'Yes, but not very well.'

'How close were you? Did she tell you everything?'

'Oh no, definitely not. No one tells someone everything, we're adults after all. And adults have secrets. I do too.'

Suddenly she started to cry. Sugar Man padded over to comfort her.

'So what you're saying is that Bonnie might have had a secret that you knew nothing about?' Skarre suggested.

'Yes, I suppose that's what I'm saying,' she answered, and dried her tears.

'Something in the past, perhaps?'

'Yes, although I know some things about her childhood. I know that she had anorexia, for example, and it was pretty serious.'

Skarre jotted the information down.

'So she told you that. Did she give any more details?'

'Not really. She was a teenager, though, which is often when it happens.'

'And anorexia is usually triggered by other things, you know that?'

'Yes, I know a little. Low self-esteem, pressures at school, even sexual abuse, and other horrible things like that.'

'Do you have any reason to believe that something like that may have happened in Bonnie's childhood?'

'I don't know. It certainly wouldn't have been Henrik, because I know him quite well, and he worshipped her.'

'But could it have been someone else, perhaps?'

'Of course,' Britt said. 'There are always nasty uncles.'

Chapter 22

December 2004

When Christmas finally arrived, Simon danced around clapping his hands. He was delighted by everything, the tinsel, the gifts, the smells from the kitchen. He had made some of the Christmas decorations himself at nursery, with Kaja's help: baskets, and shiny paperchains and red felt hearts. Granny and Grandpa were sitting on the sofa; his mum was wearing a dress and had flushed cheeks from standing over the cooker for so long. It was Simon who handed out the presents. He had a red hat on, and saved his presents until last. He placed the presents in their laps one by one and waited with glee. Grandpa Henrik didn't really know what he was doing, but Bonnie helped him with the ribbons, and a pair of brown leather gloves appeared. He put them on and held his hands up to his face, smelt them.

When everyone else had opened their presents, Simon sat on the floor with his gifts, there were five in total, the tip of his tongue peeping out of his mouth as he tussled with the paper. Bonnie folded it up neatly so it could be used again. In the evening, she drove her parents home.

The lock cylinder had been changed and everything was working again, at least for the moment. The car should have been in for a service a long time ago, but she couldn't afford it. These were happy days, and there were still some to come. They stayed up as long as they liked, slept as long as they liked, and ate cake every evening.

Chapter 23

January 2005

The holiday passed all too quickly, and in January, Bonnie had to go back to work and Simon had to go back to nursery. He was slow and uncooperative in the mornings, banged the table with his little fists and shouted that he didn't want to go. Bonnie gritted her teeth; she half carried, half dragged him out to the car with an aching heart.

Then, one morning in the middle of January, she woke up with him calling her. She leapt out of bed and ran into his room, turned on the light, and asked if he'd had a bad dream as she stroked his hair. Then she noticed something strange on his face, several big blisters; she pulled his pyjamas off in a panic to have a look. His whole body was covered in blisters, and she was terrified, she had never seen anything like it and couldn't imagine what it was. She got him out of bed and into some clothes, then she called the office to say that she had to take her son to the doctor, but that she would be at Erna's as soon as she could.

'Will I need any injections?' Simon asked from the back seat, once they were in the car.

'I don't know,' Bonnie said. 'You might just get some medicine. Pills or some cream. We'll have to wait and see what the doctor says.'

'Will I have to go to nursery after?'

'No, not as long as you've got those spots. I'll ring Granny, so she can look after you while I'm at work.'

When they got to the doctor's she was relieved to see that there weren't many people sitting there waiting. There were only two others in front of them in the queue, and she did everything she could to calm Simon who was frightened. As they waited, her mind was racing and she thought that perhaps it was some kind of allergy. Even though Simon had never been bothered by anything like that before, and nor had she. When they went in to see the doctor, she took off his clothes, and the doctor ran his fingers over the angry rash.

'It came up overnight?'

'Yes.'

'Has he had it before?'

'No.'

'Will I need to have an injection?' Simon whispered.

'No, no,' the doctor said reassuringly. 'You won't need an injection, little man. This is quite harmless and easy to treat.'

'But what is it?' Bonnie asked.

'Hives,' the doctor explained. 'I'll give you some prednisolone, and that should make it disappear fairly quickly.'

He stroked Simon on the head and wrote out a prescription.

'Do you think he might be suffering from stress?' the doctor asked.

Bonnie felt like she'd been punched.

'I guess he might be. It's just the two of us, Simon and me, and he's not very happy at nursery. But we don't have any choice.'

She took the prescription, thanked the doctor and then she and Simon walked down the corridor to the hospital entrance where there was a chemist's. They got the medicine, and then drove to Bonnie's mother, who met them at the door. Simon had no objections to staying there, and finally Bonnie was free to drive to Erna's.

'It's about time,' the old woman said grumpily. 'I've been waiting for an hour and a half. Punctuality is a virtue, you know. You won't have time to do anything now.'

Bonnie stood quietly and took a deep breath.

'But you did get a message from Ragnhild to say that I needed to take Simon to the doctor?'

'Yes, I got the message. In my opinion, single mothers with small children shouldn't actually work at all, they have to take so much time off.'

Bonnie went into the bedroom as usual and picked up the basket of socks. She put the socks on the legs of all the chairs and tables, while Erna sat in her chair and watched her like a hawk. As she worked, Bonnie thought about Simon. That of course he was stressed, just like the doctor said. And she should do something about it, only she didn't know what. Of course it wasn't good that he had practically no contact with his father, she had robbed him of that. She often regretted it, but she was so proud. And Olav had a daughter now, he was happy with Kathrine, and every time she thought about it, she boiled with rage. She washed the floor and hoovered as well as she could. Then she did the bedroom, changed the bed and, as usual, looked up at the photograph of Erna as a young girl. It was hard to imagine that the radiant girl in the picture had become the flinty woman out in the living room. What does life do to us? she thought. When she was finally finished, she went to say goodbye, and Erna followed her to the door so she could lock it.

'And next time, I expect you to be punctual,' was her parting shot.

Over Christmas, Ingemar had finally been given a place at Hallingstad nursing home, so Bonnie went to visit him later on in January.

He was sitting in a chair by the window, but there were no horses to be seen outside, only a car park with long rows of cars. There was a box of chocolates on the table, still wrapped in cellophane, no doubt from his family. Bonnie thought to herself that the chocolates were an insult to a man who only wanted soured milk, sausage and cod liver oil straight from the bottle.

'It's Bonnie,' she said as she went over to him. 'How are you?'

He turned his head and looked at her. He definitely recognised her, but he did not give her a smile. He turned his gaze back to the cars outside the window, his grey, bushy eyebrows knitted.

'You don't need to speak so loudly,' he said. 'There's nothing wrong with my hearing.'

Bonnie looked at his large white ear, and thought suddenly that it reminded her of a beautiful conch shell. She wondered, if she put her ear to his, whether she would hear the sound of his long life. Which was over now. The memory of life in his old house with the horses outside the window was all that he had left. Ahead, there was nothing.

Then she did something she had never done before. She gave his cheek a gentle stroke. And that teased it out, a little smile.

When she was in the car driving home again, she thought to herself that she never wanted to be old, she couldn't face the deterioration, the helplessness. She didn't want her hair to go grey, and her jowls to sag. She thought about her father; he was like a child now, his life was over too, even though he was only seventy-five, and he was in another world. But he was in good physical health and might live for years yet with serious dementia. She had seen an Alzheimer brain on the TV once, and it was as full of holes as a Swiss cheese.

That evening she sat on the sofa with Simon and looked through a photograph album. She had to point out and explain who was who all the time.

'That's Granny and Grandpa,' she said, 'on their wedding day. Isn't Granny lovely?'

Simon agreed. There wasn't a picture like that of his mother and father, because they never got married.

'Look, that's me,' she pointed and laughed. 'I was just a baby there, and I was pretty fat. And there I'm ten, we're at the beach. I remember that swimming costume, because I had it for a long time.'

'And that's me and Daddy.' Simon looked up at her. 'And I've got a sister.'

'A half-sister,' Bonnie corrected him. 'It's not quite the same.'

She helped him to brush his teeth and tucked him into bed, switched off the light. She felt utterly exhausted, went back into the living room and sank down in an armchair. She tried to find something to watch on television. Where was her life going? What was going to happen? Sometimes, like now, she felt that something was close, something she couldn't articulate.

Chapter 24

Every winter, on the night before Christmas Eve, Eddie went to bed first. When the door closed behind him, Mass swung into action. She filled an old red stocking with sweeties, then hung it above the door to her son's bedroom. He would lie awake in bed and listen to the hammering, and early the next morning he would empty the contents of the red stocking out onto the table, and munch his way through it in no time. And now it was already January, Mass had tidied Christmas away and all the pine needles had been swept up.

Eddie had been working on the crossword for some time, chewing the pencil which was now about to disintegrate. *Intrigue*. Plot. When he had finished, he sat and pondered. And when he had pondered for a while, he went and sat down at the computer. Mass took over the newspaper, but kept an eye on her son staring at the screen. After a while, he turned and looked at her.

'When was Dad born?' he asked.

'Oh, darling, I've told you so many times before.'

'Well, tell me again,' Eddie insisted. 'I need to get it absolutely right.'

'The sixth of the eleventh, 1945,' she said with a frown.

Something about her son's behaviour made her uneasy.
There was a determination about him that she had seen
on a couple of previous occasions; it meant he was up to
something.

'Do you have his personal ID number as well?'

'No.'

'And where was he born?' Eddie wanted to know.

'In Bergen.'

'And when did he leave us?'

Mass sighed in exasperation.

'Eddie, darling, why do you want to know all this?' she
asked anxiously.

'When did he move?' Eddie persisted.

'In 1987. On the twenty-seventh of May.'

He looked at her in surprise.

'Crikey, you even remember the date?'

'Women remember things like that,' she said wearily.
'Men don't always pay attention to the details.'

'And when did he die?'

'In '92. But don't ask me the date, because I don't know.
And I don't know where he's buried, and I don't know if
he had any children with his new wife. And I don't want
to know. He was a coward.'

'Why do you always say he was a coward?' Eddie
wondered.

Mass thought for a while before she reluctantly replied:
'Well, when you were little, you weren't very easy to deal
with.'

Eddie looked at his mother with piercing eyes.

'Why? What do you mean?'

'You didn't want to do anything. You didn't want to go
to nursery, you didn't want to be with other children. You
clung to us all the time, you suffered from what's called

separation anxiety. So even though we managed to get you a place at nursery, we couldn't use it. I'm just being honest now. And Anders was at the end of his tether, he didn't think you'd ever amount to much. He called you a snivelling brat, and fathers shouldn't say things like that about their own children, it's just not right.'

'But if you weren't in touch, how did you find out that he'd died?'

'His wife wrote me a letter.'

'His wife?' Eddie exclaimed. 'Wrote you a letter?'

'Yes.'

'But she didn't say where he was buried?'

'No, and I didn't particularly want to know either, because I had no intention of visiting his grave.'

'But if you got a letter –' Eddie was excited now – 'then you know her name, don't you? And then I can find out.'

'I don't remember much of the letter,' she admitted.

'Nothing?'

'Good Lord, Eddie, you do bang on. You're starting to annoy me now.'

'But you do remember her name, don't you?' he nagged. 'You can remember the date he moved to Copenhagen, so that means you've got a good memory, just like me.'

She closed her eyes and a considerable amount of time lapsed before she opened them again.

'Well, since you're obviously not going to give up, her name was Inga.'

'Inga what?'

'Inga Margrethe.'

'What else?'

'I can't remember.'

'But it must have been written on the back of the envelope,' he said. 'Have you still got the letter?'

'Of course not,' she snapped. 'Why would I keep it?'

Eddie thought about what his mother had told him, that he was a difficult child. Even though it had never been said so directly, it was something he already knew. He turned back to the computer screen and opened a new document. He sat for a while and thought before he started to write.

To the Tracker Tore production team,

My name is Eddie Malthe, and I am writing to you because I need help to find my father's grave in Copenhagen. He left my mother and me on 27 May 1987, then remarried and moved to Denmark. My father was called Anders Kristoffer Malthe, and he was born in Bergen on 6 November 1945. His new wife is called Inga, but I don't have a surname, I'm afraid. They settled in Copenhagen. I know that he died in 1992 but I don't have the exact date. I watch your programme every week, and I know that you have found people all over the world. It would mean a lot to me, because then I could go to Copenhagen and lay flowers on his grave. All I have is an old photograph that hangs over my bed. I hope that you will be able to help me find him.

Yours faithfully,
Eddie Malthe

He posted the letter the same day.

He had printed it on good paper; he thought that it might be more personal that way. No doubt they got heaps of letters. He didn't want his to drown in them all. He had written his address and telephone number at the bottom, and, to be on the safe side, had stuck on two stamps. The long wait started. He would sit by the kitchen window and watch for the red post van, and as soon as he saw it, he would rush out into the snow. Ansgar often came out at the same time with the cat at his heel. Presumably he stood by the window waiting as well, but Eddie just grabbed what was in the mailbox and disappeared back into the house as fast as he could. Sometimes he had Shiba with him. Her legs were getting worse and worse, but every time he mentioned it to his mother, she got upset. Some days she laid out a newspaper by the front door, so the dog could shit there. But Shiba also had good days, and then Mass held on to the hope that she would get better. She couldn't bear to accept the inevitable. And all the time, Eddie waited for a letter from Tracker Tore. His body ached with anticipation and he was constantly in and out of his room to look at the photograph. His father really was a handsome man, he thought, with broad shoulders and thick blond hair. He had forged a steely determination to find his father's grave. He would look day and night for months if he had to.

Chapter 25

August 2005

Sejer and Skarre went back to see the Haydens; they had some more questions. They saw that the chair by the window was empty as soon as they came in.

'Is he at Hallingstad?'

'No, he's in bed. I can't always get him up,' Henny explained. 'And it doesn't really matter where he is. He just sits with his hands in his lap and hardly ever speaks, and when he does, it's just nonsense.'

'And how are you?' Sejer asked with concern.

'I take it hour by hour,' she said in a tired voice. 'Sometimes I go into her old room and lie down on the bed. And it feels like there is no reason in the world to get up. Have you found anything? Is that why you're here? Have you got some more information?'

Sejer had to admit that they didn't.

'All you have is a footprint,' she said despondently. 'And that's not going to get you very far.'

'I'm afraid we have to talk to you about something,' Skarre said. 'There are things in Bonnie's life that we need to investigate more closely.'

'I see.' She didn't look at them when she answered.

'Bonnie was bright,' Skarre started, 'and her dream was to become a doctor. Instead she ended up as a home help, which is not quite the same. Why was that, do you think?'

'I suppose it was just one of many dreams that weren't fulfilled,' Henny sighed. 'That's what happens sometimes. And she liked her work as a home help; she put her heart and soul into it.'

'Was she in any way disappointed that she never fulfilled her dream?'

'I don't think so. She certainly never said anything about it. But life was a struggle for her, especially after Olav left. I will never forgive him. Fortunately he had the sense to stay away from the funeral. If he had shown up I would definitely have told him what I thought. That a grown man can fall for a teenager and give up all he has is more than I can understand.'

'I need to ask you some difficult questions,' Skarre ventured. 'But please remember we are on your side. Do you have any family secrets that we should know about?'

'Don't all families have secrets?' Henny replied. 'I think perhaps you should show a little more sensitivity. Things are bad enough as they are, we're in shock.'

'But a murder is a matter of public concern,' Skarre told her. 'In fact, you are duty-bound to answer our questions. Only when the witness is a close relative of the accused are they absolved of that duty. And that's not the case here, is it? I think you should let us decide what is important or not.'

She didn't say anything. She looked down at her hands, then at the empty chair. They could see she was struggling.

She had no doubt imagined the scene in the caravan, the raised knife, over and over again. She had heard their screams in her head; she would hear them now until she died. Sometimes Sejer was filled with despair at all the questions he had to ask, but he was also used to the family being keen to help.

'I've got something else on my mind too,' he said.

'I'm terribly tired,' she said. 'I just want to be left alone.'

'I understand that, and we'll leave you in peace very soon. But it's been brought to our attention that Bonnie suffered from anorexia when she was a teenager. And we have to talk to you about it. Now, you might not think that it has anything to do with the case, but we ask you to bear with us. So, can you tell us about it?'

She straightened her back as though she were about to defend herself. As though she wanted to say that she had nothing to hide when it came to her daughter's illness, and that she and her husband were not to blame in any way.

'She was seventeen when she went on a diet,' she explained. 'She weighed sixty-seven kilos, which wasn't much for Bonnie really, as she was quite tall. And then it got out of control and the weight fell off her. She sat and picked at her food and withdrew into herself, as if she wanted to disappear altogether. She went down to forty kilos within the year and we went to lots of doctors for help. She couldn't have cared less, she even started to lose her hair, and she had pressure sores, as if her bones were trying to break out of her skin. It was awful to see. She was in hospital several times and the doctors were worried about organ failure, so it was extremely serious. We were terrified we were going to lose her. Neither Henrik nor I could sleep at night.'

'How did she manage to turn it around?' Skarre asked.

'Eventually we found a doctor who she connected really well with. It was as though he found the key. And then slowly but surely she started to get better. I've never been more relieved in all my life than when she started to eat again. At first she only ate soup and porridge because she found chewing hard. But then finally it was all in the past. And she's never had any problems like that since.'

'I imagine that you and Henrik gave considerable thought to what might have caused the illness,' Skarre said. 'What was your conclusion?'

She looked as if she was about to cry.

'It wasn't our fault,' she said, distraught. 'But we often felt that that was what the doctors thought, that they judged us, and the way we treated Bonnie.'

'And how did you treat her?'

'We were rather strict, I suppose. Especially Henrik, he was very overprotective. He would stand at the window every time she went out, and watch her go to the gate. Sometimes we worried that someone with a big motorbike might be waiting for her on the main road. And that she might not have a helmet. Isn't that what all parents think?'

'Yes,' Sejer smiled. 'I have a daughter too.'

'He always told her to be back by nine at the latest,' Henny carried on. 'And generally she was home on time, because she was a good girl. But every now and then she was late. Henrik would stand by the window and wait, and when she finally came home, he would bombard her with questions. Why didn't you come home when you were told to? Who were you with? Where have you been and what did you do, and are you going to see him again? Have you been drinking or taken anything else? Can we trust you? And Bonnie would get really upset. She'd say she'd been with her girlfriends and forgotten the time. And she would apologise a thousand times, then scuttle off to bed to get away from it. Some girls who develop eating disorders do it to gain some kind of control over their lives, that sort of thing.'

'Do you think Bonnie had lost control of her life?' Sejer asked.

'No teenager is in control, really,' Henny replied. 'They're still so unprepared. And Bonnie was the sort of girl who couldn't say no.'

'Do you think there's more?' Skarre asked later. 'Is there something she's not telling us?'

'Perhaps. But she's started processing it now, so we'll just give her space. I'm sure she'll tell us in her own time. Maybe she's ashamed of something. And shame is a powerful enemy.'

They drove into the car park in the basement, and then walked up to reception. There was a girl waiting there. She looked around eighteen, maybe twenty, and her hair was bleached by the sun.

'I've been on holiday in Spain, and just come home,' she said. 'I went out on the sixth of July, at seven in the morning. It's about what happened at Skarven Farm. The papers are full of it and I've read everything. And, well, I've been thinking.'

'Did you see something?' Sejer interjected.

'Possibly.'

'Come up to the office and tell us about it.'

She followed him into the lift and up to the fifth floor, and when they came into the office, Frank got up from under the desk. She greeted him enthusiastically, admired his wrinkly head and black eyes.

'I was in the car park at Geirastadir on the fifth of July,' she said. 'A friend and I wanted to get out in the good weather and go for a walk. We thought we'd go up to Saga.'

'Carry on.'

'Well, I was sitting in the car waiting, because my friend had called to say she was running a bit late.'

'When had you arranged to meet?'

'At one.'

'And what did you do while you were waiting?'

'I sat in the car and listened to the radio. I had the engine running because I needed the air conditioning on. The car park was almost full, but then, a while later, another car came. It was an old red estate car, I think, I don't know much about makes, but it was definitely not a small car. And the driver struggled to find a space to park. But eventually he managed to squeeze in.'

'So it was a man?'

'Yes.'

Two red cars, Sejer thought, one at Skarven Farm and one at Geirastadir.

'Then he got out of the car,' the girl continued. 'I thought he was probably going to walk to Saga or Svarttjern, but he didn't, he disappeared down across the fields instead. Towards Skarven.'

'Did you notice what he looked like?'

'Well, I wasn't paying much attention, but he certainly wasn't a lightweight, let's put it that way. He was tall and pretty big. And he was wearing black clothes.'

'But there was something else about him that you remember, which is why you're here now. Am I right?'

She smiled.

'Yes, you see, the fifth of July was a really hot day. And while the rest of us were melting, the man was wearing a jacket and gloves.'

Chapter 26

February 2005

Eddie never got a reply from *Tracker Tore*. He felt utterly overlooked. He was obviously not important enough, and nor was his father, so he would have to do it himself.

One day his mother asked him to give Shiba a bit of TLC. To cut her nails and put some cream on her paw pads. He sat on the kitchen floor with the dog between his legs – she didn't have the energy to protest – and while he was doing this, he thought intensely about his dead father. When he was finished and the dog had lain down again, he went over to the computer, because he was sure he could find the answer if he just kept looking. The National Registry, he thought all of a sudden, I can try there. Because his father would be registered, and he had some years and dates now. But he soon discovered that the information he was looking for was subject to data protection, and when he tried the Danish National Registry, he got the same answer. He sat and thought for a while. Maybe his father was registered in the church records – a lot of people found their ancestors there – but that idea didn't lead anywhere. Instead, he clicked onto the population census website, and felt a glimmer of optimism. It turned out you could search using several different criteria: first name, surname, sex, civil status, profession, date of birth, place of birth and domicile. He filled out the search fields with his heart in his throat and then pressed go, but to his great disappointment, there were no hits. He couldn't understand it. His father had lived in this world, he was registered and he had worked, and everyone was tracing their ancestry these days. I've done something wrong, he thought, but what? He went to get a Cherry Coke from the fridge, and wondered whether he could call the National Archives to ask for help. I demand to be heard, he thought, this is important.

Full of renewed determination, he got the telephone number from directory enquiries, then picked up the phone and dialled the six digits. Only to be bitterly disappointed again. Died in 1992? Then the information is subject to data protection for the next sixty years.

Eddie was on the verge of giving up his important project. But an iron will burned inside him, it filled his body and made his head warm. He turned and studied his mother who was pottering around in the living room with a duster. Maybe, just maybe, she hasn't thrown away the letter from Inga in Copenhagen, he thought.

Later, when they sat down for supper, he helped himself to four meatballs and a big portion of his mother's home-made mushy peas.

'I have to talk to you about something important,' he said, and looked at her across the table.

'Not so much salt, Eddie,' she chided. 'It's not good for you.'

'Something important,' he repeated. 'Inga.'

His mother looked down. He saw her mouth tighten in that all too familiar way.

'Yes, what about Inga?'

'I need to know her surname.'

'I've told you, I've forgotten it,' she said impatiently. 'And I don't know why you're so interested in her – she stole your father from you.'

'But she knows where Dad is buried. I'm sure you could remember if you just tried. Sometimes I think you're hiding things from me on purpose.'

Mass pushed her plate to one side, and looked him in the eye in an attempt to be strict. But she feared it was a lost battle.

'Maybe I have good reason for that,' she said. 'I have to look after you. And there are also some very good reasons why you're still living at home. You need to be protected.'

He thought about this for a while. Then suddenly he was filled with rage at all the obstructions and he flared up. He hit the table with his fist, which made all the crockery jump.

'Her surname!' he shouted. 'Now!'

Mass look at him in dismay, because the outburst had scared her. A kind of reality finally dawned on her, she didn't have the right to stop him in his efforts.

'Nilsen,' she said quietly. 'Inga Margrethe Nilsen.'

The air seemed to go out of Eddie, but the information brought colour to his cheeks. He leaned forward and asked for the address.

'I threw away the envelope, I promise. And I shredded the letter and threw it on the fire. I had already lost him.'

Eddie was keen to get on now. Inga Margrethe Nilsen in Copenhagen, he was sure he could find her. He shovelled down the rest of his food at great speed, then went over and picked up the phone, and asked for international directory enquiries.

His heart was hammering as he gave the name.

'How does she spell Nilsen?' the operator asked.

Eddie didn't understand her question. Surely he didn't need to spell Nilsen.

'In Denmark they often write Nilsen with an extra "e",' she explained.

That hadn't occurred to Eddie.

'Look for that one,' he instructed her. 'You're probably right.'

It only took her a few seconds, and then she could tell him that there was no Inga Margrethe Nielsen in Copenhagen. Eddie was holding the receiver so hard to his ear that it hurt. Was there no end to the obstructions to his search?

'She might have moved,' the woman suggested, wanting to be helpful. 'I could do a search of the whole of Denmark. It's such a small country.'

'Yes,' Eddie replied. 'I need to find her. It's very important.'

He drummed his fingers on the desk as the seconds dragged out. Where could Inga have gone?

The woman only found five hits in the whole of Denmark. In Silkeborg, Holstebro, Kolding, Århus and Odense. Eddie wrote the numbers down; now all he had to do was try – one of these five women must have been married to his father, he was sure of it. Before he dialled the first number, he prepared what he was going to say, he wanted to introduce himself in a polite manner and explain why he was calling. But he didn't get an answer in Silkeborg; he let it ring for what felt like an eternity, but had to give up in the end and try the next number in Holstebro. A child answered the phone there. Eddie had problems understanding his Danish, and so spoke as clearly as he could and asked to talk to an adult. 'Mum,' he heard and then some footsteps across the floor.

Finally the mother came to the phone, and Eddie said what he'd prepared. He asked if she had lived in Copenhagen and if she had even been married to Anders Kristoffer Malthe from Norway.

'No, I haven't,' she said. 'I think you've got the wrong number.'

He put down the phone without saying goodbye and immediately dialled the third number in Kolding, but he got the same response. As he dialled the number of Inga Nielsen in Århus, he looked out of the window; the white light on the bare trees made him uneasy. But when he mentioned his father's name there was silence at the other end. For some time.

'Yes,' she said. 'That's right. But he died in '92.'

'I know,' Eddie said, his breathing shallow. 'I am his son, Eddie Malthe.'

Another deadly silence. Eddie waited.

'He talked about you. Is there something you want to know?'

For a moment Eddie considered sending praise to God, even though he wasn't a believer. He turned in triumph to his mother, who was sitting on the sofa. She looked very pensive.

'Yes,' Eddie said eagerly. 'I want to know the exact date that he died. And I want to know where he's buried.'

He had paper and pen at the ready.

'He died on the first of October 1992,' she told him. 'He's buried at Vor Frelsers Cemetery in Copenhagen. It's in Amagerbro.'

Eddie nodded to himself. He recognised the name from the long list he had found on the Internet. Before ending the call, he exchanged a few words with Inga Margrethe, and any bitterness that he had felt towards her evaporated. She was nice. And his father had often talked about him, but the fact was that Thomasine had been difficult after the split, as she put it.

'Dad is buried in Amagerbro,' he said and turned to face his mother. 'And I have a brother. He's called Mads and he's studying in New York.'

Eddie started to search again. He immediately found Vor Frelsers Church, but to his surprise he discovered that the address for the church was different to that of the cemetery. The church was in Sankt Annæ Gade in Christianhavn. He called international directory enquiries again and asked for the number, because now he had the full address, and the operator told him that there were several numbers, which one did he want?

'Who deals with the graves?' he asked.

'Presumably the sexton,' she replied. 'It says here that he's called Povel Koch.'

Eddie said goodbye and then dialled the number straight away, 004532546883, and after four rings he had the sexton on the line.

'I want to visit a grave,' Eddie explained. 'In Vor Frelsers Cemetery. But I don't know where it is, and I don't want to just wander around the graveyard looking for it.'

'If you have the date of birth, and date of death, then I can help you,' Povel Koch told him. 'We've got an electronic map.'

Eddie almost wept with joy. He had a brother called Mads in New York and he would find his father's grave. But he also had to face up to some painful truths. His father had left him and started another family, and all he had was the photograph of his father on his bedroom wall. He had practically no memories, and absolutely no love in the years that followed. And Mass had been difficult. There was a lot to think about. Eventually he turned the computer off and sat down on the sofa; he had to order all the thoughts that were tumbling around in his head.

His mother had nothing to say. She got up and went to the bathroom, filled the bath, got undressed and lowered her body into the warm water. She had always known that she wouldn't get away with it, and now it was about to happen. Eddie had found the man who had betrayed them. She grabbed the sponge and started to wash her body. She noticed a large bruise on the inside of her thigh. She thought it odd, because she couldn't remember bumping into anything, and when she put her thumb on it and pressed gently, there was no pain. Then she saw another one, further down towards the knee; they were so dark they were almost black. But she quickly forgot them when her thoughts returned to her son.

Chapter 27

August 2005

They were standing outside Simon's nursery at Blåkollen.

The big playground was green and well equipped with climbing frames, swings and sandpits, as well as an old boat with a small cabin on top. Someone had painted 'Captain Sabeltann' in black letters on the bow. This is where Simon played, Sejer thought. He could picture the little boy on top of the climbing frame, or onboard the old boat, pretending to be a pirate. They went in. The head came to meet them, showed them Simon's coat peg under the snail.

'What have you told the children?' Sejer asked.

The head was now sitting behind her desk.

'Well, we certainly gave it lots of thought, I can tell you. First we called a meeting with the parents, so they could all say what they thought, but there was no agreement. Some thought that the children should be spared, and others thought it was better to tell the truth, because children have such lively imaginations.'

'And you?'

'I wanted to tell them the truth. Not all the gruesome details, of course, but that they had been killed with a knife. I consulted a child psychologist from the Educational and Psychological Counselling Service over at Haugane School, and she supported me in wanting to tell the truth, so that's what we did in the end.'

'But some parents disagreed?'

'Yes.'

'So, how did it work when you told the children?' Sejer asked.

'We took them all into the quiet room, where there are mattresses and pillows and no one is allowed to shout. No one shouted that day. It's never been so quiet in that room.'

'How did they react?'

'With silence. The youngest ones put their thumbs in their mouths.'

'Did they ask any questions at all?'

'Yes, they wanted to know who had done it and why. We explained that he had probably been angry about something, but the police would find him and put him in jail. And that he would stay there for a long time, perhaps forever.'

She smiled when she said the last word.

The office was full of little statues and there were paintings on the wall. Sejer had a salt-dough figure on his desk lamp in the office, a small constable in a blue uniform, and over the years it had got drier and more cracked. He didn't dare to touch it any more, because he guessed it would just crumble.

'Did you notice anything different about Bonnie's behaviour in the weeks before they were murdered? Did she mention any particular incidents?'

'No, nothing like that. But it was just heart-rending every morning when Bonnie had to leave. Simon was a nervous little boy and he was always devastated when she disappeared out the door.'

'He didn't have much contact with his father,' Skarre remarked. 'Do you know why?'

'Bonnie never talked about things like that. If we broached the subject, she was dismissive. But I believe that children should have a father.'

Sejer and Skarre didn't say anything. There was nothing new to be learned at the nursery, but they hadn't really expected there would be. The visit was on their list as it helped them to get a picture of how Bonnie and Simon had been before they were killed. Just as they were on their way out, Kaja stopped them.

'There was one thing I noticed, a little thing, so it may well mean nothing,' she said. 'But a few days before it happened, I noticed a car outside the gate, it stopped as close as it could. It looked like they were waiting for someone, but no one got out, the car just stood there. It was just after Bonnie had picked Simon up and was about to pull out. For some reason, I stayed at the window and watched the car, because when you work in a nursery I suppose you're always a bit more vigilant. There are so many stories about fathers who have lost custody and kidnap their own children. We have to keep an eye out.'

'When Bonnie drove off, what did the other car do?' Sejer asked.

'It turned round and followed her.'

'And you saw the car only once?'

'No, it came back again the next day. I got the feeling that if they weren't following Bonnie, whoever it was was looking for someone, or watching a house further down the street.'

'Did you mention it to Bonnie?'

'No,' she said, distraught. 'Maybe I should have done. But Bonnie had so much on her plate already, I didn't want to make things worse. And I didn't want to overreact either. But you said you needed to know everything . . .'

'Can you remember the dates?'

'No.'

'OK. But a few days before the murders, you saw this car twice. And both times it turned and followed Bonnie?'

'Yes.'

'Are you a car person?'

'No, not at all. The only thing I can say for certain is that it was red.'

They prepared a statement about the red car for the press. The hope was that observant people may have seen it in the area. Sejer knew that the switchboard would be inundated with sightings, of course, and that was precisely what he wanted. When they got back to the station, they once again sat for a long time and studied an enlarged photograph of the footprint. The front part of the sole had left a number of small circular prints, as if it had buttons. The heel had the same circles. It was a big foot, about a size forty-six. Who did it belong to? A furious or raving lunatic, a man who had been wronged in some way, a man whose mind was full of revenge or delusions, a man who perhaps heard voices, a man who was out of his head on something. A man full of demons and fiends, a man who might not even be able to explain to himself, let alone to anyone else, why he did what he did. A man who drove a red car and had left a footprint on the worn linoleum floor and then fled through the woods.

Chapter 28

March 2005

Bonnie always felt sad in March.

She had often wondered why, but in March it was as if she was in no-man's-land: it was no longer winter, not yet spring or summer. The weather was unpredictable and the light was grey with rotten snow and the roadsides were dirty, as forgotten rubbish from the previous autumn emerged once again. One day it was freezing and there were snowstorms, the next the sun shone generously and all the snow melted again. It was hard to know what Simon should wear; he had to take his winter clothes and rain gear, waterproof boots, and a hat and mittens. There was a spare set of clothes in his bag, and some more on his hook under the snail.

One morning in late March, she stood outside Erna's door and rang the bell. Even though Erna was always up, and often unlocked the door before Bonnie arrived, she still gave three short rings to announce her arrival, to say it's me, Bonnie. But that morning, the door was locked. She realised that Erna hadn't been sitting in the window watching out for her. She stood on the step for a while, baffled and worried. She might have fallen and broken her hip, or worse. Or perhaps one of the children had been to collect her and had forgotten to notify Ragnhild in the office. Bonnie put her ear to the door and listened in case the old woman was lying on the floor, calling out, but there wasn't a sound to be heard in the house. Maybe she had overslept and was sleeping so heavily that she hadn't heard the doorbell. Bonnie gave three more short rings and stood there waiting. Then she did what they had agreed, an agreement she had with practically all her clients. Erna had a spare key, so Bonnie went round to the back of the house and found it under the flowerpot where it was always kept.

She let herself into the hall. Stood there and listened. Erna was not in the living room, nor was she to be seen in the kitchen, although the light was on. Bonnie's heart started to thump and she called her name – quietly and carefully at first, then louder. She was most scared to go into the bedroom, but when she did it was clear that Erna was already up. Or, had she not gone to bed the night before, could that be it? She might have fallen down the steep stairs into the basement, tumbled down onto the cement floor with her fragile bones. No, that didn't seem right. So she turned to the only other place: the bathroom. The door was ajar. At first all she saw was the white tiles, the ones that Erna insisted she scrub with a toothbrush, so that she could clean the grey, discoloured grout as well. Erna was lying on the floor beside the bath. She was wearing an old lacy yellow vest, but her thin body was naked from the waist down. The strip light on the ceiling was flickering and it made Bonnie feel dizzy. Was she about to faint? Erna's feet were big and swollen. On the inside of her thigh she saw a web of blue veins. She was lying on her stomach with her arms out, and a great gash was visible on her forehead. A small amount of blood had pooled on the white tiles.

Bonnie leaned against the door frame for support. She saw that there was water in the bath and realised that Erna must have fallen and hit her head on the edge of the bath.

She got down on her knees to feel for a pulse, but there was nothing beating under the thin skin. So she went into the living room and took the crocheted blanket from the sofa, went back to the bathroom, and put the blanket over the dead body. She had never seen Erna naked, so pitiful and exposed. All her energy gone. I'm going to die one day too, Bonnie thought, someone will come into the room and find me when it's all over. I hope to God I'm never found in this state.

In the evening, she had to explain to Simon why she had come to collect him so soon after she had dropped him off. She wanted him to know the truth about life and death. But she was careful all the same.

'You know that she's going to be buried in the ground, don't you?'

Yes, Simon knew that, because they'd talked about death at nursery. Kaja had tried to explain that dead people weren't there any more. They weren't sleeping, they weren't dreaming, they couldn't see, they didn't breathe, and they would never wake up again. She said that death was another country and that anyone who was alive could only imagine it.

'The coffin is very beautiful,' Bonnie explained. 'It's got silk and velvet inside, and the person is all dressed up for their final journey.'

'Where are they going?' Simon wanted to know.

'To eternity,' Bonnie replied.

'Where's that?'

'We don't know. But I think it's very beautiful there. I think it's a bit like a big garden full of flowers. And you get to meet all the other people who are dead.'

'But how do they know how to get there?'

'Oh, they just know,' Bonnie said. 'But when we're alive, we don't know. It's like a special surprise for all of us, don't you think?'

Simon was happy with that. But after he had gone to bed that evening, Bonnie sat up thinking about her own death, which of course she knew nothing about.

Chapter 29

'What are you doing on the phone?' Mass asked. 'You haven't said anything.'

For English, press 5, Eddie heard, as he played with the photograph that Inga Nielsen had sent him. It was an enlarged colour print of his father with his arms around Inga and their son, Mads. It was taken in 1991, only a year before he died. It was obvious to Eddie that Inga Nielsen was beautiful; she was much younger than Mass, with blonde wavy hair, and she was wearing a spotty summer dress. It was easy to understand why they had fallen in love. Why his father, tall and handsome as he was, had chosen this beauty over them. His mother had been reluctant to look at the picture when he held it up for her to see. His brother Mads was just a little boy, and he could tell that his father was much older in this picture than the one above his bed.

No, he didn't have a Eurobonus card, but he continued patiently to tap his way through the menu to book a return flight to Copenhagen. *This phone call may be recorded*, he heard. Jesus, as if I care. And then, having waited for what seemed like forever, he finally heard a voice asking if it could help him. He had doodled all over the notebook as he waited. The doodles didn't mean anything, they were simply an expression of his excitement and tension. This was perhaps the most important decision he had ever made in his whole life.

'I have flown before, you know,' Eddie muttered, when his mother expressed her concern.

'But I was with you,' Mass pointed out. 'How will you find out where to go?'

'I'll ask,' he said curtly. 'Everyone at the airport will be in uniform.'

'I mean to get to the cemetery,' she said. 'Copenhagen is a big city.'

'I'll take a taxi,' he replied. 'It's not that difficult, is it? Stop going on.'

Mass wanted to cry. Her son, who she loved so much, was going out into the big, wide world, alone, to find a father who had deserted him. And then showered all his love on a second son.

The flight was at ten past seven in the morning and his mother drove him to the airport express train. She stood on the platform and watched the train pull out with a sense of foreboding and an uneasy heart. Eddie. Dear Eddie. He had a rucksack on his back that contained the few things he needed, and as the train whizzed him out to the airport, he sat and thought. It didn't bother him in the slightest that his mother didn't want him to go.

When he got to the airport, he went to the check-in desk with his reference number. He didn't dare use the automatic check-in, in case he got it wrong. He was given his boarding card, went through security, and then he had to take off his heavy boots and go through again. He went straight to the gate, where he sat and waited patiently. Dad, he thought, I'm only a few hours away. He boarded the plane, found his place by the window, and collapsed into the narrow seat. The person before must have been a real skinny malinky, so he had to adjust the seat belt. He concentrated on the safety demonstration, keeping his eyes on the air hostess, and picked up on the oxygen masks, the life jackets and whistle, and the four emergency exits. He would have to struggle out through the doors if they crash-landed. He would crawl down the aisle, over the other passengers if necessary. The plane might explode in a ball of flames. And all that his mother would be given was the remains of some scorched bones. Eventually he relaxed and settled. The pilot wanted to get home in one piece too, he probably had children waiting for him. So he had to land them all safely.

When he got to Kastrup, he didn't know where to go. He followed the other passengers to the luggage hall, but he didn't need to wait for anything as he had his bag on his back. So he headed straight for the exit and found a taxi.

'Amagerbrogate 33,' Eddie said, and leaned forward between the seats.

He got his wallet out of his bag and had his Visa card at the ready.

'You got someone there?' the driver asked.

'My father,' Eddie explained, as he sat back in his seat.

The driver steered a steady course through the Copenhagen traffic. He had a ring of silver hair round the back of his head, and his crown shone like a globe. Eddie was almost there, for real; the sexton was going to meet him at the main entrance. When they found each other, they shook hands. It had started to rain, so they would get wet.

'So,' Povel Koch said, 'let's go and find your father. As I told you, he's in a very nice place. You might find that his grave is a little overgrown, but you said yourself on the phone that his family had moved away.'

The sexton was heavy and waddled through the maze of beautifully kept graves. It was an enormous cemetery and Eddie was astounded that the sexton could find his way anywhere, even if he did have a map. His heart started to pound inside his wet jacket, and he felt very proud of himself as he followed behind. Tracker Tore could eat dirt.

And then all at once he was standing there alone in the rain. The sexton left him in peace, and he stared at the name, Anders Kristoffer Malthe. Peace be with you.

Eddie noticed immediately that his father's gravestone stood out. The other stones were black or grey, whereas his was white. It stood there gleaming among all the other dark stones, as if it were calling out to him. The stonemason had carved a wreath under the arched top of the stone. Now that Eddie was finally standing in front of his father's grave, after endless years of frustration, anger and longing, the emotions overwhelmed him. He was furious and happy and proud, but he was still bitter. There was nothing growing on the grave, as it was March, and Eddie suddenly realised that he should have brought flowers. Think of travelling all this way and forgetting the most essential thing. He bowed his head in shame, and looked around at the other graves. Many of them did not have flowers either. He had a little wander, but made sure he didn't stray too far, for fear of not being able to find his way back. When he had been walking about for a while, he spotted a gravestone with an angel on it and a bunch of fresh flowers on the ground in front. There was a candle beside the flowers that had been extinguished by the rain. He read the name on the gravestone, Martin, who only lived to be four years old, which was probably why he had such fresh flowers. Presumably his mother came to the grave every day. He picked up the flowers and inspected them, they were white and blue. He took the candle too and said to the grave: 'You'll get new ones tomorrow.'

He went back to his father's grave and laid the flowers on the ground.

He stood in front of the white gravestone for a long time, so many thoughts in his head. It felt good to be there, but there was a certain sadness too, and as he was about to leave, he pressed his hand against the stone, and the rain trickled down under his collar and made him shiver.

You shouldn't have come. Mum is raging.

For the rest of the day, he wandered around Copenhagen.

He went into a cafe and had some chicken for lunch, then a little later he sat down somewhere else for a Coke and some cake. He went into the shops, looked for things from New York, and thought about his brother Mads. I'm going to find you too, he thought, now that I've started. By the time he was on the flight home again at eight, he felt deeply satisfied. He had done what he'd set out to do, it had been an important project, and he had not let anything stop him, not the authorities or his mother's doubt. He was served coffee and a roll, the sky outside was dark, and his mother would be waiting for him at the station. He would give her a detailed report, though he would omit the fact that he had stolen the flowers from four-year-old Martin.

She was there waiting and gave him a big hug, was relieved to have him home again in one piece, hoped he would calm down now and be himself again. When she thought about it, it was only right and reasonable that he'd gone. I clipped his wings, but they've grown out again. She had bought some cinnamon rolls for him and Eddie munched away happily. She had also been to the shopping centre and bought him a new sweatshirt. It was black, but it said something different: *Survival of the Fittest*, with a picture of a Rottweiler baring its teeth. He liked it a lot. He told her about the rain in Copenhagen, the friendly sexton. The enormous double wrought-iron gate at the entrance, the beautiful white stone with a wreath on it. About the chicken he'd eaten and the cakes, all the people in the rain. Later that night, he finally put the photograph of the Malthe family up on the wall, and slept more soundly than he had done for a long time.

Mass sat under the reading light. It warmed the top of her head. She had a constant ache in her back now, and had found more bruises. Her right wrist was sore as well. What on earth was the matter with her? She leaned her head back and closed her eyes. There could be no doubt any more. Something was seriously wrong with her body.

Shiba was no longer fat as a stuffed sausage, but instead a weak, skin-and-bones bag of a dog, with a lot of pain. She was riddled with cancer, so there was no hope. Mass could sit in the corner with her for ages, stroking her head and back while mumbling words of affection. She drew in the smell of her, buried her face in her fur, rubbed her big paws. Eddie watched them from the living room. He knew where it was all leading, and could tell that his mother was putting it off for as long as she could. One day, he went into the kitchen, leaned against the windowsill, and said: 'Enough is enough. She can hardly walk. And there's no dignity in shitting on a newspaper.'

Mass looked at her son.

'I know. But I can't face it. It'll be so empty without her. No one waiting for me in the morning.'

'I'll be waiting,' Eddie said.

'But to stand there and watch him give her the injection, I can't even bear to think about it,' she said, distraught. 'I just can't do it.'

Eddie made a big decision. Buoyed by his visit to Copenhagen, he felt that he could now do anything, and what's more, he really wanted to help. He liked the fact that his mother needed him.

'I'll take her to the vet,' he said firmly, 'so you don't need to. I'll sort everything out. Just call Munthe to say that I'm coming.'

Mass thought about it for a while.

'Do you think I'm a coward?' she asked.

'Of course not,' Eddie assured her. 'You've never been a coward. You can say goodbye to Shiba here, and then I can carry her out to the car.'

'OK,' she said eventually. 'Thank you. Let's do that then.'

Now that the decision had finally been made, she picked up the phone and called Munthe. She explained that Eddie would come with Shiba, that she couldn't face it, and that she would like it done as soon as possible.

'I'll go and buy some smoked sausage,' she said to Eddie afterwards. 'So that she finishes with something nice.'

'Buy some for me too,' Eddie said. 'I'm starving.'

When the day finally came, they were both up early. This was no ordinary day. Mass couldn't bear to look her son in the eye.

Shiba had been given the first appointment of the day, because Mass didn't want to wait for too long. She had transferred three thousand kroner to Eddie's account, to pay for having the dog put down and cremated. She would go to the vet at some later point to pick up the urn, which she wanted to keep by the wood burner. It was a quarter past seven when Eddie carried the sick dog out to the car, and then it was time for Mass to say goodbye. Eddie gave her plenty of time, he sat patiently at the wheel and waited. For some reason, he was excited to be part of this. He felt that he was on an important mission. But also, Shiba's death meant that he would no longer have to share his mother's attention with anyone.

He drove the thirty kilometres into town, parked the car and got out, opened the boot and lifted her down. She stood there on shaky legs and looked at him dolefully. 'Come on,' he said. 'You're not getting out of it.'

She pulled herself across the car park to the steps. Then Eddie had to lift her up and carry her into reception, where he put her down on the floor before going to the counter.

'Malthe,' he said. 'I'm here to put my dog down.'

'What's your dog called?'

'Shiba.'

The veterinary nurse nodded. 'Mr Munthe is ready for you,' she said. 'He'll be right out.'

Eddie sat down. The only other person there was a young girl, with a basket on the floor in front of her. Maybe it was a cat, or a rabbit. 'There's always something wrong with pets,' he whispered to the dog, 'you're expensive.'

Shiba had closed her eyes. He wondered if she had sixth sense, if she knew what was about to happen. Generally dogs seemed to understand an awful lot. Humans know that they're going to die, he thought, so dogs must do too.

Munthe stopped in front of him.

'Good morning, Eddie. So you've come, eh?' he said.

'Mum couldn't face it,' he explained.

'So I understand,' Munthe said. 'It's a good thing she's got you.'

Eddie felt pride swelling in his breast. He followed the vet into the room, pulling Shiba behind him for those final steps. Then they put her on a bench that could be raised and lowered.

'I know this is hard for you,' Munthe comforted, 'but in terms of her health and well-being, it is absolutely the best thing for all three of you.'

'I know,' Eddie replied. 'I've told Mum hundreds of times.'

He put his hand on the dog's head, tried to catch her eye.

'Would you like some time alone with her?' Munthe asked.

'No,' Eddie said immediately. 'Just do it.'

Munthe got some small ampoules and a syringe. Then he put his hand on the dog's neck and explained the procedure to Eddie.

'First I'll give her an injection in the neck skin here. It's an opiate, so it will make her drowsy and calm. Once she's had that, Shiba won't worry about much any more.'

'Sounds good,' Eddie said, keen to get on with it.

Munthe put the needle into her skin and emptied the syringe. He looked across at Eddie.

'We have to wait for fifteen minutes now. She'll fall into a light sleep. So I'll leave the two of you alone now.'

Eddie leaned down over Shiba and thought about what was about to happen. He lifted her paw, it was completely floppy. He pulled her tail as he normally did, but she didn't react. He lifted an eyelid and stared into her black pupil. She was dribbling. Then he sat down again and waited for the executioner. He heard a little dog yapping out in reception, could be a poodle or a chihuahua; a telephone was ringing furiously but no one answered. There were people sitting out there who needed help with all kinds of things, maybe their dog had worms or eczema, or a double set of teeth like Shiba had had when she was a puppy. When he got home he would have to report everything to his mother, exactly what had happened, because she would no doubt ask about all the details. After a while, Munthe came back. He got another syringe.

'I inject this one into her front leg,' he explained. 'It's intravenous. So it works very fast, only takes a minute. It paralyses her brain first, then her breathing. She won't notice anything. She's already out of it.'

Eddie thought about Mass. She would be waiting with her hands in front of her face. She might have cleared the kitchen corner already, put away the two dishes and the old blanket. She might even be vacuuming the floor to get rid of all the dog hairs.

You should have been an Alsatian, he thought, you weren't much good as a guard dog, just barked no matter who came. The yappy little dog out in the waiting room had stopped yapping and there was a deafening silence.

'When you get home, please tell your mother that everything went well,' Munthe instructed him.

Eddie nodded.

'What about getting a new puppy, Eddie?'

'Mum says no. So it'll be just the two of us, which is OK. You can just do it now,' he added, because he was waiting. He was thinking about his own death. Not that he was going to be given an injection. His mum wouldn't even be there. To grieve. No one would grieve. No one would come to his grave with flowers, and his coffin would be carried out of Geirastadir Church by six minions from Securitas. Three handfuls of dry earth over the coffin, and the priest might just sing alone with majesty. The hymn he hated more than anything else. Lead, kindly light, amid th'encircling gloom. Or, as he often thought to himself, help me through the mist.

The hypodermic needle was as thin as a sewing needle. Shiba did not move at all, but Eddie could see that she was breathing. Munthe looked for a vein in her front leg, then pressed the contents slowly in. There was not even so much as a tremor in her thin body. Eddie watched the dying animal with great intensity.

Once Shiba had been put down, he went to the CC shopping centre and had a smoked salmon and scrambled egg sandwich. When he was finished, he went back to the counter and ordered a custard slice and another Coke. For one reason or another, he felt light-hearted. But now he had to prepare himself for going home and to decide what to say. Before getting into the car, he wandered around the shopping centre, looking at people and things. He was glad that he didn't know anyone, glad that he didn't need to talk. About the weather and other stupid things, such as how he was. Almost everything people said to each other was rubbish.

When he pulled up in front of the house, he saw his mother's pale face in the kitchen window. He lifted his hand and waved, but she didn't wave back.

That night, as Eddie lay awake in bed under the picture of the family in Copenhagen, he thought about Kennedy the cat. What if he put down a line of rat poison from Ansgar's mailbox to the house? The cat would no doubt be tempted by the tasty little pink grains. And then, the next morning, all he would have to do is pick it up, put it in a plastic bag and throw it in the rubbish. Eddie knew that rat poison contained strychnine. And strychnine poisoning was a horrible way to die, with internal bleeding and cramps. As always, when he had these fantasies, he felt calm. Like after a cup of hot milk and honey.

Chapter 30

After Erna's funeral, Bonnie was given a new client, and as she waited outside the door, her body filled with a strange anticipation. A man opened the door and held out his hand, and his handshake was so firm that Bonnie almost whimpered. She entered into a large hallway and took off her coat.

'You can call me Alex,' he said. 'No one calls me Alexander.'

'I hope I can be of use,' Bonnie replied. 'Just tell me what to do.'

She looked at him with curiosity, because he was so different from her other clients. He couldn't be more than twenty-something. He was wearing a black T-shirt, and her first impression was that his upper body was very muscular, especially his upper arms. He must have been training for years. Otherwise, he had fair hair and a ring in one ear, and even though it was only March, he was a healthy colour. He rolled his wheelchair into the living room, and she noted that he was obviously financially well off, as he had good furniture and an impressive flat-screen on the wall. There were large loudspeakers in every corner of the room and a lot of green plants.

'Do you play chess?' Alex asked.

Bonnie had to confess that she didn't.

'I'll teach you,' he said, without hesitation, and rolled over to the table. He got the black and white pieces out of a drawer under the tabletop, and then explained to Bonnie how they could move across the board.

'We're at war,' he said. 'You have an army and I have an army, and we're both out to capture each other's king. The point is that you constantly have to think ahead. If you move the knight like this, or this, what space does that leave for my king? Does that make sense?'

She nodded.

'I should really use my time on other things,' she said cautiously. 'You see, we have to follow regulations. So in terms of what you need, why did you apply for a home help?'

'Sod the regulations,' Alex said sharply. 'It's me who decides. You take the white pieces, which means you start.'

Bonnie moved a piece. She had no idea what she was getting herself into. She looked around the room, and her eyes stopped at a photograph of Alex and a beautiful girl with red hair. Alex was standing on his own two legs in the picture, no wheelchair to be seen.

'My girlfriend,' he explained. 'She comes every day after work. And with a bit of imagination we manage to do most things.'

He smiled at Bonnie and she smiled back. She was always happy when people didn't let each other down, in the way that she'd been let down.

'How did you end up in a wheelchair?' she wanted to know.

'Car accident,' he told her. 'Head-on collision with a Polish lorry.'

'Oh,' Bonnie said, horrified, as Alex moved his first black piece.

'Whose fault was it?'

'Mine.'

'Were you driving too fast?'

'A hundred and forty.'

He waited for her to make the next move.

Bonnie found it hard to concentrate.

'What about the guy in the lorry?' she asked. 'Was he injured?'

'No,' Alex replied. 'Lorry drivers are pretty safe. But if he had been injured or killed, I don't know how I would have managed to live with the guilt. He didn't even break a finger. He came to visit me in hospital. And now, Magnus Carlsen, it's time for you to play.'

Before she left, she was allowed to run the vacuum cleaner over the floors in the adapted, easy-to-care-for flat. He rolled out into the hall with her to say goodbye.

'What are you doing this evening?' she asked. 'Is Elisabeth coming?'

'Yes. We're going to the Apollo gym. We go there every other day. You should start training too,' he said. 'It makes you better equipped, you know, for life and things.'

Bonnie shook her head.

'Will you babysit for me then?' she said. 'I'm a single mother.'

'I think you should get yourself a man,' Alex told her, because he saw that she was beautiful and thought that wouldn't be hard.

'A shame you're taken,' she retorted, and opened the door. 'I can hardly beat Elisabeth.'

They both laughed. And she knew that her days with Alex would be good days.

That night she had a terrible dream.

She dreamed that Olav came to get Simon, that he wanted to take him out to Gullfaks. The father and son sat close together in the helicopter and the sea below was grey and stormy. She stood on the quay and waved as the helicopter lifted, then she sank into despondency. And as she stood there watching, it plummeted into the sea, and Simon disappeared forever into the churning water. She woke with a gasp, lay there for a while with a hand on her racing heart. Later she went into Simon's room and stood at his bedside for a long time. She stroked him gently on the cheek, then crept back to her room. She often went to bed in the evening with an enormous sense of relief that nothing had happened. It could not be taken for granted that they were both healthy and well. She read in the papers every day about catastrophes that had struck other people's lives, and she offered a quiet prayer to God that she and Simon would be spared.

Chapter 31

One morning, Mass woke with such pain in her back that she was seriously worried. She managed to crawl out of bed and sat down on a chair in the living room. Her wrist was still sore. As soon as she knew the medical centre was open, she rang and made an appointment. It was urgent, she said, she was in a lot of pain and she needed painkillers. She got an appointment the following day, but said nothing to Eddie, because she didn't want to worry him.

When she arrived, she told reception who she was, and sat down to wait with a magazine. But she couldn't concentrate, and put it down again. After half an hour, she was called in. She sat down on the patients' chair.

'Good morning, Thomasine,' her GP said. 'It's a long time since you were last here. How's Eddie?'

'Oh, you know how he is,' she said. 'Stubborn as a three-year-old and still on incapacity benefit. But he's good company. Without him, I'd be all alone.'

He pulled up her medical records on the computer screen, read through the last consultation notes.

'So, how can I help you today?'

'I've got these terrible pains in my back. And for some reason, my right wrist is sore as well.'

She put her arm down on his desk, and he lifted it gently and examined it carefully.

'No swelling,' he confirmed. 'Have you fallen or hit it in any way?'

'Not at all. I'm still steady on my feet; I'm only fifty-six, you know,' she exclaimed.

'Quite,' he nodded. 'Have you lifted anything heavy?'

Mass started to laugh. 'I've got Eddie. And he's as strong as an ox.'

'How long has it been hurting?' he asked.

'Quite some time now. It wasn't much to begin with, but it's gradually got worse.'

'I see,' he said, and paused for thought. Then he turned back to the screen and added some notes in the records.

'And otherwise?'

He looked at her. She was sitting with her handbag on her lap and looked as though she wanted to take flight.

'Well, I've got some bruises,' she had to admit. 'There seem to be more and more of them and I've had them a long time.'

'Where are they?'

'On my thighs. I notice them when I shower. And I have no idea where they come from.'

'Let me have a look,' he said.

Mass stood up and pulled her trousers down. She was shy, but she knew the GP, had been his patient for many years, and she really needed to find out what was wrong. He put his finger on the bruises one by one.

'Are they tender?'

'I can't feel anything, that's the strange thing.'

She pulled her trousers up again. The doctor sat and pondered; she wanted him to say something, but he was just silent.

Then he took out a small torch and rolled his chair round so he could get closer, and shone it in her eyes. First one, then the other. Mass had no idea what he was looking for.

'We need to take some tests,' he said. 'You'll have to sit and wait outside the lab. We need to check your blood. And I also want you to go to the main hospital for some X-rays. I'll send a referral and you'll get an appointment in the post.'

'Will I have to wait long?'

'No,' he said promptly. 'I'll say it's urgent.'

'Is it urgent?' she asked, horrified. 'Should I be worried?'

'Probably not,' he said and smiled. 'But we need to find out what it is. And in the meantime, I'll prescribe tramadol, which is good for back pain.'

She took the prescription and thanked him.

'Say hello to Eddie,' he said as she got up. And she promised to do so.

'I don't see much of him,' he commented.

'Eddie's never ill,' Mass replied.

She took a queue number outside the lab; there were obviously a lot of people in front of her and she found it impossible to relax now. When she was finally shown in, she didn't dare ask about anything. But when they were done, she did ask if they could send a letter when the results were ready.

'We'll send the results to your doctor,' they said, 'and he will contact you.'

She thanked them for their help and went out to the car. She stopped at the chemist's to pick up the painkillers. When she got home, Eddie asked where she had been.

'I had a few errands,' she said. 'You know, the bank and things. And the post office.'

'Jeez,' Eddie whistled. 'Does it take that long to go to the bank?'

She didn't answer. Instead she went out into the kitchen and out of habit glanced down into the corner, but Shiba was gone. Neither of them mentioned the dog any more.

Only a week later, she got a letter from the hospital with an appointment. When she got there, she made her way through the main entrance and up in the lift to the X-ray department, full of hope. This time she didn't have to wait before she was shown in and the examination didn't take long. They took X-rays of her back and wrist.

Once again, the results would be sent to her doctor. She took Eddie out for a Chinese meal later in the afternoon. She hadn't told him about her visits to the doctor and hospital yet. She kept telling herself that it was nothing serious. In any case, the tramadol was working so well that she almost forgot the pain. And when her GP then contacted her to say that all the results had come in, she was certain that it would soon all be sorted.

He sat with his hands in his lap and looked at her, took off his spectacles.

'I'm going to explain to you what we've found so far,' he said, 'but I'm afraid you're going to have to go for further tests at the hospital.'

Mass didn't dare respond; her eyes were glued to the doctor, and she was gripping her handbag so hard that her knuckles were white.

'We have found something in the blood tests and X-rays,' he explained. 'And when I examined your eyes, I saw that you had jaundice.'

'What?'

She stared at him, nonplussed.

'Yes,' he confirmed. 'The whites of your eyes are yellow. You perhaps haven't noticed yourself.'

'What does that mean?' she wanted to know.

'That's what we need to find out, and that's why I'm referring you on for more tests. But there's something else as well, and this will probably surprise you. It turns out that you have a fracture at the base of your wrist. Radius. And I initially thought osteoporosis, as it's a common symptom and injury.'

Mass closed her eyes in dismay.

'I've heard about women who get fractures just by turning over in bed,' she said. 'Or banging into something, like a door or piece of furniture.'

'Yes,' the doctor said hesitantly. 'That's right. But I'm not entirely sure that is what's wrong with you. When is the pain in your back worst?'

'When I'm lying in bed. Not when I'm moving about. It seems so illogical.'

'Fractures can actually happen spontaneously,' he told her. 'Which might be the case here.'

'But how can that happen? Is it an illness?'

'I don't want to comment on that really, I'll leave it to the experts,' he said. 'I'll give you a referral. They'll probably take some more blood tests at the hospital. Ultrasound, an MRI and a CT scan. And maybe a couple of biopsies.'

The worry was eating at her now. What was wrong with her, and should she tell Eddie? She decided not to say anything until she knew for certain.

When she got home, she tried to distract herself with domestic chores, but it was impossible to concentrate. She sat down with the paper, but didn't read it; she ate some food, but didn't taste it; she turned on the TV, but it was nothing more than images that flickered by. She hardly slept that night, took more and more tramadol, and even though it would soon be spring, she couldn't muster any enthusiasm.

Eddie thought she was in mourning for Shiba. It worried him that she was so restless. One day he suggested that they could get a new puppy, but Mass gave a definite no. 'This time you're not going to persuade me,' she said.

She went back to the hospital where she went through endless tests. Everyone was friendly towards her. She wondered if that was because they realised how worried she was, but then thought probably not, because they had to deal with so many people and were practised at it. When she was finally done, she put her clothes back on and took the lift down to the cafe. Now she just had to wait for another letter. In the past few weeks, she had started to experience stomach pains and had lost some weight. Even though that was something she had wanted for a long time, she knew this weight loss was due to something else, which wasn't good. She sat there with a cup of coffee and studied the other people. She thought they were moving so slowly, that all the voices just merged into a hum that rose and fell. Then she drove back home to Eddie. She didn't tell him anything about what she had been through.

One day he came in with the newspaper and put the post down on the kitchen table.

'There's a letter for you from Vestre Viken Health Authority,' he said. 'Are you going in for a mammography?'

He could just imagine his mother's heavy breasts pressed together between two glass plates, and he was sure that she didn't like standing half naked in front of strangers.

'No,' she said evasively. 'It's something else.'

She picked up the letter, then put it back down on the table.

'Aren't you going to open it?' he asked. 'What is it?'

She sat with the envelope in her hands.

'Can you get me a knife?' she said wearily.

He fetched a knife for her, and she opened the envelope, read the few lines on the page. They asked her to come to the hospital for a consultation with Dr Bromann, in connection with the examinations and tests that had been done.

'It's just the results of some tests,' she said bravely to Eddie. 'I have to go in on Friday and talk to the doctor.'

'I want to come too,' Eddie said swiftly.

He didn't like the white envelope and his mother's evasive eyes.

'No, I'll go on my own,' she said. 'You don't need to hold my hand, I'm a big girl now.'

'I know. I just thought you might like the company.'

She shook her head and put the letter down. She couldn't look her son in the eye.

The shelves were filled with books and there were great piles of paper everywhere. Bromann was sitting on a high-backed chair. He had a large melancholy face, and some thinning tufts of fine white hair. When Mass entered his office, he got up to greet her.

'Please, sit down,' he said kindly. 'We have a lot to talk about.'

She put her handbag down beside the chair, and waited for the judgement.

'So, Thomasine,' he started, 'you have had a series of tests done, and you are probably quite tired of it all. And no doubt a little confused.'

'Yes,' she said, 'I'm exhausted.'

'But we had to make sure it was a thorough examination, and we've found a number of things. I'll go through them one by one, and will try not to use too much terminology, so you can understand.'

She didn't say anything. She realised that something was about to happen, something she had always feared.

'First of all, you have jaundice,' he said. 'You have pains in your stomach and you've lost weight. You also have pain in your back, which is worst when you are lying down. Your blood counts are all over the place. And we noticed something in your bones when we did the MRI scan. And the ultrasound.'

'Gosh, that doesn't sound good,' Mass said in an anxious voice.

'Well, it isn't entirely good,' Bromann said, and looked her straight in the eyes. He didn't blink.

Mass noticed the most absurd things, that his glasses were smeared, that there was a dent on the bridge of his nose. She felt as if she were standing on the shore and a wall of water was rushing towards her.

'I'm afraid I have to tell you that you have full-blown cancer of the pancreas,' he then said.

Mass gasped.

'You mean tumours? Malignant?'

'Yes. Several of them.'

'But they can be taken out?'

'I'm afraid not.'

'Why not?'

'Normally, we can operate,' he told her, 'but not in this instance.'

'But dear God, why not?'

He sank into his high-backed chair.

'Because unfortunately it has already spread to your bones. You have been ill for a long time without realising it. This particular cancer has only a few and rather diffuse symptoms.'

The tidal wave engulfed her. In a matter of seconds she understood she was going to die. She thought she might collapse on his desk, and that Bromann would gather her up in his strong arms.

'But what about Eddie?' she sobbed. 'He can't cope alone.'

'Your husband?'

'No, he's gone. I've only got a son. He lives at home with me because he needs help and he's on benefits.'

Bromann nodded. The sympathy he felt for the woman sitting opposite him who was soon to die was in danger of making him lose his professionalism.

'What is his diagnosis?'

'He doesn't have one,' Mass wailed. 'But he can't work. He's incapable, he doesn't fit in. But he manages fine at home with me.'

'Can you tell me what sort of things he can do and what he can't?'

'He's very slow and cautious, but his brain is good. He gets anxious when I leave the house. When he was small, he suffered from separation anxiety, and he's still frightened of strangers even now. He seldom goes out. He's twenty-one years old and he will live at home with me until I die. And now you've told me that I'm just about to die. Because that is what you're telling me, isn't it?'

She looked at him in desperation.

'Can I not have a marrow transplant?'

'No,' Bromann said. 'I'm afraid it's too late.'

'But when am I going to die then?'

'I understand that you ask. The cancer is quite far advanced, but you know, even doctors can be wrong. You will be given chemotherapy.'

'And then I'll lose my hair?'

'Do you think that's so bad?'

'No, I've never been that vain. But Eddie will be scared.'

She picked up her handbag, opened it and looked for a tissue, but she didn't have any, so she put the bag down again.

'Is it a matter of months? Or maybe a year?'

'We would normally reckon on three to six months. But in your case, unfortunately, it may be sooner.'

Mass sat with her eyes closed. She was sinking, sinking, sinking. Eddie alone in the house, it would never work. He had no concept of cleaning. Would he even be able to make himself food?

She felt sick. Her mouth was dry.

'Can I die at home?' she asked in a faint voice.

'Yes,' Bromann said. 'If that's what you want, but it won't be easy. You will be supported by the palliative care unit at the hospital. They will visit you at home. And as far as your son is concerned, we'll make sure he gets all the help he needs from the social care services. We'll send a request to the council as soon as possible.'

'No,' Mass said wildly. 'You don't know what he's like!'

He asked if she had someone she could talk to, other than her son. She said no. She got up, but her legs would scarcely carry her.

'What am I going to say to Eddie?'

Bromann followed her to the door.

'You have to tell him the truth. Don't leave him in the dark. Given what's coming, you have to work together. And you might have important things to say to each other.'

*

When Mass finally got home, she found Eddie on the sofa under a blanket. An old American film was flickering on the TV screen. He was eating an enormous bar of chocolate. She dropped her handbag on the floor and disappeared into the kitchen, where she opened a cupboard. She got out a glass and filled it with ice-cold water. Her mouth was like sandpaper and she swallowed it down in greedy gulps, filled the glass again and sat down at the kitchen table.

'Were the tests OK?' Eddie asked from the doorway. He stood there looking at his mother with big eyes.

'Yes, yes,' Mass reassured him, without looking at him. 'I'm anaemic and my ESR is high. I need to take some medicine,' she mumbled. 'Let's make supper.'

She stood up and opened the fridge, took out a packet of three pork chops, two for Eddie, one for her. As they ate, she suggested that they drive up to Geirastadir Church to tend to Eddie's grandparents' grave. He was keen to go. It was April now and they could finally plant some flowers, because the snow had melted and there was some warmth in the sun. They stopped at the garden centre on the way. Eddie carried the box with four small plants out to the car and then they drove up to the churchyard. Mass walked between the graves, breathing through her mouth – she couldn't get enough air. She would be lying here herself in a few weeks. She couldn't believe it. Eddie followed her with the plants, and his mother was carrying the trowel. They were going to plant the flowers. She kept her eyes on the slab path. She looked down at her feet, as if they somehow were not hers any more.

'Look at that!' he exclaimed when they got to the grave. Mass looked in horror at the heavy, tilting stone with her parents' names on it. She put down the trowel and went over to it, placed her hands on the stone to see if it would move. It didn't.

'What are we going to do if it falls?' Eddie asked, appalled. 'Do you think someone has pushed it?'

'I can't imagine why they would; it just happens sometimes. We can talk to the sexton.'

Mass plumped down on her knees and pressed the trowel into the ground with considerable force. Earth, she thought, darkness. In a few years, only bones left. Eddie lifted the blue flowers out of the box, held them up to his nose; they smelt sweet. When the plants were in place, Mass stood up with her hands on the small of her aching back. Even though she wasn't in front of a mirror, she knew she was pale.

'There's no way that's just from cleaning,' Eddie said.

Mass gave a brave smile. Then they went back to the car. Fastened their seat belts and drove home. Mass's head was teeming, she knew she didn't have much time and there was so much to be done while she still had the energy.

Chapter 32

August 2005

Sejer and Skarre told Henny Hayden about the red car that had been observed near the scene of the crime. She had already read about it in the papers, which she pored over every day now.

'Do you know if anyone in Bonnie's circle of friends and acquaintances drove a red car?'

'I'm afraid not,' she replied. 'And in any case, I really don't think it's anyone who was close to Bonnie. Goodness, who would it be?'

'Well, we'll see,' Sejer said. 'We'll keep you updated.'

'So you think the red car is a clue?'

'Yes, I suppose so.'

'But no one saw who was sitting inside?'

'Yes, there was one sighting, when the driver got out of the car. And there's something about the man that interests us.'

'What's that then?'

'The way he was dressed made him stand out. And he was seen walking down towards Skarven.'

'You mean on the day they died?'

'Yes, and around the same time.'

'But tell us how you are,' Skarre encouraged. 'Do you have good friends who can support you?'

'Yes, I have some very good friends. But I can't face talking to them at the moment, so I haven't been in touch. And they don't know what to say to me, can hardly look at me. When I bump into them in the shops they look the other way, try to avoid me.'

'You mustn't underestimate them.'

'I don't, I just can't face it!'

'And what about Henrik, how is he?' Sejer wondered.

'We're losing him more and more,' she said. 'I don't know what to do.'

There wasn't much the two men could do to comfort her. So instead they asked some more questions about Bonnie, because they realised that it was her daughter she wanted to talk about.

Did she have any particular interests in the period before she died? Did she mention anything unusual, anything that made you think? Or was she worried about anything?

'No, nothing. And if there was, she didn't say anything to me. She was often worried about Simon, he was such a nervous child. She was concerned for the old people that she looked after every day. And for her father.'

'And what about the people we've already spoken to,' Skarre asked, 'for example her ex-partner, Olav? You haven't remembered anything that might be of interest? She took the break-up very badly, and could hardly bear to see him.'

'That's just the way Bonnie was. When she got attached to someone, it was till death do us part.'

Sejer noted her use of the words 'till death do us part'.

'She had been betrayed once before,' Henny told them. 'But she was only a teenager then. It was her first boyfriend and she was over the moon. Stood in front of the mirror all the time and we weren't used to that. But then, he finished it. And she was devastated, inconsolable.'

'Did you know him?'

'No, she never brought him home. I thought that perhaps it was because Henrik was so strict. He thought she was far too young to have a boyfriend, and sometimes I got the feeling that he was just waiting for it to be over, and then he could relax again. You know what fathers are like.'

'Do you remember what he was called?'

'Jørgen.'

'Did he ever contact her again?'

'Not that I know of. He simply disappeared into the big blue. Just like Olav.'

Sejer suddenly thought of something.

'She was a teenager when she developed anorexia,' he said. 'Did you ever connect that with the break-up? With Jørgen?'

'Yes, I did, as a matter of fact. But at the time we were just relieved that she'd managed to get over it without any lasting damage and started to eat again. We fretted that she might not be able to have children, because the doctors had spoken to us about that. You know, because of the illness. Malnourishment. But then after some years, she had Simon. Sometimes having a child can give us new life.'

Chapter 33

April 2005

One day Bonnie Hayden received a letter. She stood by the mailbox and studied it, because she didn't often get letters and this was fortunately not a bill – at least, she didn't think it was. She felt immediate relief. It was a rather posh yellow envelope, and on the bottom left-hand corner it said in blue script 'Falck Solicitors'.

Solicitors? She did a double take. She had no idea what solicitors might want with her. For some reason it made her feel uneasy, and she went back to the steps where Simon was waiting, unlocked the door and went in, put the letter down on the kitchen table. At first she wanted to rip it open, but then she got nervous. There was something ominous about a letter from a firm of solicitors. Why did they want to get in touch with her? She sat down on a chair and looked at the envelope in her hands. Simon was standing in the doorway watching her.

'Do we have to pay more money?' he asked anxiously.

'I don't know,' was her curt reply.

'Open it.'

'Later. Let's have something to eat first.'

She put the letter on top of the fridge and started to make supper. After they had eaten, they cleared the table and settled down on the sofa. Bonnie held the letter up to the light, as close as she could to the bulb, so she could see. But the writing inside the envelope remained unintelligible black scribbles. Eventually she tore open the envelope and read the letter.

With reference to the death of Erna Margrethe Vibe on 17 March this year, and her signed and attested will, you are requested to attend our offices at your earliest possible convenience. Please call to make an appointment.
Yours sincerely,
Christian Falck

The full address and business hours were given at the bottom.

Bonnie lowered the letter into her lap. It was certainly unexpected. But Erna's will, what could that mean? She had only worked for her, they weren't related. She was struck by an amusing thought, perhaps she had inherited something, some coffee cups or silverware. If it's silverware I'll sell it straight away, she thought with a smile. Simon saw his mother smiling. It was time for her to read him a bedtime story.

That night, Bonnie lay awake thinking about Erna. She had sometimes wondered if the old woman actually belonged in a mental hospital of some kind, what with the socks on the furniture legs. Whatever the case, she had children and they would be her legal heirs. When she eventually fell asleep, she dreamed about Alex, whom she had grown so fond of in such a short time, and she was getting pretty good at chess. She hadn't managed to beat him yet, but she had promised herself that one fine day she would.

The offices of Falck Solicitors were in Engene, and Bonnie stood outside and looked in through the arched windows. She was wearing her good clothes and smelt of Chanel No. 5. The doors were made from oak and had heavy brass doorknobs, and when she went into the waiting room, she walked across thick carpets and sat down in a nice leather chair. There were paintings and diplomas on the walls and several healthy-looking plants in the windows. She had been thinking of Erna all day. She wasn't the first client she had lost, but she had been one of the most difficult, the one she always dreaded going to most. As she sat there and waited, she started to feel ashamed. What did she know about getting old? She might become an old battleaxe herself when the time came. If it ever does, she thought, because not everyone lives to be that old. She took a box of IFA lozenges out of her bag and popped one in her mouth. When Christian Falck opened his door, she was amused to see that he looked a bit like the man on the IFA box, the opera singer Ivar F. Andresen. He might break into an aria at any moment. He seemed like a nice man, tall and dark and well dressed, a good deal older than herself. She crossed the thick carpet again, her sandals sinking into the deep pile – it felt like she was swaying. She shook his hand and followed him into a very grand office. She had never seen a desk like it, or such beautiful leather chairs. They were black with dark wood. On the desk, there was a green lamp that gave off a soft glow.

'Now, I'm sure you're wondering why I wrote to you,' he said.

'Yes. To be honest, it made me a little nervous,' Bonnie admitted. 'I thought that maybe someone was after me.'

'You have no reason to be nervous,' he said. 'You knew Erna far better than I did. But I understand from her family that she could be rather difficult. I believe it was you who found her?'

'Yes,' Bonnie said. 'She was in the bathroom. I don't know what the cause of death was, but she had hit her head. I went to the funeral because I felt I should.'

'Did you talk to her family?'

'No, I'd never met them. They wouldn't have known who I was and there were so many people there. I didn't go to the reception afterwards either, because I had to get to a client.'

'And when you lose one client, you are immediately given a new one?' Falck asked.

'Yes, you can say that again. We've got long waiting lists.'

She looked around the office. There were shelves and shelves of books, and lots of plants in here too that were far nicer than her own. She spotted a fern, a Swiss cheese plant and a succulent.

'Now, let me tell you why I've asked you here,' Falck said with a smile. 'Not everyone writes a will, but Erna Vibe certainly had. It was done long before she died, and is very detailed. And signed by several legal witnesses, so no one can contest it. Because, as I'm sure you know and have heard, that does sometimes happen. Inheritance is not to be taken lightly. And the fact is that you are a beneficiary of Erna's will.'

'I see,' Bonnie said, shaking her head. She had never felt loved by Erna in the way that she did by Gjertrud.

'As regards the house, furniture and other movables, they will of course go to the family,' he explained. 'But she has also left money, and some of it has been left to you.'

'Money?' Bonnie said, astounded. 'I didn't know she had any money, she was very frugal.'

'All old people are frugal,' Falck smiled. 'No matter how wealthy they are. Perhaps that is why they are wealthy. And Erna had a lot of money.'

'Right,' Bonnie said quietly. 'I had no idea. Did she inherit it from her husband? He died a long time ago now.'

'Yes,' Falck said. 'He was a successful businessman. And Erna looked after his money well. Some wealthy pensioners give their money to various foundations, but Erna gave a lot to the local social services. Which you are part of. But some of the money is directly for you. Your son Simon is also mentioned. She thought of you both.'

Bonnie had never been so surprised in all her life. She remembered the five bottles of perfume, and how thrilled she had been to get them.

'Are you sitting comfortably?' Falck asked.

Bonnie looked at him, baffled.

'Yes,' she said with a little light laugh. 'Your chairs are very comfortable.'

He leaned forward over the desk; she noticed that he had a thick gold band on his finger, and not a tie, but a bow tie. He smelt good too. There was something familiar about the scent. Olav.

'Erna has left you two million kroner.'

You could hear a pin drop. His smile was roguish.

'No,' Bonnie said automatically. 'No, I don't believe it, there has to be a mistake.'

She felt like the ceiling was floating down, and a gentle breeze was playing in the plants.

'A mistake?' Falck grinned. 'Why do you say that?'

'She's got children. She's not allowed to deny them their inheritance – aren't there laws against that sort of thing?'

'The children are also inheriting a fortune; like I said, she was very wealthy. They have no reason to complain and nor have they. In fact, they have asked me to pass on their regards and thanks for everything you have done for their mother over the years. Erna talked about you all the time, it seems. And how good you were. You were irreplaceable – reliable and good in every way.'

He looked at Bonnie's astonished face. She kept shaking her head. It was more than she could comprehend, this sort of thing happened to other people, people who had rich uncles in America.

'You must have meant a lot to her,' he went on. 'And you have no doubt earned every single penny. That's what the family say too. Congratulations,' he added, chuckling. 'Two million goes a long way. It might take some time before the money comes through though, but I will let you know as soon as it does. In the meantime, I will need your account details. And now I think you should go out and buy yourself a bottle of good champagne.'

When Bonnie got up from the comfortable chair, her legs would hardly hold her; she took his hand but felt she had no strength. A little dizzy, beside herself.

'It will sink in at some point this evening,' Christian Falck assured her. 'You may not even be able to sleep tonight. You'll be floating a metre above the mattress.'

Bonnie had to laugh at that. She thanked him and went back through the waiting room, opened the heavy oak door and stepped out onto the street, into the blue afternoon. I will never again judge anyone in my life, she promised herself. Erna was probably just shy and afraid to show her feelings. Old school, the war generation, the ones who never got anything. They kept it all bottled up. She decided to go to Sydney Grill. She ordered a cheeseburger, struggled up onto one of the high bar stools by the window and looked out. Suddenly she loved this town more than anything in the world. The river and all the bridges, the riverside walk. St Hallvard and his woman in the boat, the old theatre. The old run-down pubs, Lauritz and Dickens and Kongens Våpen. The old brewery that was illuminated at night. When you saw it on the other side of the river from the station, it looked like a dream palace. A pigeon had strayed into the road, presumably from the main square. It strutted down the grass divide, lithe and beautiful. It wasn't a grey pigeon with blue feathers. It was a white dove with golden flecks. Didn't they symbolise peace?

'Old people often save up all their money,' she explained. 'And then when they die, the money is given away. And you and I have been given a lot. We don't have it quite yet, because it takes some time before it's in the bank.'

'How much did we get?' Simon asked, wide-eyed.

'A lot,' Bonnie said. 'So we can buy ourselves nice things. You can get a new bike, and I can get a new car.'

'Oh,' he squealed with delight, 'is it really that much?'

'We might even be able to go to Gran Canaria,' Bonnie added with a laugh.

Simon sat with his mouth open. What he was hearing was making his head boil and he was flushed to the roots of his hair.

'I want to go to Africa,' he said, full of hope.

Bonnie gave it some thought.

'Yes, let's go to Africa and see the lions,' she said. 'But we'll have to get vaccinations first. You know, injections, so we don't get ill.'

'Yes,' Simon whooped and clapped his hands. 'I'll have loads of injections!'

He started to run around the room with a plastic lion in his hand, and Bonnie went out into the kitchen to open the champagne. Just as Falck had said, it really hadn't sunk in yet, and she certainly wouldn't be able to sleep, never, not on a day like today.

Chapter 34

'One day, I'm going to die,' Mass said seriously. 'The house will be too big for you on your own. Perhaps we should move into a small flat?'

'Die?' Eddie rolled his eyes. 'But that won't be for ages! So we can at least wait until you're old.'

Mass looked at her son's brown curls. His big white hands and double chin. If only he had a brother or sister, but that had never happened and it was too late now. She wanted to go out for a drive with him, sit close to him in the car, enjoy the good weather. They drove out to Tangen and Frydenlund. Mass pointed at the blocks of flats and residential complexes, said how nice they were, and look at the big balconies, I could have flower boxes there. And you wouldn't need to clear the snow. They got back into the car and drove across the river and up the hillside. There were lots of big detached houses here, but they were just out for a run in the car and Mass liked driving. Eddie had bought himself a Coke at a kiosk and sat beside her, burping every time he took a sip. It had always irritated her before, but not any more. He was the son she had been given, and she had always been patient with him.

She was overcome by waves of angst and then struggled to breathe. Eddie drank from his Coke bottle and looked out at the scenery; everything was shiny and nice in the golden spring sunshine.

'The crocuses will be out soon,' he said happily. 'And the tulips. You'll have plenty to do.'

Mass thought about all the flowers she would see for the last time. Everything was for the last time. The last spring, the last summer. She had told Dr Bromann that she would like to die in her own bed. But the more she thought about it, the clearer it became that that simply would not be possible. Eddie wouldn't cope at all. Take one day at a time, she told herself, as long as the pain isn't too bad. She thought about her final days, lying in a hospital bed screaming, with a terrified Eddie sitting beside her. Suddenly she wanted to go home. The angst overwhelmed her; she wanted to make supper for him, something nice. Everything had to be kept as normal as possible.

In the evening, they sat and watched television. She had been to the shops and bought a big bag of Twist chocolates, which her son was now guzzling. The colourful empty wrappers lay in a pile on the table. Eddie picked up the newspaper, leafed through to the crossword and then grabbed a pencil.

'I'm so glad that you've got hobbies,' Mass said. 'The crossword. Your computer. You're a whizz.'

'I know,' Eddie said proudly. 'I've always known that. And you're a whizz in the kitchen.'

Yes, Mass thought, we have to remember to say nice things to each other while we can. He needs self-confidence, as much as he can get. But deep down she was afraid that he would not cope. That the world would come tumbling down and he would hide somewhere in the dark and not reach out to other people. And then anything could happen.

'Buy a flat,' Eddie said. 'Crazy idea. You must be losing it.'

Mass balled her fists in desperation, because it was true. The disease was like a blow from a hammer and she felt dizzy. And soon, soon enough, the pain would take over.

Chapter 35

As the days passed, Bonnie got used to the idea that she was now a millionaire and she realised that her life had changed forever. Simon scarcely recognised his mother. She laughed all the time, walked with a light step, and put on nice clothes even though she was just going to clean someone's house. And she laughed about the old Opel that would soon go to the scrapyard. Kaja had shown him Africa on the globe. It was made up of lots of big and small countries, and he wasn't sure where they were going to go. We won't be travelling alone, his mother had explained.

'Will Granny and Grandpa be coming?'

'No, we have to go with a tour company. And then we'll get a guide who shows us around. In a safari car without a roof.'

'How long is it until we can go?'

'Not long, I don't think,' Bonnie said. 'As soon as the money comes, we'll go.'

'But when is it coming?' Simon was getting impatient.

'They said it might take a little while. Come on, let's go window-shopping, and if we find something nice we can go back and buy it later. OK?'

She started the old Opel and Simon was allowed to sit in the front for once. The seat belt cut across his neck, which wasn't good, but normal rules and regulations didn't apply any more. This was a new world.

The snow had melted and the blue wheelchair signs were clearly visible now, so she parked in one of the other empty spaces. As soon as they went into the shopping centre, Simon smelt the bakery. Bonnie bought him a raisin bun, which he ate with gusto. They took the escalator up to the first floor and started to wander around. They spent a long time going in and out of shops, and Bonnie realised that in a few weeks she would be able to buy whatever she wanted for herself and Simon. She looked at dresses. She looked at jewellery and bags and shoes. She looked at carpets and cushions and bedlinen; everything they had was worn, and she was looking forward to renewing it all. Simon also found several things, but he understood that he had to wait. When they were full of plans and ideas, they went back down to the ground floor and carried on their wandering. They popped into a pet shop and Simon fell in love with the dwarf rabbits.

'I want two of them,' he said decisively.

Bonnie had to laugh.

'I think we can do that,' she said. 'They're so cute.'

They went on to the sports shop. This was where Simon really went to town. His mother had never been so accommodating, and he was simply overwhelmed. They had bicycles and skateboards, knives and torches, helmets and small scooters, trainers in bright colours and cool rucksacks. On the back wall, there was every kind of fishing rod you might want. Then they went through to the clothing section. Bonnie fell for an outdoor jacket and Simon found a good tracksuit.

'We'll have to wait,' she reminded him.

'But then someone else will buy it,' Simon objected. 'Please!'

Bonnie stroked his hair.

'All right,' she smiled. 'But we'll have to eat porridge for the rest of the week.'

When they got home, Simon took the tracksuit out of the bag. He found some scissors and cut off the tags, put it on in front of the mirror in the hall, and then paraded back into the living room.

'You look great,' Bonnie said. 'Just like the Norwegian flag, all red, white and blue.'

Chapter 36

August 2005

Sejer and Skarre continued to visit Henny Hayden at regular intervals. They had investigated the circumstances surrounding Bonnie's inheritance, but there was nothing to indicate that the two had been killed for the money. Erna Vibe's other heirs had been duly questioned, but it led nowhere. And according to Henny, very few people actually knew about the inheritance.

'I read all the papers,' she said, distraught, 'and they're saying it's a very difficult case.'

'That's true. But that doesn't mean we won't solve it. We first have to find the man who was observed near the scene of the crime. A big man driving a red car. And then we have to prove he went to Skarven Farm. And then we can find out the motive.'

'There are foreigners working there, you know,' Henny hastily informed them.

'Yes, we know. We questioned them some time ago now. You look tired,' Sejer added. 'Are you getting enough sleep and eating properly?'

After their visit to Henny, they drove on to Skarven. Woiciech, Stanislav, Jürgen and Thomas were sitting on the grass in front of the outhouse eating their lunch, which comprised thick slices of bread and ham and strong coffee from a Thermos. They had taken off their shirts in the warm sun, and were all strong, muscular men.

'Woiciech,' Skarre said, 'have you ever seen the red car again?'

'No, just that once. We went to visit the graves,' he added. 'They were good.'

He had a pair of black-and-yellow braces on to keep his sturdy work trousers up, and they were all wearing heavy leather shoes. The soles had long since been checked and none of them had the characteristic pattern found on the floor of the caravan.

'When will you be going back home?' Skarre asked.

'In November,' Woiciech told him. 'My kids are waiting for me. We're going to build a house.'

Later, Sejer and Skarre walked down across the fields to where the caravan had stood. Randen had finally towed it away. They wandered around somewhat aimlessly, each lost in his own thoughts. There were other unsolved cases, of course there were, but not that many. Some cases would always gnaw at them.

'He'll be following what's happening,' Skarre said, looking at the inspector.

'Obviously,' Sejer replied. 'And he may not be sleeping at night.'

When he got back to his flat on the twelfth floor, he was ambushed by Frank, so he knelt down and took one of the dog's soft paws in his hand. The dog's eyes, which were barely visible amid all the folds and wrinkles, were black.

'You need a facelift,' he said affectionately. 'But it would cost a fortune.'

He went out into the kitchen, started to rattle around with the pots and pans, and Frank immediately trotted in to beg for titbits. Sejer hesitated before giving him a bit of sausage. I never learn, he thought sheepishly. If only Elise had seen that.

Chapter 37

April 2005

Bonnie wanted to tell anyone who would listen about her inheritance, she was so full of it. But something made her hold back. Many of her clients only received a minimum pension, and struggled financially just as she had. However, young Alex was let in on the secret. When he heard about Erna's generosity, he was thrilled.

'So are you going to take me to Bagatelle?' he asked hopefully. 'Or an eleven-course dinner?'

'Of course,' Bonnie agreed. 'In the autumn. And Elisabeth can come too. But first I have to clear my debts.'

They were in the middle of a chess game.

'I wish I had a pawn on wheels with right of way,' Bonnie laughed.

He immediately responded with a very smart move. Leaned back in his wheelchair and looked at her. He wanted to tell this beautiful woman, who was only three years away from forty, and who came to his door to help him, that she was the highlight of his week. But he was far too proud and shy to show his devotion.

'I've got an old aunt who lives on a small farm,' he said instead. 'And her Border collie is called Bonnie, and she's an impossible dog.'

Bonnie laughed again.

'What's your greatest wish for the future?' she asked him.

'To have my own child,' he replied without hesitation. 'I want what you've got. A son. He would run riot, but he'd also do things for me. And he would of course be a genius at chess. And I would make it perfectly clear that when it comes to bad driving, he had to stay alive.'

'What's wrong with a girl?' Bonnie asked.

'Nothing, I just want a boy.'

'And you know that you can have children?'

'Oh yes, we're planning to. And what's more, we have you,' he said with a little smile. 'I hope that you'll be around for a long time, and that you won't desert me, just because you're rich.'

'Never,' Bonnie assured him, and moved a knight.

Alex brushed his fringe away from his face. He was clean-shaven and smelt good.

'You better watch your queen,' he warned her. 'Let's take a break. Put the pizza in the oven.'

Simon Hayden was like his father Olav, he had the same slim body and thin ankles. The same blue eyes and the same restlessness. When he was big, he wanted to work at sea, like his father. Every morning when he sat on the bench under the snail at nursery, he looked up at his mother and said: 'Do you think the money will come soon?'

'Yes,' Bonnie told him. 'It won't be long now.'

'It will definitely come, won't it?'

'Yes, we'll definitely get it. Because Mr Falck promised. And he knows things like that, because he's a lawyer.'

Simon had already told Märta the big news, and about everything he was going to get and the trip to Africa. That he would have to have lots of vaccinations and that he would come home with photographs of lions. Märta retorted that he might get eaten, but then Simon told her that the person driving the safari car had a gun. Kaja noticed that he had blossomed, that he opened up to the other children and that the desperate scenes when his mother left had stopped. He would now run around and at times couldn't be stopped. She had to admit that she was a little envious: there was no likelihood of her ever inheriting anything like that amount of money. But she was pleased for Bonnie.

Britt was also delighted by what had happened. Bonnie's life was back on track and she hadn't seen her so happy since she had been with Olav. She could never have dealt with all those difficult old people. She liked the drama of her work with the air ambulance, the first decisive minutes in which she could save a life, it made her feel important. But what Bonnie did was important too, only in another way. They saw each other more often now than before. Bonnie had more energy, she got her mother to babysit and they went out on the town.

Bonnie didn't mind staying out late, and when the alarm clock rang in the morning, she jumped out of bed straight away to wake Simon, often with a song. He was also quick out of bed. They were both looking forward to the summer that would soon be there.

Chapter 38

The cancer had really started to ravage her body. The pain increased, especially in her bones, and she continued to lose weight. She still hadn't said anything to Eddie. There was fear in his eyes as he watched his mother getting thinner and thinner, but Mass reassured him that it was just age.

'You know,' she said, 'old people are never fat.'

'But you're not old.'

'Yes, I am. I will be soon enough anyway.'

One day, when Eddie was sitting at the computer, Mass came into the living room with two plastic bags of food and drinks, newspapers and fruit, and chocolate for Eddie, even though it wasn't good for him. She had been out for some time because she'd had a few errands to run. She was suddenly reminded of the winter she turned thirteen. She had nagged and nagged her parents until they let her get a perm, because other girls in the class had curly hair. She had straight hair. It was long and thick, to be fair, but not even a wave in a single hair. So after going on and on about it, she was eventually allowed to do it, only to come back from the hairdresser with what could only be compared with black sheep's wool. When she went to school the next day, the boys in her class flopped over their desks, howling with laughter; they shouted and yelled and pointed, baaing like sheep. They punched her and threw rubbers at her. Sambo! Hottentot! After the last class, she slunk off home, burning with embarrassment. She sat down at the fireplace in despair and cut off all the curls, as close to her head as she could. She threw them into the fire, and could still recall the smell of burnt hair. When she looked in the mirror afterwards, she looked like a plucked chicken. And as if that wasn't enough, she then tore off her clothes and threw them on the fire too. She remembered the episode now, standing in the middle of the room with a green scarf round her head. Eddie looked at her in astonishment, because his mother had never used a scarf before.

'Is that in fashion now?' he asked.

'Yes,' Mass said. 'Let's hope so.'

'But you've got such lovely hair, you shouldn't hide it.'

He turned back to the screen, his fingers racing over the keyboard.

Mass collapsed into her chair; she looked at her son's broad shoulders, at his brown hair that curled so beautifully at the neck.

'Where have you been?' he asked, turning round again. 'You were gone for ages. If you're going to be that long, you have to say. Otherwise I just sit here waiting and not knowing.'

'I went to the hairdresser,' Mass said in a feeble voice.

'What?' Eddie couldn't believe it. 'But you've got a scarf on. Did she make a mess of it?'

'No.'

She turned away. She knew that she couldn't avoid it any longer. It was as if there was a wolf between them, snarling. Get to the point. Coward.

'I don't have hair any more,' she said, and looked straight at him.

'What do you mean, you don't have hair?'

'I've shaved it off,' she explained, 'because it was starting to fall out.'

'But why?' he asked, horrified. 'Are you ill? Will you get a wig?'

'I'm not going to get a wig, Eddie. It's the medicine I'm taking that makes my hair fall out.'

Finally Eddie understood. He gasped once, took a deep breath, then two, three more, and his voice, which was usually so loud, was thin and reedy.

'Right, but it will grow back, won't it?' he asked nervously. 'I've heard that it does.'

She shook her head.

'No, that's not going to happen.'

'But why not? You'll get better again.'

He tried to stay the panic that was rising.

'Cancer?' he said slowly.

'Yes,' she said, 'cancer. It started in the pancreas, and has now spread everywhere.'

'Seventy per cent of people who get cancer survive,' he said doggedly. 'That's what I read on the Internet.'

'Yes,' she said. 'I know. But I don't belong to that seventy per cent. I'm going to die, Eddie, and quite soon.'

'No,' he said feebly.

'Yes.'

'The doctors often make mistakes,' Eddie tried. 'And you're strong. I know you're strong. You're like an ox.'

He punched the table.

'But the cancer is stronger. You're going to have to live on your own, Eddie, and you'll need help. You will have to accept all the help that's offered. People will come to the door, and you must cooperate. You know, home helps and people like that. People from the council.'

He stood up without turning off the computer, just stood there in the middle of the room.

'I've got some savings,' Mass continued. 'But from now on, you're going to have to get by on your incapacity benefit. And that means you can't live on Coke and cinnamon rolls. You're going to have to make yourself proper food, or you'll get ill. Are you listening to me?'

'You're wrong,' he said, desperate. 'People get it wrong all the time.'

Mass struggled to get up. The pain in her bones was intense, and she knew it would only get worse. That it would spread to every single cell. She couldn't bear to look her son in the eye, everything felt so heavy, her heart, her head.

She went into the kitchen and opened the fridge; she had thought of frying some eggs and bacon for them both. Eddie followed her in his tartan slippers. He sat down and put his hands on the kitchen table, swallowed hard. Every time a thought started to form in his head it was interrupted by another, just like when a bonfire burns at night and the sparks fly up into the sky, a shower that will only last as long as there are flames. His mother dead and buried. Strangers coming to the door, people demanding impossible things of him: that he should get out and meet people, that he should try to find a supported workplace. He thought about all the things his mother had done for him over the years, all the things that he had taken utterly for granted. She had cleaned and tidied and made food, she had done the shopping and kept things in order, changed the beds. She had made sure there was toilet paper, taken the car in to be serviced. She had paid the bills and done the tax returns, about which he knew zero; she had kept a check on his spending.

'Do you have to go to hospital?' he asked anxiously.

'Yes, soon. I've thought about it long and hard, because at first I wanted to stay in my own bed. But you can't look after me here; it would be too much for you.'

'But I can do the shopping and things like that,' he said, 'and I can go to the chemist for you. And you can tell me how to do things from the bed, and I'm sure I'd manage.'

She went over and stroked his cheek.

'I would do anything in the world if it meant you didn't have to go through this,' she told him. 'You are my greatest joy, and have been my greatest comfort, especially after Anders left. But now you have to be stronger than ever before. You simply have to manage. You just have to take one thing at a time, and you will have to get people to help you. You'll have to arrange the funeral and all that, and don't use Jølstad, they're too expensive.'

Eddie couldn't speak any more. His father had left him and now his mother was about to do the same.

'To be honest, Mum,' he whispered, 'I don't think it's going to work.'

'Don't say that,' she said in anguish. 'That's not what I need to hear when I'm dying. You went to Copenhagen on your own. Just remember that.'

'Maybe there's something after,' he said, trying to be hopeful. 'We don't know for certain.'

'That's one thing I know for sure,' she said firmly. 'I will not live on, neither here nor there. Only in your thoughts,' she added, to soften it. 'You will have to manage alone.'

They ate their eggs and bacon in silence. Eddie dipped his bread into the egg yolk, his feet fidgeting under the table. After they'd eaten, he went back to the computer, and started to search. He got lots of hits. He sat for a long time reading about pancreatic cancer and how it spread to the bones and marrow. The symptoms were described in detail, and he recognised them. Some people could be operated on, but not everyone. And often it went unnoticed until it was too late. The last thing he read terrified him. Among doctors, this form of cancer was known as 'The Silent Killer'.

Chapter 39

June 2005

He got up, put on some clothes, then opened the door to his mother's room and asked if she wanted a yogurt for breakfast; she could have strawberry or melon. He could take the top off and find a spoon. She said no. She managed to get herself out of bed and tottered across the floor. He could see her sick body through the fabric of the nightie. The evening before, they had packed some things into a bag that was now standing ready by the door. While his mother was in the bathroom getting dressed, he sat on a chair and waited. He thought about trying to find a doctor other than Bromann, someone who was better. They could go to China, for example, because he'd heard that the Chinese knew everything about medicine. Then he pulled himself together. Don't be a fool, Eddie, China's too far away and too expensive. She wouldn't be able to cope with it, she's too weak.

Eventually she emerged from the bathroom and they went out to the car. She didn't even look back at the house, her eyes were trained on the road ahead.

*

An hour later, Eddie said goodbye. He found the car in the car park and drove carefully out of the gates. He stopped by the mailbox when he got home to pick up the papers. Ansgar appeared with Kennedy at his heels.

'Been out driving, Eddie?' he asked, bursting with curiosity.

'Yes,' was Eddie's curt reply.

'Yes,' Ansgar followed up. 'A lot to be getting on with now that summer's round the corner.'

He already had his papers, but he stood studying Eddie.

'It's been a while since I've seen your mother,' he said. 'Is everything all right? She's not ill, is she?'

Eddie glared at Ansgar – he had always hated him. His dark, nearly black eyes, that loathsome grin. His skin had a yellow tinge. Eddie knew that he'd done service in Afghanistan and was ridiculously proud of it.

'Yes,' he said. 'Mum is ill.'

'Oh dear,' Ansgar stammered. 'Is she in hospital?'

'Yes, I took her there this morning.'

'I hope it's nothing serious,' he responded, looking serious.

Eddie clutched the newspaper in his hand.

'It's very serious. She's dying.'

For once, Ansgar said nothing. He picked Kennedy up and looked at Eddie, dumbfounded, then turned and hurried back to the house to tell his wife the shocking news.

Eddie let himself in. He put the post down on the kitchen table and carried on into the living room. The house was horribly silent. He thought he could hear a low, ominous humming, as if some great machine had started up. There was gurgling in the pipes, a banging at the windows, and heavy doors slammed shut, never to be opened again.

*

June was cold and blustery. Simon still wore a thin hat when he went to nursery. There was a lot of rain and he had to wear gumboots as well. He had stopped asking about the money; in fact, he had almost lost hope. In the evenings he sat glumly in front of the television while Bonnie tried to cheer him up as best she could. But that was the nature of children, they couldn't wait. Not for Christmas, not for birthdays, not for the summer holidays. So she took him to a travel agent, where they each sat down in a chair, then Bonnie explained that they needed help to plan a trip to Africa.

'We're not actually travelling quite yet,' she said, 'because we're waiting for some money, and I don't know when it's going to come. Sometime soon anyway. But what kind of price are we looking at? For the two of us? A fortnight's safari?'

The consultant clicked on his computer.

'I would recommend Tanzania or Kenya,' he said. 'Then you'll only have to change at Heathrow for a direct flight to Nairobi. You'd have the first week on safari with an excellent guide, and the second week you would be left to your own devices, but would stay in a very good hotel in Mombasa. Which is by the Indian Ocean.'

'That all sounds very expensive,' Bonnie laughed, feeling extravagant. 'How much should we reckon on spending?'

'Around fifty thousand, I should think. But everything is included. Food, everything.'

'Will we be camping?' Simon asked hopefully.

'No, you'll stay in small huts, which are very nice. They've got straw roofs and you have to go up a ladder to get in. So the animals can't get in too. And you mustn't feed the apes,' he said in a stern voice. 'It's forbidden.'

'Why – do they bite?'

'They bite and they steal food. And they can make you ill. Remember, if you go to Kenya, you have to do a lot of things beforehand, like vaccinations, et cetera. And there are some places where you're not allowed to take photos, but the guide will let you know about things like that. She'll be with you all the time.'

He gave them a thick catalogue and that evening they sat on the sofa together looking through it. Bonnie pointed and explained. Simon was full of hope once more that the inheritance money would soon come; he could just imagine Falck the solicitor staggering to the bank with a big bag of money. He was so excited that he didn't want to go to bed, and Bonnie had to read him several stories before he calmed down. Bonnie was also excited. I must be mad, she thought, travelling so far away with a five-year-old. But then she reminded herself that they would be part of a bigger group. Every step would be planned.

Before going to bed, she called Britt and they talked for a long time about the summer. Britt and Jens were going to go to Crete. They had been there many times before and Britt was always tanned when they came back.

For Bonnie, the days just raced by. She drove from client to client and listened to the weather forecast, hoping that the warm weather would come soon. The meteorologists promised a fantastic July; there was even the prospect of some tropical nights. She told Simon that everything would be better in July, especially as it was his birthday, on Sunday the tenth.

'And you're going to be five,' she said, 'and that's halfway to ten. To think that you're that big already. This winter you'll have to help me clear the snow, I'm sure you can manage that now, I think your muscles are growing bigger already.'

She squeezed his upper arm. Yes, he was very strong. Granny Henny had once said that he was the man of the house and he had to help Mummy with whatever he could. So he strutted around the house, like a man, while he waited for the African heat.

One evening, when Eddie came home from sitting by his mother's bed, something happened that terrified him. He stood in the doorway to his bedroom and saw something odd hanging from the curtain rail. It was dark in the room because the blinds were always down. He turned on the light, but he still couldn't understand what the thing was, it was totally unknown and alien to him. It made him think of rotten fruit, or a dead bird. He thought he could make out a pair of legs and some big ears. It hung there immobile, and he reversed back out into the living room and slammed the door. He realised that the windows in several rooms had been open all day, and the hideous thing must have come in through one of them. He had no idea what to do. Should he sleep in his mother's bed and just wait until it disappeared by itself? But what if it didn't disappear, and just hung there like a bad omen? He mustered his courage and went into the kitchen, found a torch in the drawer and went back to his bedroom. He stood in the doorway for a while staring at the thing, then approached it slowly, one step at a time, and turned on the torch. The beam of light slid over the curtain and then he understood. A bare animal with no feathers or fur, but noticeable ears and folded wings. It was a bat. Eddie knew that bats were wild, that they could bite if they felt threatened, and that they could carry rabies. He had to get the beast out, and his mother was not there to help him. He didn't dare get any closer, so he backed out of the room again. He got the mop from the cupboard. He opened the door and windows, approached the bat with care and then nudged it with the mop handle. Suddenly there was movement everywhere. Eddie pulled back in fright; the bat flew frantically round the room, in tight, fast circles – he'd never seen anything so fast. He stood in the middle of the room, with the mop raised in defence. Why couldn't the mad animal find its way out? – all the windows were open. Suddenly it flew straight into his face. He waved his arms around wildly, but then, to his great relief, it vanished out through the open living-room window. He immediately rushed over to close it. Never again, not even in summer, would he have the windows open, because there weren't just bats out there, there were wasps too. Afterwards, he sat in his chair and studied his wrists under a lamp. The veins on his left wrist were thin, and spread out to the palm of his hand like a three-pronged fork. But it was completely different on the other wrist – the veins seemed to be bigger, perhaps because his right arm was stronger. A thick blue vein ran from left to right; he put his finger on it, felt his pulse, the gentle thud.

They weren't looking forward to the holidays, because then Bonnie wouldn't come and they would have to put up with a temp who they might not like. Gjertrud thought that she would hide her bottles of eau de vie – you never knew who might come. And Alex wouldn't have anyone to play chess with. Bonnie tried to do that little bit more for them, and promised with her hand on her heart that she'd come back, but when she then told them that they were going to Kenya, many of them got even more anxious.

'They have the death penalty down there,' Alex said. 'A student once stole a computer from the university and he was hanged.'

'That's terrible,' she said, but then had to laugh. 'I'm not exactly a criminal,' she added. 'I promise not to steal so much as a coconut. We'll stay on the straight and narrow.'

In the evenings, she and Simon sat writing long lists: everything they had to remember, everything they had to take with them. Britt had given her some good advice, and promised to call every evening until they left. Her mother Henny was less enthusiastic.

'Why couldn't you just go to Majorca, like everyone else?' she said. 'It's perfectly nice there.'

'I wanted Simon to choose,' Bonnie told her. 'He hasn't had that many of his dreams fulfilled.'

Eddie would sometimes go for a walk round the garden and look at the things that were growing. His mother had taught him the names of all the flowers: primula, flox and tulips, bleeding heart and freesia. Sometimes he would squat down to pull out some weeds. Even though he didn't really manage, he tried to keep it as tidy as he could. Indoors, he had problems with the washing machine, which wouldn't start, even when he pressed all the buttons. Often all that he produced was a red flashing light. So he wore the same top with a Rottweiler on it day after day. He wondered if he should tell Inga Nielsen; he could always ask his mother but she would probably say no, so he did nothing more. It was 20 June and the promised summer weather had still not arrived. A cold wind blew over the country.

His mother was now in so much pain that she couldn't move. Some small, clear drops of morphine dripped from a bag straight into her arm. They didn't talk much any more. Eddie sat lost in his own thoughts and Mass lay completely still with her eyes closed.

There wasn't much time left.

Eddie barely left her side; he held her hand tight, sat leaning forward in the chair, making his back ache. The nurses were in and out all the time, and always had a friendly word for him.

'Would you like to be alone?'

'Yes,' Eddie replied.

'Are you frightened?'

'Yes.'

Sometimes his mother opened her eyes as if she wanted to check that he was still there. She felt him squeeze her hand, but her own lacked strength. Her lips were dry and cracked, and her hairless head was the colour of wax. Eddie prepared himself for her imminent death. When the evening drew in, she clearly had something on her mind. She tried to turn her head to catch his eye.

'Eddie,' she whispered. 'There's something I have to tell you.'

'Yes, Mum,' he replied. 'I'll do whatever you say.'

'No, it's not something I want you to do. It's something that you should know. And I don't have much time left.'

Eddie leaned even further forward.

'Anders,' she whispered. 'Anders Kristoffer. He's not your father.'

Eddie dropped his mother's hand as if it were burning coal.

'Don't be ridiculous!' he said, alarmed. 'I went to his grave.'

'Yes, but he wasn't your father. Not your real father.'

Eddie felt himself swaying on the chair. He thought about the two photographs hanging on his bedroom wall, the ones he looked at every night before falling asleep. His father and him. Inga and Mads. She had taken everything away from him in the space of a second.

'But who was my father then?' he asked.

Mass closed her eyes.

'You'll never find him, Eddie. Let it lie.'

'Is he dead as well?'

'I don't know. I don't know where he is. Let it go.'

'Does that mean you slept around?' he asked.

'No, it's not what you think.'

The thought of having to look for a new father winded him. No father, no brother in New York. But what bothered him most was the fact that his mother had lied to him. He had lived a lie all his life and he didn't know if he could forgive her, but then perhaps she had her reasons for keeping it secret. His mother looked like she was sleeping. He thought she was perhaps already dead.

But a little while later she came to life again. She coughed without any force, and a single trickle of blood appeared in the corner of her mouth.

'You have to forgive me, Eddie,' she whispered. 'I only ever wanted the best for you. And the truth isn't always the best. And we've had a good time together, you and I. Don't you agree?'

'Yes.'

'So please take what I'm about to say with composure.'

Eddie didn't know if he dared to listen.

'I'm not your mother, Eddie,' Mass told him. 'Not your real mother.'

He sat on the chair for a long time, as though paralysed.

Then he got up and went over to the window. He could see the car park and all the cars far below. And behind, the green hills where people went for walks in both summer and winter. He had been there as well, with Mass, for the first time when he was a baby in a blue Simo pram. Then on his own two feet. To get to the top, they had to drive through a tunnel called Spirallen, and there was a big troll in the middle of the tunnel. He turned back to the bed.

'I couldn't have my own children, Eddie,' Mass explained. 'Anders and I were foster-parents, and initially you were supposed to go back to your real mother. But then that didn't happen. And after a year we formally adopted you. And I want you to know that I was over the moon, Eddie. You've always made me so happy.'

Eddie stepped closer and bent down over the bed.

'But my real mother,' he asked, confused. 'Why didn't she want me?'

'There were lots of reasons. It's not easy to explain.'

'What was her name? Where does she live? Or don't you know that either? I have to know, Mum, you have to tell me!'

Mass clawed at the duvet cover. The blood was barely flowing through her veins, her heart was barely beating.

'I'm not so sure that you should try to find her,' she said. 'It's not always such a good idea. Remember Adelina-Susann who went all the way to Lahore.'

'But why wouldn't it be a good idea? Is she poor?'

'Not that I know of.'

'Why wouldn't she be pleased to see me then?'

'She was only fifteen when she fell pregnant,' Mass explained, 'sixteen when you were born. She gave you away, Eddie; she couldn't keep you. She was far too young.'

Eddie flared up. For a few mad seconds he lost control. Mass didn't recognise his voice, it was hoarse and dark. He leaned down over the bed and put a hand on either side of her head.

'Tell me who she is!' he shouted. 'Now!'

Mass died so quietly. One moment she was there, the next she was gone – no fight, no movement, just a small sigh. Her eyes were open, but she no longer saw him.

He contacted Eiker funeral directors and asked for help.

He would rather go to their offices, because he didn't want to open the door to strangers at home, and they promised they would organise everything, and that all he needed to do was say what he wanted. He sat and looked through the catalogues, then made a relatively swift decision and ordered the cheapest white coffin, which cost six thousand kroner. And the cheapest gravestone from the stonemasons. He didn't want any kind of wake after the funeral, as it would cost money and he couldn't afford it. Not many people would come anyway. He didn't know much about hymns and he didn't want to follow the coffin to the grave, someone else could carry her out. He would drive straight home and lick his wounds. They told him that he could apply for financial assistance from the social services and said that they would help him fill in the forms and notify all the necessary authorities of his mother's death. Eddie accepted their help. He asked them to order a simple wreath with no card, as there was nothing he wanted to write on it. There was no need for any singers; he just wanted the whole thing over and done with.

In the evening, once everything had been decided, he sat in a chair at home. His cheeks started to burn. When he touched them with his hand, he could feel the heat, and after a while he got up and went to look in the mirror.

His face was red and it was spreading down his neck. What Mass had told him had started to burn him up inside. His real mother had given him away because she didn't want him; she had given him away like some package, pushed him around like rubbish, and no doubt she now had other children she loved. He turned off all the lights and sat down again. His cheeks continued to burn and sting. It was an unfamiliar feeling for someone who never went out in the sun. He sat there quietly, alone in the dark, and felt the fire burning.

Ansgar came to the funeral, but he had the good sense to sit at the back. Eddie didn't so much as look at him. He was having trouble enough looking at the white coffin. He knew that Mass was lying inside, but he still couldn't comprehend it. As the organ released its sad tones, he felt that the church was closing in and he bowed down as far as he could on the hard pew. He thought the priest was meanly dressed, in a simple cassock with a belt around his waist. You don't know Mass, he thought, you don't know what you're talking about. God has nothing to do with this.

When the service was over, the priest wanted to shake his hand. It was weak and half-hearted and Eddie turned and walked down the aisle and then out. As he stood by the car, Ansgar came over and seemed to want to say a few words. Eddie pursed his lips, opened the car door and got in. His neighbour bent down and looked into the car.

'How awful for you, Eddie,' he said. 'What's going to happen to you now? Will you manage alone, or will you have to go into care?'

The temperature started to rise at the end of June; people had been waiting for the summer and looking forward to the best time of year. It was what they dreamed of during the long, cold winter months. One day Bonnie received an important phone call. Christian Falck rang to say that the inheritance money had finally been transferred. He wished her all the best and Bonnie lifted Simon up and swung him in the air.

'Finally,' she said and danced around the living room. 'Tomorrow we'll go to the travel agent and book our trip to Africa.'

She opened the doors and windows. She couldn't resist phoning the bank to hear her balance. Then she went into the bathroom and stared at the happy Bonnie in the mirror. She thought that she might even tell Olav – her new-found wealth appeased her, she could forgive everything. But then she changed her mind. I can manage without you, she thought, just you wait and see.

They booked their trip to Africa for the middle of August, so she only took the first week off in July. She went to the bank, paid off all her debts. She bought a bike for Simon and an expensive dress for herself, which was white with ladybirds on it. In the autumn, she would go to the car dealers and buy a new Opel. She went to the hairdresser and had her long fair hair styled. Olav had always liked her hair, and whenever she wore it in a plait, he would pull off the band so that it tumbled down over her shoulders. Now it was her turn to shine.

Eddie got into the car and drove to Blåkollen. He had been given the exact address when he enquired. A short distance from the house, he pulled in to the side and stopped. It was a small, yellow house with green window frames, and it looked old. There were two bikes leaning against the wall and an old Opel parked in the drive. I'm here, he thought. You didn't expect this, did you? He didn't let go of the steering wheel. He could hear his own shallow breathing. As he sat like this, thinking, a little boy came out of the house with a helmet under his arm. He went over to the bikes and put on his helmet, then a beautiful, blonde woman appeared in the doorway.

She stood there. Like an angel. She was a harp, she was a flame, she was a jewel. She came down the steps and walked over the gravel, swaying as she went. She put her hand on the boy's head with the same love and reverence as a priest would bless a baby. It looked as though she was giving the boy instructions on where he could cycle. So he did have a brother, a little brother. Who now had something that was his. Bonnie Hayden.

The two of them, close as close can be; they would always be together. She would never give away that little boy. She went back indoors. The boy pushed his bike out onto the road, and just as he was about to get on, Eddie got out of the car. He walked over and looked him up and down.

'What's your name?' he asked.

'Simon.'

'And your mum is called Bonnie?'

'Yes.'

The boy looked as though he was about to cycle off, but Eddie put one of his big hands on the handlebar.

'And how old are you?'

'Nearly five.'

He turned and stared back at the house as if he wanted his mother to come and rescue him, but Eddie kept his hand there. He glared down at the anxious little face, took in every detail, the curls, the blue eyes. He was blond like his mother. Eddie shook the handlebar. The boy struggled to keep his balance, his face white with fear. Eddie continued to shake the bike, looking at the boy with black eyes. Then suddenly he let go and went back to the car, sat there and watched him. The bike wobbled a bit as the boy hurried away.

He went back again the same night. He parked some distance away and walked to the house, imagining them both lying asleep, maybe cuddled up together in the same bed. Just as he had cuddled up with Mass when he was little. He went up the steps and read the nameplate. It looked handmade. Bonnie and Simon live here. Then he walked round the house. There was a rabbit cage at the back with two tiny rabbits in it. They looked just as scared as the boy had been, and he hit the chicken wire with his hand a couple of times. The rabbits huddled together in a corner. He looked up at the dark windows, wondered which one was her bedroom, it was impossible to see in. Then he went back round and sat down on the steps. He felt he had a right to sit here; this house should have been his. He sat there until it started to get light, and they would soon be up. Then he drove to the end of the road and waited. At seven o'clock, the pale blue Opel drove by. He caught sight of them as they passed, and he followed the car at a safe distance.

It wasn't far to Simon's nursery. He stopped right by the gate and watched Bonnie get out of the car; she undid the seat belt and Simon clambered out of his child seat and they went in together. Mass had always stayed at home, he thought, she looked after me.

Five minutes later she came back out. It was warm and she was wearing a white dress and sandals. He followed her into the centre of town where she disappeared into a house, and after he had sat there waiting for an hour, he drove home again. He went into Mass's bedroom, opened her wardrobe. He stared at the coats and dresses, and the neat row of shoes at the bottom. He stood for a while breathing in the smell of the clothes, and when he'd had enough, he closed the wardrobe door. Her bed had been left as it was since she went into hospital, and he decided to make it up. He did the best he could, smoothed the sheet and puffed the pillow, then put the quilt on. He would never go into the room again, never. He concentrated on Bonnie and his brother, Simon. He followed them for several days, learning their habits and routines. He always made sure to park at a distance, even though he was not afraid of being discovered. He could stand in front of her and tell her the truth, that he was her son. And he could ask her why she had given him away, and he would see the confusion in her eyes. The shame and embarrassment. Just like Adelina-Susann's mother by the River Ravi.

He soon understood that she was some kind of helper, as she went from house to house; maybe she was a cleaner, he thought. When she finished for the day, she went to collect Simon from the nursery, then they went to the shop to buy food. Simon often came out with a bun in his hand. It was just the two of them. Bonnie was always touching Simon, ruffling his hair, stroking his cheek, and sometimes she lifted him up and gave him a hug. There was something caring and sincere about her that made him bitter and sad. His cheeks burned constantly. It was worse than ever. The fire had spread to his head and heart.

It was Sunday, and Bonnie had the day off. She drove up to Geirastadir with Simon. He had a little backpack on and they disappeared up towards Svarttjern. Eddie sat in the car and watched them go.

Chapter 40

August 2005

One day towards the end of the month, Randen appeared in the outhouse and wanted to talk to Woiciech. The sexton from Haugane had called because he needed someone to paint the long fence around the graveyard. The man who had originally agreed to do the job had put his back out and was on sick leave, and the wood was now drying out and needed some attention. Woiciech immediately accepted the job, he needed every krone he could get, and he liked it up at Haugane Church. He liked working outdoors as well, and he started straight away. The fence was to be painted white like the church. He got down on his knees in the green grass and worked hard, as he always did when he took on a job. Woiciech was a happy man, his life was good. He was strong and healthy, had a family, there were no obstacles as far as he could see.

People came and went in the graveyard at regular intervals, tending the graves. They brought watering cans, trowels and plants. He noticed an elderly woman who came every day to the graves of the mother and child who had been killed up at Skarven. He watched her walk slowly between the graves, her head bowed and her back bent as she went out through the wrought-iron gates.

He was just getting ready to leave one day, when a man drove up and parked beside him, got out of the car and went down into the graveyard. Without knowing why, Woiciech sat and watched him. There was something about the way he walked. A heavy, slow man dressed all in black. He didn't have anything with him either, no flowers or trowel or watering can, but he was not just out for a potter, he definitely knew where he was going. Woiciech waited. When the man got to Bonnie and Simon's graves, he just stood there and stared, as though he didn't really know what to do with himself. A lot of people had visited their grave, they were presumably curious. The case was so gruesome that it had attracted attention beyond the country's borders. Woiciech looked at the car that was parked beside his. He had read about the details in the newspapers, like everyone else, so he used his eyes. The man by the grave stood with his hands deep in his pockets, and occasionally kicked at the soil. Eventually he turned back to the parking place, got into his car and drove off down the avenue of trees.

Woiciech went straight to the police station. He had nothing else to do, he had the time. There he asked to speak to Sejer, and he was shown into a bright office, where he was greeted by Frank.

'I've got something to report,' he said shyly. 'I'm working up at the church, painting the fence. People come and look at the graves. Of those two, I mean. And today a man came.'

'And he drew your attention?' Sejer said. 'That's why you're here. What did you see?'

'He was big. Tall and solid. He stood there for a long time, and I sat in the car and watched.'

'Did he realise he was being watched?'

'I don't think he noticed.'

'And what about his age? How old do you think he was?'

'Under thirty. No grey hair. Black top and boots. I thought it was strange to be wearing boots in this heat. His car was parked beside mine. I waited. Then he drove slowly off down the avenue.'

'In other words, you got a good look at the car, close up,' Sejer said. 'This could be very important to us.'

'Yes,' Woiciech agreed. 'The car was similar to the one I saw up by the farm. I had a close look before he came back.'

Sejer nodded. He couldn't keep his hands still, he opened and folded them, sat drumming his fingers on the map of the world that was on the desk in front of him.

'What kind of car was it, Woiciech?' he asked.

Woiciech seemed to be pleased with himself.

'An Opel Omega estate,' he said. 'Red.'

Sejer knew that they would solve the case now. But he had known that all along. He felt neither joy nor triumph, just relief and satisfaction. He felt that it was something important, significant. For Henny and Henrik Hayden. For everyone who had been affected, for all the local community in Haugane. For the organisation he was a part of, and for Bonnie and Simon. Woiciech got up, pulled his mobile phone from the pocket of his green work trousers. He tapped on some buttons and then put the phone down on the map, on Krakow.

'Here,' he said. 'I took the registration number.'

Henny Hayden was quick, she understood people. She picked up on details and nuances, she had intuition. And as soon as she saw the two detectives, she knew something significant had happened.

'What is it?' she asked.

'We'll soon find out,' Konrad Sejer replied.

She showed them in.

They told her about the car up at the church, that they had the registration number, that it was one of several red cars that had been seen in the area. And that via the registration number, they had found out who owned the car.

Henny's husband, Henrik, was at home, sitting by the window in a red-and-blue-striped dressing gown. When they came in, he turned to look at them with a tentative smile. Like a child who doesn't know what the adults want. He was pale and thin and vulnerable. The silk dressing gown had opened slightly at the top to reveal his chest, which was covered in fine, white hairs. He had been muscular when he was younger, but this had now turned to fat. A transparent tube, as thin as a thread, disappeared into his ear, indicating that he used a hearing aid.

They sat down, and then focused their attention on Henny.

'Do you know the name Malthe?' Sejer asked. 'Thomasine Malthe?'

Henny looked at them, confused. She couldn't believe what she'd just heard. Malthe? No, it couldn't be true.

'We had expected it to be a man,' Sejer explained. 'We couldn't imagine that Bonnie and Simon had been killed by a woman. But perhaps Thomasine has a husband. Our witness saw a man up at the graveyard. He was relatively young, probably in his twenties.'

Henny was still confused. She shook her head every now and then, as if what was happening seemed unreal, that they were on the wrong track. But something that came from way back in the past broke over her like a storm.

'Do you know Thomasine Malthe?' Sejer asked again.

'No, not really.'

'But you know who she is?'

'Yes.'

'Is there something that you've been keeping from us that you'd like to tell us now?'

'Do I have to?'

'Yes.'

'But it's got nothing to do with the case.'

'Let me be the judge of that.'

'She has a son,' she said with trepidation.

'A son?'

'Yes, Thomasine Malthe has a son. He's twenty-one.'

'And do you know anything about this son?'

'Yes, if it's important.'

'It is important.'

'Should I have told you straight away?'

'Yes.'

She couldn't look at them any more. She seemed to be disconsolate and ashamed, desperately trying to get out of the situation.

'Tell us about Thomasine and her son.'

She took a deep breath. 'Bonnie had a boyfriend when she was fifteen. I think I've already told you about him. He was called Jørgen. We never got to meet him, she never brought him home because Henrik was so strict.

He broke off their relationship after a few months and Bonnie was distraught. We couldn't understand why she was taking it so badly. She wouldn't have any trouble getting a new boyfriend because she was so pretty. She was more beautiful than any of the other girls. We thought it all very odd. Girls have boyfriends. I had five before I met Henrik.'

'But she didn't get a new boyfriend?'

'No, and she didn't try either. And a few weeks later we realised why: he had made her pregnant. That was why he had broken it off; he didn't want to have a child, the coward. We didn't know how far gone she was.'

'Did you contact Jørgen?' Skarre asked.

'No, we didn't even know his surname. She didn't want us to know who he was. But she did want to have the child. It was almost as though she was doing it in defiance, maybe to punish him. And Henrik was furious that she wouldn't tell us who he was. He swore that if he ever found out, he would wreak his revenge. Make mincemeat out of him, was what he said.'

'But he never did?'

'No.'

'So Bonnie went to term. And how was that?'

'It was embarrassing for us to have to tell the family, and that we didn't know who the father was. As if there were several candidates, a queue of them. To be honest, I was ashamed of Bonnie. She was no longer the daughter I knew, she was possessed. She ran around the house screaming and slamming doors. Buried herself in her bed, wouldn't talk. Henrik was in shock, and we had no idea what the future held. Bonnie had so many plans. She wanted to study medicine. She wanted to work with geriatrics, and no one else wanted to do that.'

'So she gave birth to a son?'

'Yes. She was sixteen at the time. He was born prematurely and was in an incubator for a long time. Eventually we took him home. But then Bonnie didn't want to see him. She didn't want to breastfeed him, she didn't want to look after him, so I had to do everything. And then suddenly, sometime after the birth, she stopped eating. From one day to the next. Like a landslide. Henrik and I had our hands full and we quite simply gave up. It was the baby who had ruined everything and we didn't want him either. So he was sent to a foster home, not far away. And we concentrated on saving Bonnie. She was under forty kilos by this stage. Later, the little boy was formally adopted and given the surname Malthe. After Thomasine and Anders Kristoffer Malthe.'

'And did you have any contact with the boy over the years? Did Bonnie have any contact with him?'

'We couldn't bear to. It's a terrible thing to say, but we tried to forget the whole thing. I telephoned once, I wanted to make sure that he was OK, but I didn't tell Bonnie. Only he wasn't OK, he had some kind of undiagnosed personality disorder. He would never manage on his own. His father found another woman and moved to Copenhagen. So it was just the two of them, Thomasine and the boy. And my conscience weighed on me even more, as if it were a punishment for what we had done.'

'But did you perhaps christen him before he was fostered?'

'We went to the town hall,' Henny told them. 'It was a humanist name day. Bonnie came, but she didn't dress up. She wore an old anorak and she didn't say a word.'

'But she gave him a name?'

'No, that was me. He's called Eddie.'

'Eddie Malthe?'

'Yes.'

'And the father?' Skarre asked. 'Did you ever find out who Jørgen was?'

'Oh yes,' she said. 'I found him in the end. I had to see who he was, to know who had ruined so much of our lives. And when Bonnie finally met Olav, was happy and pregnant with Simon, she was able to tell us everything. She eventually told me his name, albeit reluctantly. He lived locally and of course he had his own family, so I got his number and phoned him straight away.'

'What did you say to him?'

'That I wanted to meet him. That I wanted to talk to him about something important.'

'But you didn't say what?'

'No, because then he might not have come. But you know, people are curious, so we arranged to meet in the shopping centre, in Christiania Cafe. I got there early, and was wearing a red silk scarf, so he could see me as soon as he walked in. And I sat there and waited. People came in all the time, but I didn't see anyone who I thought might be Jørgen from all those years ago. I sat there a while longer, with a cup of coffee, and eventually a man came over to the table. He was calm enough, as though he had thought through all the possibilities. But I was shocked when I saw him. He was much older than Bonnie. And after we had spoken for a while and he understood who I was, it emerged that they had started a relationship when Bonnie was only fifteen and he was over thirty. He was already married and had two children. He hadn't told her that, so he had betrayed her in every way. He'd promised her that it would be the two of them, but she had to be patient, because he had some things he needed to sort out first. Then she got pregnant, and he panicked and left her. He said that he hadn't realised that she had taken it all so seriously, but that he had often wondered whether she had given birth to the child. You are a coward, I told him. Irresponsible. Arrogant and egotistical. And he agreed. He asked me to give his best wishes to Bonnie, and I said that there was no way I was going to do that, and that he should stay away.'

'What was his name, Henny?'

'Jørgen Jonsson. He lives at Gimle. Do you need to talk to him?'

'Yes.'

A silence fell in the living room. Henny seemed nervous, but relieved. She had no idea what the consequences of all this would be, but she knew that she had told them something important. She could see that they were on to something and that she had held them back. With her shame and her pride.

'He turned up at the funeral, didn't he?' Sejer asked. 'And you told him where to go. You were angry. What did you say to him?'

'That he should bugger off. That he had no business there.'

'Does Eddie know that he was adopted?'

'I hope for goodness' sake that he does, he's not exactly a child any longer. That's the sort of thing parents should tell their children. And even if they don't, they often find out. It's their right to know, don't you think?'

She went over to her husband by the window and stroked his hair. He turned towards her, but he had no idea what was going on, he wanted the strange men to leave, he didn't know them. There was a tension in the room that he didn't understand, something unfamiliar.

'Is it my fault?' Henny asked.

'No. But we have to talk to Eddie Malthe. Please take care of yourself and Henrik. And look after the graves.'

Chapter 41

July had brought with it the longed-for summer heat. Bonnie and Simon were out walking in the fields around Geirastadir. They chose a path that ran along the edge of the woods, and Bonnie picked a bunch of wild flowers, dog daisies, bluebells and clover. She had helped Simon to make a big calendar with a square for every day from now until they went to Kenya in August. Each evening he put a cross in the square, and watched the time shrink. It was even more exciting than an advent calendar. He held his mother's hand firmly, as he always did when they were out walking; her hand was big and warm and safe.

They were getting close to Skarven Farm when Simon spotted the caravan between the trees. He stopped in his tracks and pointed, asked his mother if anyone lived there, but she didn't think so. The caravan was in poor condition with lots of rust around the windows, and a couple of small steps up to the door. She could see some ripped curtains in the windows. Simon tugged at her hand, he wanted to go and look. Bonnie had to laugh. It was so typical of Simon, he loved small houses, he loved making tents with blankets, and he loved the little snail above his peg at nursery, with its house on its back. They opened the door and peered in. On the left there were two narrow sofas with a table in between. In the middle a tiny kitchen space with a gas cooker and shelves and a cupboard, and on the right, two beds with no bedclothes. The caravan had six windows and they were all dirty. It smelt stuffy and damp. Not particularly inviting, Bonnie thought, but Simon was not of the same mind.

'Can we spend the night here?' he asked. 'Just one night?'

Bonnie knew he was going to ask that. And all she wanted to do at the moment was please him, her little munchkin.

'But it's not our caravan,' she said.

She looked up towards the farm at Skarven.

'Maybe it belongs to the farmer. They're probably waiting for it to be towed away, because it's just been abandoned here. Come on, let's go and ask.'

The light blue Opel swung into the farmyard, whereas Eddie stopped and watched them from a distance. He thought that perhaps they wanted to buy some vegetables or berries, and he decided to wait, for a while at least. But when the car door opened, he saw to his astonishment that Bonnie had two duvets in her arms. The farmer came out to speak to them. The boy jumped and danced around, tugging at his mother's sleeve. He had a teddy bear under one arm and a small pillow with a blue case under the other. And then, for some unknown reason, they started to walk down across the fields and soon they were out of sight. Eddie slipped out of the car, found a path that ran past the back of the house and then spotted them again, his mother and brother. I don't care if they can see me from the windows, he thought, and looked up at the big white house to his right. When he got to the corner, he stopped. There, by the edge of the woods, was a caravan, and Bonnie and Simon opened the door and went in. They were going to spend the night there, he realised. Each on a narrow bed, the boy with his brown bear under the duvet. Maybe they would lie there and whisper to each other while they waited for it to get dark. She would probably tell him stories and they might even make great plans for the future.

When he got home, he stood in front of the mirror for a long time. There were now lots of tiny blisters on his flaming cheeks, and he had a belt of the same hellfire around his waist. As though someone had thrown a pan of hot oil over him. He tried to ignore it, but it couldn't be ignored, even though he was driven by his own project. Determined, he turned and went into the kitchen. He opened one of the drawers and rummaged through the contents. Then he thought carefully before selecting a filleting knife with a wooden handle. There were brass rivets in the handle and the blade was long and sharp. There was an electric knife-sharpener lying beside the knives, which he plugged in at the wall.

Chapter 42

August 2005

Sejer and Skarre went to Malthe's address. First they went to the garage to look for the car. Skarre went in a side door, came back out and said there was a red Opel inside. They saw a face at the window and a curtain drawn to one side. It took a long time before anyone opened the door. A man stood there. Tall and solid, dressed completely in black. The first thing they noticed was the violent rash across his face, which looked like a burn.

He said nothing, just stood there. His sweatshirt was unwashed and his slippers were tartan.

'We've come to talk to Thomasine Malthe,' Sejer explained. 'Is she in?'

'No,' was Eddie's blunt reply. 'She's dead.'

'Oh,' Sejer said hastily, 'I'm so sorry, we didn't know. Is that recent?'

'Yes.'

'Are you her son, by any chance? Are you Eddie?'

'Yes. I am Eddie Malthe. I live here alone now, I've always lived here.'

'May we come in?' Sejer asked. 'We have some questions we'd like to ask you.'

Eddie didn't answer. He left the door open and retreated into the house. They followed. There was complete chaos in the living room, mess everywhere, clothes on all the chairs, and bags of rubbish. Even though it was summer and very hot, all the windows were closed and the smell was awful. Skarre popped into the kitchen where there were great piles of dirty plates and glasses on the worktop. On the floor, an unsteady tower of empty pizza boxes. And a few withered plants on the windowsill.

'You know why we're here?'

'I know.'

'You have to come to the station with us. We need to have a serious discussion.'

Eddie Malthe nodded. His movements were cumbersome and he was constantly on his guard. Every now and then he put his hand to his burning cheeks. When they were standing out in the hall, Skarre noticed a pair of heavy black leather boots. He lifted one of them up and recognised the pattern on the sole.

'We need to take your boots too, Eddie,' he said. 'Do you have anything else?'

'Only slippers.'

'You'll have to wear them then.'

Eddie got into the back of the police car and pressed his face to the window. As they pulled out onto the road, he saw Kennedy. The cat was sitting in the ditch by the side of the road, chewing at something, possibly a mouse. Ansgar was standing in front of his house; he stared with curiosity at the police car as it passed, his hand shading his eyes. I'll get you, Eddie thought. When I get out again. It might be ten years or more, but I'll get you.

Frank trotted up to say hello. Eddie wasn't interested – he kicked the dog away with his slippered foot. Frank retreated under the table.

'That's the ugliest mutt I've ever seen,' he stated.

'Well,' Sejer smiled, 'there's plenty who would agree with you.'

'Is he old?'

'No.'

'But he will be one day. And then he'll get put down. And you'll have to stand there and watch him die. It'll be horrible.'

'Yes, it will,' Sejer agreed. 'What's happened to your face?'

'Don't know.'

'Perhaps we can help you treat it.'

Eddie noticed the salt-dough figure under the lamp. Salt and flour and oil had been mixed to a dough, which was now disintegrating. He picked it up, studied it, held it carefully in his great hands, turned it over.

'Doesn't look much like you.'

'No.'

'It's crumbling. It wasn't baked long enough. And it should have been varnished. Amateur.'

'So you know all about salt dough?'

'Mass made it for me when I was little. I saved all the figures, they're in the cupboard at home.'

'Mass?' Sejer said. 'Your adoptive mother?'

'Yes.'

'And your adoptive father?'

'He's dead as well, in Copenhagen. I hardly remember him, he left when I was small. It's strange the way people just disappear. Cowards.'

'Is that why you stayed at home? To keep Mass company?'

'I don't cope very well on my own. I don't mind doing time,' he added. 'It doesn't really matter where I am.'

Sejer looked at the young man. His eyes didn't waver for a moment; it was as though he was simply prepared for what was to come.

'How did you find them, Eddie?'

'Mass told me what she was called and that they lived at Blåkollen. Then she didn't say any more. All that came out of her mouth was a trickle of blood. No one has told the truth. No one wanted me.'

'Do you know who your biological father is?'

'Mass said I would never find him. She said that I shouldn't even bother to look.'

'I know who he is, Eddie. He lives at Gimle and his name is Jørgen. You've got three siblings.'

'Half-brothers and -sisters,' Eddie corrected him. 'I don't need them.'

Sejer put his hands down on the big map of the world that was his blotting pad. He focused on little Denmark, on the beautiful city of Roskilde, where he himself had been born fifty-five years ago. He had often gone to the cathedral with his father, held his hand tight, knowing that his father was stronger than him.

'Would you like to meet him, Eddie?'

'No.'

'And then you lost Mass,' Sejer prompted. 'What happened?'

'She got cancer. Before she died she could hardly breathe. I could see the bones under her skin. She didn't have any hair.'

Then he was quiet for a moment. All they could hear was the hum of traffic outside and a telephone ringing somewhere in the building.

'I'm going to ask you some simple questions,' Sejer told him. 'And you have to answer.'

'OK.'

'Where were you on the fifth of July?'

'At Geirastadir.'

'Can you be more precise?'

'In the fields near Skarven Farm.'

'Did you find the caravan?'

'Yes.'

'How did you find them there?'

'I'd been following them. For a few days.'

'Did you have anything to do with the murders?'

'Do you really need to ask?' Eddie said. 'You know that already.'

'Can you remember what happened?'

'Yes.'

'Can you tell us why?'

'You don't need an explanation. We're sitting here.'

'Yes, you are being charged,' Sejer explained. 'You will have the right to a lawyer and you will be remanded in custody for eight weeks. A panel of forensic psychiatrists will examine you and observe you to determine whether there is a case for diminished responsibility.'

'I am of sound mind.'

'Then your case will be heard in court and you will either be sentenced or be found innocent. Imprisonment or detention, or forced psychiatric care. If there is any doubt about your criminal responsibility, that will fall in your favour, and they will have to acquit you. In this instance, if you admit culpability, it will probably result in summary proceedings on the basis of a guilty plea. Do you understand?'

'I'm not an idiot,' Eddie replied.

'I don't for a moment suppose you are. Are you thirsty? Would you like something to drink?'

'Cherry Coke,' Eddie said. 'But I don't know if you've got that here.'

'Cherry Coke? Is that Coke that tastes like cherries? Sounds awful.'

'You wouldn't know about things like that. I'm happy with water. If you haven't got anything else.'

'We'll get you some water then. But first, I want an answer to something. When you were standing inside the caravan, when you were standing there looking at the two of them at the table, when you had finally found your mother and brother, what did you say to them?'

Eddie looked Sejer in the eyes without any difficulty.

In fact, he raised his chin, as if he wanted to make one last point.

'You must have said something. You must have wanted to explain in one way or another. What did you say?'

Still no answer.

'Who did you kill first?'

'Simon. He was standing by the door.'

'And what did you say to Bonnie?'

'You can ask as much as you like. It's none of your business what I said to them.'

Chapter 43

5 July 2005

A man walked briskly across the fields at Geirastadir.

His eyes were fixed on the path and his heavy boots left no mark on the dry earth. His arms were swinging like oars in water, his cheeks were stinging and burning, and his mind was boiling over. There were flocks of fat, black crows all over the fields, and they lifted as he approached, squawking and shrieking. He eventually got there. His mouth tasted of blood and iron.

'Can we stay here one more night?' Simon asked.

'No, we have to go home to the rabbits. Granny will pick dandelions for them when we're in Africa.'

'What are the black spots?' he asked, and picked at the surface of the folding Respatex table.

'Fly poo,' Bonnie said. 'But don't worry about it. Look, I brought some cards, I'll teach you to play Crazy Eights. It's easy. And you're smart, aren't you, Simon?'

'Yes,' he said proudly. 'I'm smart and rich.'

Bonnie had to laugh.

'First you need to know the four colours and suits,' she said and spread the cards out over the table.

'But there are only two colours,' he said. 'Red and black.'

'No,' she explained, 'we say there are four. Red hearts and diamonds, black spades and clubs. You see?'

He nodded.

'So the aim is to get rid of all your cards,' she told him. 'You lay them out on the table, matching numbers or suits. So heart on heart, OK? And clubs on clubs. And you can change a card to another suit, but only after an eight. And then you should change it to the suit you have most of, so you get rid of as many cards as possible. You get it?'

'I get it.'

'Right, I'll deal out the cards then,' she said. 'I'll keep you straight as we go along. You mustn't show me your cards, I shouldn't see them, they're secret.'

Simon was wearing his new tracksuit in red, white and blue. He had hung up his calendar page counting when they were going to Africa by the window. Copying his mother, he made as big a fan as he could with his little hands. The cards were smooth and worn, and he held them up to his nose, they smelt good. His head was full of lions in Africa and his mother in her white dress with ladybirds on.

He arranged his cards as best he could, but they kept slipping out of his hands and several fell onto the grey linoleum floor.

'Don't look,' he said to his mother, 'I'm going to pick them up.'

She waited while he got down on his knees and picked up the cards. When he had got them all, he clambered back up onto the sofa. That was when he noticed the man walking down across the fields.

'There's someone coming,' he said. 'It's a man.'

Bonnie nodded.

'He's probably just out for a walk,' she said. 'He'll have come down from Geirastadir.'

Simon knelt on the sofa and watched the man approaching. He knew that he'd seen him before, by the house. The man had tried to push over his bike, had stood in front of him like a troll and scared him.

'He's coming here,' he told his mother. 'He's coming here to us.'

Bonnie nodded happily. She wasn't frightened of people coming to the door any more. She had nothing to fear and it might even be good news.

'It'll be one of the Poles,' she said. 'He must have a message for us.'

She smoothed her dress and straightened her back.

'Open the door, Simon, and see who it is!'

Karin Fossum has won numerous awards, including the Glass Key Award for the best Nordic crime novel, an honour shared with Henning Mankell and Jo Nesbo, and the Los Angeles Times Book Prize. Her highly acclaimed Inspector Sejer series has been published in more than thirty countries.